BOOK STORAGE

✓

Epstein, Seymour, 1917-
     The dream museum. Garden City, N.Y.,
Doubleday, 1971.
     297 p.
     The carefully planned & constructed world
of a successful New York writer is shattered
when he discovers that after twenty years of
marriage, he doesn't really know his wife &
son at all. His belated coming of age is achieved only after a long period of self eval-
uation &, ultimately, a drastic change in
personal values.

1c   I. Title.

The Dream Museum

Books by Seymour Epstein

THE DREAM MUSEUM
CAUGHT IN THAT MUSIC
A PENNY FOR CHARITY
LEAH
THE SUCCESSOR
PILLAR OF SALT

The
Dream Museum

Seymour Epstein

Doubleday & Company, Inc., Garden City, New York   1971

All of the characters in this book are fictitious, and any resemblance to actual persons, living or dead, is purely coincidental.

For
ANNETTE AND WALLY

If just to answer back the voices,
    echoing from sleep,
Of ancient reptiles munching bones:
    though maybe
Something to be trusted will yet spring up
And save Art Evergreen, who, somewhere in my heart,
    is dying.

The Last Will and Testament
of Art Evergreen
                        Robert Pack

David

1.

I'm alone for the first time in my life. . . . . Strictly speaking, that isn't true, but effectively speaking it is. For instance, there's a young lady living with me on a somewhat provisional basis, but her presence, while delightful, has done nothing to alter the situation. I thought it might at first, but it hasn't. What I mean is that since coming here I have found myself subject to no need, habit, or responsibility that would serve to distract me from myself, and I suppose it's the absence of one, or all, of these lifetime companions that accounts for my peculiar aloneness.

This apartment is very nice, incidentally. It belongs to a well-to-do friend of mine who has gone to live in Europe for several months. A fortunate coincidence that his business affairs, or restlessness—I'm not sure which—should have fallen in so conveniently with my short-circuiting life. This is not Ralph's home, mind you. Actually, Ralph is more than well-to-do, he's damn rich, and there's another labyrinth of rooms in Westchester that's subleased, swimming pool and all, to someone who can afford it. This apartment is a place Ralph keeps for evenings in town, or an important client, or an occasional woman.

There's a lot of teak and rosewood, and metal frame fixtures finished in dull black. The open bookshelves display new books in their glossy jackets. Heavy books on art and travel. The curious thing—as I've mentioned to Kathy, the young lady referred to before—is that this is precisely the sort of place I used to dream of when I was young and foggy with longing. A place to be when the mauve haze settled on New York, and the heart opened like a night flower toward a million possible pollinations.

Right now it is nearly four o'clock. Kathy is with her friends. I'm waiting for my father, who wants to talk to me. He phoned me during the day. "David?" he said, after hearing my voice. Everything is a question to Sam Lang, even paternity. The whole world of human relationships has somehow become obscured in his life, and he must reach out tentatively with each contact to reassure himself.

"Hello, Pop," I said.

"What are you doing?" he asked.

"Nothing."

"On this you can make a living?"

"It's very relaxing."

"I want to talk to you," he said.

"Talk."

"I can't talk to you over the phone. Later I want to talk to you. Can I talk to you?"

"Of course you can talk to me. Do you want to come here?"

"Where's here?"

I gave him the address. He said he'd be over about four. That's quite safe. I'm not expecting Kathy back until after dinner. My father will be prompt. It's impossible to imagine what would detain him. He is a man whose life has been thoroughly purged of incident. . . . If I am to begin at all, it might as well be with Sam Lang, my father:

A man gifted with his hands. Apprenticed at fourteen to a tailor who traveled the Dnieper on a riverboat, docking at cities and towns and taking orders from local merchants, civil servants, and minor nobility. I never knew whether that mythical team carried with them bolts of cloth and did their cutting and stitching in a cabin in the boat, or whether they went into the towns and hired a room where they completed their itinerant business. I don't want to know. All good myth should be left unanchored in space.

Kings and mountains, rivers and worktables, detached and freed forever from the shrinkage of time.

In the city of Kiev, Samuel Lang got mixed up with a crowd being fired on by government troops. He ran into a cellar and hid. Then he turned west and didn't stop until he reached New York. He's been hiding ever since. Is it possible for a man to live three quarters of a century and not acquire a single friend? There's something extraordinary about such isolation. When you consider the human varieties on earth, there's bound to be someone to match every shade of lightness or darkness in another's soul. But consider: apprenticed at fourteen; caught in the Duma riots; escape to America . . . let's say that he was scared at an early age and everything that happened since gave the wheel a turn.

Sam Lang built himself a permanent cellar, coming out long enough to grab himself a wife. The arrangement he made with life was that he would work and make money fulfilling his own needs and his obligations to others. I think that's all there was to it—except if that was all there was to it why should he have telephoned? His financial responsibility to me ended decades ago, and his fatherhood never began. So why the reflex of concern? I don't know. Or perhaps I do. Perhaps he was always concerned, in his fashion. Perhaps this dull, dark, derelict father who set me up in the lifetime career of looking for a father had always felt beneath the rhino hide of his habits an itch he couldn't reach, an itch needing the friction of another to be scratched.

At any rate, he is coming. It was somewhat over a week ago that I informed my mother and father that I had separated from my wife, and I've been more or less expecting an emissary from the old country.

There's really only one significant window in this apartment. It gives me an unobstructed view of the Jersey Palisades. The view is coincidental. I enjoyed a variation of this scene somewhat south of this location, in my office, to which I no longer go. I've sold out my share of the business. Actually money is no problem. There are no real problems—except the one that blossomed in a

5

sudden noiseless blaze on the front lawn of the house where I no longer live.

There's the buzzer. My father.

He stands at the door looking at me as though I am expecting from him some sort of password that will admit him into my life again. "Hello," I say. "Come in." He enters looking at me steadfastly. One might think he is studying me to see what effect recent events have had on his son, but I know better. He looks at me in this manner in order to avoid looking into the apartment. This place, to him, is furtive and illegitimate, and he intends not to recognize it, as nations sometimes do not "recognize" each other.

"You know, David—" he begins.

"Why are you standing here?" I interrupt. "Come in. How do you like this apartment?"

I wish he hadn't begun that way. "*You know, David—*" doesn't sound very promising. I'm afraid this is going to be a typical meeting between Sam Lang and his older son. I take him by the arm and together we proceed through the foyer and into the living room.

"A friend, you say," he says, referring to the owner of the furnishings he barely glances at.

"Ralph Friedman. I think you've met him. I'm sure you have. Tall fellow."

"The one in the textile business?"

"No, that's Dan Marcus. I haven't seen Dan in years."

Now he advances on the chrome-framed foam-rubber-cushioned sofa on which he at last sits down circumspectly, keeping on his impeccably cut overcoat of midnight blue.

"Take your coat off," I invite.

He holds up a hand. He wants to remain insulated, transient.

I say, "Ralph is the fellow who owns the advertising agency. You and Mom met him at my house about three or four years ago when I had that big Thanksgiving dinner."

"How come he lets you live here?" my father wants to know.

"Why not?" I say. "He's not using the place. He's in Europe."

6

"Well, that's nice. At least you won't have to pay two rents." Then abruptly: "Mama spoke to Duddy."

"Did she?"

"Duddy talks about divorce."

"That may be true."

"But you didn't say that," he reminds me crossly. "You said you weren't getting along."

"People who don't get along sometimes get a divorce," I point out.

He nods. He's well aware of that. But he is also aware of other disorders like gambling, thievery, and murder. It is my belief that he has never experienced a nerve beat of sympathy for aggravated passions, and therefore they have no application to himself or anyone that he knows. "Duddy," by the way, is his pronunciation of "Dodie," my wife's nickname, the one she is known by in the family, derived from Dorothy. It was not I who named her thus but herself, as a child, mispronouncing her name and giving her parents one of those verbal amulets to jingle the rest of their days.

I sit beside my father and wonder what on earth he has come to say to me. What advice. What little piece of wisdom he has been hoarding all these years—seventy-four of his, forty-seven of mine—to give me at that moment in my life that his fatherly instinct would recognize as critical. I know that people are fanatically unchanging and that life is largely a series of accidents, but I persist in the notion that here and there, in the proper circumstances, there can be insights and revelations. It happened to me. Why shouldn't it happen to him?

"Now listen—" he says.

Now listen! We are about to talk sense!

"—let's talk sense."

"All right," I say.

"People have disagreements—"

"They do."

"That doesn't mean they have to get a divorce."

"That depends on the disagreement."

7

Slight grimace. What disagreement? What do a man and a woman disagree about? Money! What else?

"Whatever the disagreement," he says.

"What do you think Dodie and I disagreed about?" I ask him on impulse.

"How should I know? Is it my business?"

"Well, what do you think it was?"

"David, I don't know. I know you're making a good living. What's happening with the business?"

"I sold out."

He raises his head like an animal scenting danger. His brow furrows. His mouth opens. He can't believe that I'm telling him the truth, but if it's a fib then the fib has a very categorical sound. Some instinct informs him that I will not retract what I said, but his imagination cannot for the moment accept both the possibility of divorce and the loss of my business.

"To Rich?" he asks, naming my partner.

"To someone else," I tell him. "To someone by the name of Buchholz. Ted Buchholz."

"Why?"

"It seemed like the right thing to do."

"But how will you make a living?"

"I get quite a lot of money on the sale. I can go into business again. I can get a job."

"But to sell your business!" His looks narrow. "Does Duddy know?"

I smile. "She knows," I say. "But we were talking about something else. We were talking about Dodie and me. Our disagreements. They had nothing to do with business, with money. I really would like to know if you have any idea what we might have disagreed about."

Now he is suspicious. He senses that I'm baiting him—and I am—and perhaps I shouldn't—but what virtue has Sam Lang ever practiced that he should be spared everything but the one great gray menace of money? No one in the family has ever brought his problems to Sam Lang, because it is known that Sam Lang

8

doesn't believe in the seriousness of any problem that doesn't begin with, grow by, and find solution in money.

"About Lenny?" my father ventures, naming my son.

"No."

He turns his head away impatiently. "Please! I don't like to play games."

Oh, don't I know! But it's true. He doesn't like to play games, and he will never take part in this one.

"You know," I say, "it isn't necessarily Dodie who wants to divorce me. I may want to divorce her."

He looks at me askance. "Why?"

"Why do you think? Why would a man want to divorce his wife?"

He says nothing. Only waits. I can see by the retreat of his eyes that he wants out of this, wants to claim the long privilege of his immunity. And I should let him have it, for God's sake! He can't help me, and what earthly use would there be in scattering blame?

"Mama said I should come and talk to you," he says.

But, you see, this is how he infuriates me! This is how he has infuriated me my whole life!

"And you?" I ask. "Don't you want to talk for yourself?"

He heaves around protestingly on the sofa. "Please, David, don't give me a cross-examination. I don't know what you got on your mind with all these questions. Why, I know what went on between you and Dodie? You kept me informed?"

"I'm telling you now," I say. "Dodie was sleeping with another man."

"Sleeping?"

I doubt if five seconds elapsed in the crazy circuitry that zipped between us. Let me put it this way: in his desire not to know, Sam Lang pressed on the damper of his mind so hard that the word "sleeping" reached him without a vibration beyond its literal meaning. Dodie, his son's wife, was sleeping with another man. I saw that he saw his daughter-in-law stretched out in bed beside a strange man, sleeping, no more. Why should his daughter-in-law suddenly find it necessary to sleep beside another man? Who

9

knows? Maybe in this strange world where the rumor of so much bizarre concern lapped in the perpetual low tide of his consciousness a new accommodation had come about. Maybe these new medicineless doctors were prescribing different sleeping companions for insomniac wives. But then why should his son, David, be so upset? Because—ah!—"sleeping" (scandal frightens his eyes) did not mean *sleeping!*

"Duddy?" he says.

"Dodie," I say.

"Duddy!"

"Dodie."

"Mama didn't tell me that," he declares indignantly, positively drawing away from me.

"Mama doesn't know," I say. "I didn't tell her. You can."

"I'm very surprised to hear this," he says. "I never expected such a thing from Duddy. Her mother knows?"

Dodie's father died five years ago. Dodie's mother now lives in Miami. I wonder if my father thinks Mrs. Phillips should be advised, like a note from school for some infraction.

"No, she doesn't," I say. "Unless Dodie told her. I doubt she would. I know I haven't."

My father is silent for several moments. Then he says, "You know, David, I'll tell you something—I'm very surprised you should tell me something like this."

"You are? Why?"

"It's not nice for everybody to know," he says.

"I grant you that," I agree, "but I didn't think you were everybody."

He lowers his eyes, looks this way and that. "How did you find out?" he asks.

"Dodie told me."

"Duddy! Told you? What do you mean? You must have asked her something first. You must have found out something."

"Yes, I did find out something," I say to my father. "One Sunday, about a month ago, Dodie had gone into the city, to a

10

museum, and when she returned home I knew she had met a man in the city."

"She told you?"

"No."

"You know the man?"

"Yes."

"He told you?"

"No."

"So how did you know?"

"I saw."

"Where did you see?"

"In my mind."

The angle of my father's head increases, and his mouth assumes a vindicative shape—a sly, wry, dry smile. He looks around the room in earnestness for the first time, seeking in its arrangement a justification for his suspicions. He nods and sighs.

"David," he says, "why are you staying here? A stranger's house. Come home with me. You'll stay in the house a few weeks, rest up . . ."

"I'm not tired."

"You look terrible. Why did you sell the business? It's all finished—the sale?"

"All finished."

"You got a good price?"

"Excellent."

"So you saw in your mind," he suddenly reverts. "How did Duddy know what you saw in your mind?"

"I told her what I saw in my mind."

"And what did she say?"

"She wanted to know how I knew."

"How did you know?"

"I'm not sure."

He nods again. Speaking of minds, I see that it's all settled in his. "Now, listen," he says, "let's talk sense. You want me to tell you what happened? You scared Duddy. When Duddy talked to Mama on the phone she said that she was scared. Of you. I

11

didn't want to say anything about this. I wanted to talk to you first, see how you were. Listen, I've seen it happen. It's nothing to be ashamed . . . You remember, about ten years ago, I was staying with that Fiori, on Forty-eighth Street . . ."

I look at him as he talks. It dawns on me that he thinks I'm crazy—or getting there. If ever in my life I were to succumb to hysterical laughter, this would be the time. I feel a wild, premonitory flutter, but then it subsides. I just sit there and remember that Fiori. He is my father's favorite tale, that Fiori, because he is a living proof and exoneration for Sam Lang. Something of the Dnieper and his beginnings must have remained in my father, for he has moved like a gypsy in the years of his trade, going from shared loft to shared loft, and leaving behind thieves and horse players and men who would not talk and men who talked too much. Always the other one. Always some crazy irregularity in the other one, never in Sam Lang. But Fiori accused my father of stealing his bolts of imported worsted, and Fiori was found one day with his head in the toilet bowl listening to the voice of his son who had been killed in the war. Did they take Fiori away or not?

"How is business?" I ask my father, because that is the kind of question he would never regard as a change of subject. "Are you getting any orders?"

"From who?" he wants to know. "All my customers are dying off. The other day I heard they took Mr. Jacobs to the hospital with a heart attack. I made clothing for that man for over forty years."

"That is a shame," I say. "Is it serious?"

"At his age it's serious."

"Maybe it's time you thought of retiring," I say.

"Who'll give me?"

He knows who'll give him. Talk of retirement is the only ironic jest of his life. His fingers have become cramped, and he can no longer manipulate the needle with the old dexterity. It is no longer an absurdity to talk of retirement, but he cannot contem-

12

plate workless days. The prospect of idleness falls into the category of jokes on impotence.

"You and Mom can take a trip," I say, just to feed him a line.

"Sure, sure! I'll go to Miami Beach. With your mother. I'll listen to her complain about her back, her shoulder, her neck—"

"I thought those new pills helped."

How easy it is to divert him from any trouble but his own! He shakes his head and says, "I wish you would talk to your mother. She drives me out of my mind. Every day it's something else. First she runs to one doctor, then to another. . . ."

He's on the right track now. He doesn't question the switch. He tells me that he has to listen to my mother's complaints, help her in the house, while his own fingers (pressing the fingers of one hand with the fingers of another, trying vainly to ball them into fists) will no longer obey him. And it's true, it's true! He has only his fingers to work with, and what shall he do now that they are betraying him, this man who has made work his tabernacle and only true companion? Perhaps he should go to another doctor. All his doctor says is, I know, I know, and gives him no medicine. Surely there must be a medicine that will loosen the joints of his fingers. All these years to pay medical insurance, and when he needs help there's no help. . . .

He can't listen to my griefs, but I must listen to his. He is talking sense. Stiff fingers are sense. Infidelity and museums and visions are nonsense. So, *adieu*, old artificer, old Sam Lang, former traveler on the Dnieper. No, not *adieu*. You'll be around and I'll be around for some time yet. But I'm returning the compliment— I'm not listening. Perhaps someday I'll listen again, but not now. I've got my own fish to fry.

I get up and he gets up. It's time to go, and he's a little confused. He has accomplished nothing, really, and he cannot believe in what he has learned.

"So what shall I tell Mama?" he asks.

"Tell her that I'm all right."

"You'll come to the house?"

"Of course I'll come to the house."

"Do you need . . ." He hesitates.

"Need what?"

"I don't know. Anything. Money?"

"No, I don't need money."

"Listen," he says, "do you want to take my advice?"

"Absolutely."

"Go see a good doctor," my father says. "Have a thorough checkup. Maybe you're worried about something."

2.

About Kathy Willens . . . She has long brown hair that falls along her face, giving her the Afghan look prized by hippies, or semi-hippies. Her eyes are hazel, her face, when seen, is broad, pretty, shining with good health, and her body is proportioned like a Maillol statue. Sometimes she will scoop her hair from her face with both hands and hook a separate mass over each ear. But her ears are small, and in a few minutes her face is covered again. Sometimes she will gather the whole business to the back and fasten it with a kerchief. She is twenty-two years old. I know that her parents live in St. Paul. Her father is a doctor. Three weeks ago, when I was visiting my son at his college in Vermont, Kathy asked me for a lift to New York.

It's now after nine o'clock. I've had my dinner—club steak, peas, a salad—and I've piled records on Ralph's expensive hi-fi machine. I remember they used to advertise these components as producing "concert hall fidelity," but I've never heard anything resembling this in a concert hall. The sound comes at you as through a rare gas that filters to a cosmic purity.

There's Kathy's key in the door.

She comes in wearing the Eskimo-hooded fur coat in which I first saw her in Vermont.

"Hi," she says.

"Hi."

15

"Did you have dinner?" she asks.

"Yes, indeed. Did you?"

"Oh, sure."

"Where did you eat?"

"Some place in the Village. I don't remember the name. I had a tremendous hamburger on garlic bread. It was so good! And beer. And a *flan*."

"A what?"

"*Flan*. Spanish custard."

"What a combination."

"Yum!"

She takes off her coat and tosses it over a chair. She's wearing a blue woolen dress that stops midway down, or up, her Maillol thighs. Kathy in motion gives the viewer the impression that she is not using energy but containing it. She has practiced modern dancing and can sit down on the floor by crossing her legs and squatting until her behind makes contact. Her movements are aborted leaps—and sometimes she actually does leap. Also, she speaks in short bursts. It is incredible, her being here with me in this apartment, but no more or less incredible than anything else that has happened.

She comes over and sits down beside me on the chrome-and-foam sofa, sliding her arm under mine and taking my hand between the two of hers.

"And what did you do all day?" she asks.

"Oh, nothing much. My father visited me."

"Your *father!* You have a *father!* I mean—"

"You mean *alive*."

"Yes . . . You see."

"I see what?"

"You're always worried about your age."

"Me!"

"It isn't a matter of years," she informs me. "I told you that before. You still have your father. I bet he's young-looking."

"Well, yes, he is, as a matter of fact. He doesn't have a wrinkle, believe it or not."

16

"Neither do you," Kathy points out. "And you don't have much gray hair either. My father is all gray."

"What's he like, your father?" I ask her.

I haven't asked Kathy this before. Nor have I asked her her father's age, although I have seen classic implications float in her wide-awake eyes. I doubt if three years separate Dr. Willens and David Lang.

"He's impossible," Kathy says.

"Really? Why?"

"You wouldn't believe."

"I would."

"He's bigoted."

"Who isn't, in one way or another?"

"He's a Republican."

"The two don't necessarily go together."

"He'd be a Bircher, an *anything,* if it didn't hurt his practice. He belongs to every snotty organization going. He hates Jews and thinks Negroes are a different species."

"Come on!"

"You think I'm kidding?"

"I guess you wouldn't kid about a thing like that. Does he love you?"

"He doesn't love anything or anybody but himself. He doesn't even love his profession. Most men love what they do, isn't that so? I swear he doesn't give a damn about making people well. He only cares about big fees and his reputation."

"Aren't you riding a hobby horse, Kathy? Exaggerating a little?"

"I'm not! If you *knew* him! Why do you think I'm exaggerating?"

"Well, maybe not exaggerating but sort of concentrating on only one facet. I read somewhere that General Patton wrote poems —or was it lyrical love letters?—to his wife."

"Who?"

"A general in my war."

"There you go again."

"You mean 'my war'?"

"Yes."

17

"In this century a man is identified by his war. Was your father in the war?"

"Yes."

"Army?"

"Navy—and he never wrote lyrical love letters to my mother."

"Were they married then?"

"No, but they were engaged. You know that my mother practically had to give up all her old friends. They weren't important enough."

"That *is* mean."

"I'm telling you! Exaggerating!"

The dirty truth is that I'm enjoying it now. At first I didn't want to hear Kathy run down her father. The obviousness is complicated. I'm a father. My father's a father. My father never got the relationship straight. I think I have. But perhaps I'm mistaken. Perhaps intelligence and effort and liberality only put a modern shape on an old-fashioned doom. My trip to Vermont was far from successful. I was hurt. No doubt I hurt Lenny. The betrayal that crashed out of New York like a river over a precipice flowed at flood tide on the Thruway, leveled off in the side roads around Vermont, and disappeared underground in the Green Mountains. I'm not a fool. Dodie has been a good mother—perhaps too good. I didn't look for partiality in my visit to Lenny. I looked for the shared sorrow of a shared loss, but like my father my son claimed an outsider's privileges. Immunity. I had no idea he considered himself an outsider. . . . Kathy, whom I met up there, a friend of my son, asked me for a lift to New York as I was about to leave.

"Let's not talk about fathers," I say to Kathy.

"All right. What do you want to talk about?"

"I don't want to talk."

Kathy moves a little away from me. A familiar look comes into her eyes, a solemn, votive look, like someone suddenly moved to piety. Then she leans toward me and runs the tip of her tongue over my lips, as though I had eaten something delicious and she is savoring the last of it. Her own breath is tainted with her Village meal, but these indelicacies are readily forgiven in the young. I try to take her in my arms and kiss her with the eagerness I have always felt and now automatically assume in the preliminary acrobatics of love, but Kathy holds me strongly by the arms, shifts into a more comfortable and commanding position (legs up on the sofa, torso facing me), and with a blink, a little nod of the head, she bids me *wait;* silently proposes an order of procedure that will teach eagerness the rewards of patience.

This girl applies her young-old art with diagnostic tenderness, as if I have long been the victim of some minor illness, one hardly needing her full curative powers, just this mild exorcism, just these occult kisses. She hasn't told me this, but I do believe she believes that older people don't know how to make love. She is solicitously instructive in the things that she does. She wants me to be better, healthier, and toward this end she has introduced an almost clinical punctiliousness into the act.

It is an exacting and exciting business. She unbuttons me, and I unbutton her. When she is all but naked, she crosses the room and opens the davenport. Then she goes to the bathroom. I silence the hi-fi set and turn out all the lights except the one small lamp that will distill the semidarkness I prefer. Light explodes from the bathroom as Kathy emerges. She comes to the bed and begins her careful, clinical search for ultimates. It is a serious, exacting, and exquisite business.

"Whom do you see in the Village?" I ask.
"Friends."
"Girlfriends? Boyfriends?"
"Both."
"Is there one particular friend?"
"There's one."
"Boyfriend?"
"Yes."
"Is it someone you knew in school?"
"He went there, yes."
"And now he lives in the Village."
"Yes."

19

"What does he do?"

"Writes. He's writing a novel."

"Aha! And does he have a mustache?"

"Don't be smartass. Nobody likes a smartass."

"And your aunt?" I ask.

"My aunt?"

"Yes, the one—"

"Oh—what about her? She's a great-aunt, really. My mother's aunt."

"Your great-aunt. Is she satisfied with your living arrangement in New York?"

"I told her I'm living with a friend," Kathy says very sleepily.

"I think you are," I say, "but—"

"Dave—" she whines.

"What?"

"Let me sleep."

"I will, in a moment. I must know some things, Kathy. I must know if you've written to your folks."

"Yes."

"Have you told them that you're in New York?"

"Mm-hm."

"They have only to pick up the phone to know that you're not living with your great-aunt."

"I told them I was living with a friend, I told you," she moans. "Please shut up, Dave. If you keep waking me up, I'll make you fuck me again."

"Why do you use that word?" I ask her.

I'm lying flat on my back. Kathy is on her side, her back to me. I hear a short, muffled laugh.

"Does it shock you?" she asks.

"Not exactly. But you know very well what I mean. Why do you use it?"

"Because I like it," she says. "It has a good sound. It begins with your teeth and ends in your throat. Fff-uck! It's the right word for what it means."

20

"Stay with me one more minute," I beg her. "Have you always been so frank?"

"Pleeeeeze!"—a plaintive ululation.

"Just tell me that, Kathy. Have you always been so frank?"

"No."

"Will you always be frank with me? I mean, as long as we know each other?"

"Mm-hm."

"I wish you would," I say. "I wish I could depend on you to tell me exactly what you're thinking, even if it's absurd or embarrassing, even if you think it will hurt me. I'd like to make such an arrangement, Kathy. . . . Kathy? . . . Kathy?"

No answer. Kathy is asleep.

3.

Soundlessly. No deviated septums or allergic swellings for Kathy. Her young nostrils easily oxygenate the secret life into which she has withdrawn, while I am left sleepless with the multiplying fantasies of myself in this apartment with the Maillol girl who has parents in another city, friends (she says) in this, relatives also (she may be lying) in this, and who has just inspired me to do three times what I have for years and years been accustomed to do only once.

Is it in the nature of youth to exact such strangeness and then go to sleep? It seems so. Well, I too have slept with strange companions in strange places. I have slept in a strange bed with a strange woman while the strange vibrations of a V-bomb passed overhead, shaking me wide-eyed awake and ripe with terror at that strange juncture of my life. But then the whole world was passing through a flaming strangeness, and I was perfectly balanced between what was and what was to be. I am not so balanced now. I am hopelessly weighted on the side of what has been. When I close my eyes, I have neither the geography of this room nor the geography of the future before me. I have, instead, the practical valet-chair that Dodie bought for me some years ago. That is to the right of the bed in which I am not lying. To the left is the night table with the pink-faced clock and the china-white Princess phone. . . . I must open my eyes quickly, because what is in *this*

22

room and what my senses arrange when I close my eyes make me dizzy. Left to itself, this scramble arranges itself as it will—present, past, fantasy, memory—but I can't leave it to itself. I know I'm not insane, although I can't explain everything. I know what happened and in what order.

It was a Sunday, a late October day of lavish sunlight that made the trees blaze in their seasonal dying. These autumn splendors have always produced a restlessness in me. I feel I should be traveling toward more and more varieties of this sad flamboyance. I never know where. Just go. Get in the car and head for some place that will be a perfect culmination of the season. But I have seldom headed anywhere. I have lived long enough to learn that the preparations to capture such a day are a guarantee of its loss.

I had finished breakfast and was sitting in the living room. Dodie was still at the breakfast-room table having another cup of coffee. The phone rang. I went to it. It was Sid Simon, a neighbor with whom I played tennis. He wanted to know how about it, last chance, the nets would be coming down for the year next week.

"It's Sid," I said to Dodie.

"Yes?" she said.

"He wants to play tennis."

"With me?"

"No, darling, with me."

"That's fine," she said.

"Did we have anything planned?"

"I did. I told you."

"Did you?"

"Yes, I did. During the week. I told you—"

"All right," I said to Sid. Then to Dodie, "You'll be wanting the car, then?"

"It isn't absolutely necessary."

"Wouldn't it be more convenient?"

"Yes, of course—"

"Can we use your car?" I asked Sid.

"Sure."

"Hour?"

"The courts are going to be crowded today," he warned.

"Make it a half."

I hung up and told Dodie I was sorry, that I was sure she'd told me but that I must have forgotten. Where was she going?

"The museum," she said.

And when she said the word "museum," there appeared in my mind a room where art books are sold. I haven't been to a museum in a long time. There was a time when I went quite frequently, but some years ago I developed a negative reaction to contemporary art, and then to museums themselves. A personal thing, a prejudiced thing, but there it is. But, as I say, I had gone frequently in the past, and therefore it wasn't so odd that my memory should select a quick emblem when Dodie uttered the word. An art book room, to the left, very definite in size and detail, with racks on which were displayed buff-colored, gold-embossed books.

"Modern Museum?" I asked.

"I see you do remember," she said.

"Some sort of special exhibit?"

"Matisse."

"Matisse is nice. Matisse is very nice."

"Well, would you like to come?" Dodie asked.

"I've already agreed to play with Sid."

She nodded and looked down at her cup. The sunlight coming through the window behind her ignited the loose strands of her auburn hair. I think it would be best if I described Dodie here:

She is tall for a woman, quite tall, and her posture is that of a woman who has never come to terms with her height. Sitting, she hangs curved over her own middle, like an unsupported plant bowing to gravity. But the arc of her spine is counterbalanced by the tilt of her head. I suppose, for the sake of some meaningless objectivity, I should say that Dodie is not pretty. She's not, but she is attractive in a special way—a qualification which has left an open wound in her life, and which she despises. Nevertheless, her features, particularly her nose and mouth, are a little too heavy, too thick. I've given these despaired-over features all kinds of

24

sexy euphemisms, but they've had little effect on Dodie's own estimation. I know she has never accepted these features as natural to her being. They are, she feels, a crude and cruel imposition, and her lovely green eyes have learned to stare at the world in a way that denies her other features.

She said, "You know you hate museums."

"Not really," I said. "I hate the atmosphere of museums."

"I fail to see the difference," she replied, quite justly.

"Did you really tell me you were going today?" I asked again.

"I really did."

"When was that?"

"I told you, David. One day last week. I don't remember exactly what day. It was the day I made the arrangement with Jean Ferguson, I think."

"Is Jean your regular museum companion?" I asked her.

"Regular," Dodie scoffed. "She's come with me before. I wouldn't say *regular*."

"Does she still wear those chippie clothes?"

"You are out of your mind," Dodie said. "Jean has—well, certainly not *chippie*, whatever that means."

"I don't know," I said. "Maybe it's the way she walks. Does she know anything about art?"

"She has a feeling for it," Dodie replied. "What's the difference? She doesn't have to share my tastes. Just as long as she doesn't inhibit them."

I smiled. "Whereas I do."

"Let's not go into that," was Dodie's request.

"You know what I would like?" I said. "I would like for us to start doing things together again."

"Like what?" she asked. "Like going to museums? That's your fault, not mine. You simply don't enjoy yourself, and there's not a reason in the world for you to go. Nor is there any reason in the world for me *not* to go. What else don't we do together?"

"Oh . . . everything. We used to play tennis."

"I'm not in your class," she said.

"I'd be happy to play with you."

"No, you wouldn't," she said. "You'd much rather have a fast man's game."

(True!)

"We used to listen to music together," I pointed out to her.

"You never put a record on the machine," she returned.

"Because you never listen."

"David, for God's sake, do you need me to listen with you? If you wanted music, you would have it without my company."

"But your not listening with me spoils it," I insisted. "I feel it's deliberate on your part. You're not rejecting the music, you're rejecting me."

"What nonsense! And your not going to museums, what is that a rejection of?"

"Then you admit it's deliberate."

"I do not. I'm just not that crazy about Bach, or Mozart, or Haydn."

"You used to be."

"You used to be interested in what museums had to offer."

It was that kind of conversation. I'm sure the words are not exact, but the trapped senses and embattled spirits are.

I went to the dining table and sat diagonally across from Dodie. I slipped my hand under the flap of her robe and put my hand on the inside of her thigh. There was no lust in my touch. I was trying in my way to conjure old intimacies and bid them good morning in the bright reconciling light of my favorite season. Things had not been good between Dodie and me. Certainly things had not been good, and while I was not at all sure how or why they had fallen so far from grace I was sure I wanted an improvement. Thus the touch. And Dodie responded by putting her hand over mine with the fabric of the robe between our hands, and she smiled a soft smile that was a miracle of steadiness. It acknowledged everything—the way things had been; the way things were; my touch; my intention. Her green eyes held everything in perfect equilibrium. I have seen many expressions in Dodie's eyes but none that traveled so far and moved so little. I have never been

26

confident about the readings that one human being can take from another's face, but this reading scared me.

I said, "I hope our fights are done with. I do believe they're done with, and it's a good thing. I believe we've reached some sort of peace. Perhaps it's that that scares me a little. I wouldn't want it to be the peace of the dead. . . . All right, you go to the museum with nice Jean Ferguson, who knows what she likes, and I'll play tennis with Sid Simon, and this evening I will take you out to dinner."

"Lenny may phone this evening," Dodie reminded me.

"Yes," I said. "That's right. I forgot." I withdrew my hand from her thigh, and I had in that instant another vision of the art book room. It was exactly as before, and I tried to remember to which particular museum it belonged. Was it the Modern Museum? Perhaps. "Well, then," I said, "we'll have dinner at home. . . . Is there a book store in the museum?"

"Which museum?"

"The one you're going to."

"I believe there is. Yes."

"To the left—as you enter?"

"No, I think it's to the right. Why?"

"Nothing. I was just remembering. To the right."

"But why did you ask?" Dodie wanted to know.

"Absolutely no reason," I replied. "When you said 'museum,' my mind flashed a picture, that's all. I just remember that art book store."

"Oh."

4.

One of life's more reliable quirks is the odd extra who shows up when the films of fateful days are developed. Usually a person of total inconsequence—usually someone who figured least to figure.

Sid Simon.

We weren't even friends. There was never a desire on either of our parts to test our connection beyond the tennis court. Sid is a wiry, sour man who owns a profitable stationery store in the Wall Street area. The town where we lived maintained its own tennis courts. Sid and I had seen each other frequently there. We were thrown together in a doubles game, and then we began to play singles. We found that we gave each other a good, hard, competitive game. In fact, nothing pleased me so much as beating the dreary bastard, which I seldom did. There's not a reason in the world why Sid should beat me, but he does. He plays a mean, pinched game full of chops and strategic little place shots, which I loathe. I play a direct volleying game. I go for the flat power shot that burns a hole in Sid's defenses. It should, but it doesn't. More often than not, I'm into the net, or way back. He beats me.

We drove to the tennis courts and played. I can't say I had had any premonition about it being a rotten tennis day for me. Sid had taken the last few sets we had played, and I was strung rather tight about beating him. But the moment we started playing, I knew I was in trouble. I was at my wooden-armed worst. Counsel myself as I would to relax, to keep my eye on the ball, to take a full swing, to do all those basic things I must do if I was not to go down to disgraceful defeat, I couldn't command the extensions of my body. My reflexes were hobbled in a potato sack, while Sid, smelling advantage, leaped ungracefully into the breach, all elbows and accuracy. He placed his shots where he pleased, and I was helpless to prevent it. I noticed how my ineptitude fed his confidence. Inch by inch, he dared, until he was right up to the net, risking what he wouldn't normally risk, discovering new possibilities out of his certain supremacy. And even while I burned in frustration, I thought of how like life this was—my loss, your gain. One man's weakness teaches another man tricks of power.

But why all of this (rage and rumination in the bright autumn air) should make the turn it did, I don't know, but suddenly there was the art book store of the museum floating through my head again. On second thought, it did have a relevance. The helplessness I was feeling with Sid had its counterpart in the helplessness I had felt with Dodie earlier that morning. It would have been such an easy thing to say to Dodie: "I'll go with you. I like Matisse"— even enduring Jean Ferguson's company, which I didn't mind so much. But, you see, there was our honesty, our terrible armed honesty, crouching behind loaded machine guns, ready to shoot at the first false gesture. That was one thing about Dodie—*honesty*. She was passionate about honesty. "For God's sake," I have heard her say so often, "let's be honest about what we like and what we don't like! It's so transparent when one of us does something just to please the other. So transparent and so irritating in the long run." Perhaps she was right about the transparency part of it, but I'm not at all sure about what would have been best in the long run.

Anyway, Sid—

I was going down badly, disgracefully. I was simply incapable of hitting the ball properly. I knew that it wasn't a question of trying harder, but rather a question of not trying at all, of getting outside my knotted self and ambling toward the contest from an-

29

other point of the compass. What I realized in that hideous moment was that I was developing the crooked smile of a loser.

I could actually feel that rubber band of a smile tug at my mouth as I prepared to execute a backhand futility against a drive that wouldn't have troubled a player of even moderate competence. I felt an icy contempt for the clown who would not only flub the return but flub it with so much effort; and feeling that, I ceased to care, truly ceased to care about the winning or losing. I took a step away from the ball I had wooed with so much clumsy ardor, gripped my racket tightly, and released a pliant swing that sent the ball skimming over the net well out of Sid's reach. On Sid's next serve, I again measured my distance and stroked the ball with caressing indifference, delivering a hard, flat drive that nicked the foul line on the far side of Sid's motionless surprise. And that's the way it went: in a passion of disinterestedness, I won the game, the set, the day.

Sid was silent as we walked to the car. In the car he asked humorlessly what the hell had happened to me "—like from one second to the next?" I told him that I had discovered the key to myself, and Sid returned that I had discovered balls. He asked whether they were still charging six bucks for a half-hour. I smiled. It had already occurred to me that Sid would entertain no other explanation but this: a couple of secret lessons with a pro. For how else does a man improve? Like that? He buys his improvement from an expert, that's how. As for the first half-hour of play—probably the difficulty of putting into practice what I had been taught. I knew that much about Sid, and that's why our acquaintance had gone no further than it had.

"Frankly," I said to Sid, "I suddenly realized that you were not the man to beat. *I* was."

He nodded. I understood that nod. It meant: *shit!*

Then we were silent for a spell. I was feeling curious and antagonistic toward the man. It occurred to me that if he were another kind of human being, I might have talked to him at that moment.

"What do you do with your Sundays, Sid?" I asked.

30

"Watch football," he answered promptly. "Professional. I don't like college games."

"Really? Is there that much difference?"

"Hell, yes. They're two different sports."

I don't know why I didn't let it go at that. I *do* know why. I've always found these sport-fan refinements a strict pain in the ass. I know they're not supposed to be taken literally, but I guess what I dislike is the self-appointed expertise. So I told Sid to come off it, that there really wasn't that much difference—same rules, same uniforms, same running back and forth from the benches. Sid retorted that if that was all I knew about it there'd be no point in discussing it, and then we both sat ridiculously contemptuous of each other. How stupid to dislike a man for liking pro football! But it wasn't the pro football, it was his awful tightassed *rightness,* the finished quality of his universe! Well, Sid Simon was Sid Simon, and I would never like him. Thank goodness the tennis season was over.

"Maybe you're right," I said. "I guess if I were a real football enthusiast, I'd see it."

"Damn right!" he muttered.

We came to my house. I got out of the car and then leaned in through the open window to offer my hand to Sid. "All in all," I said, "you're the better player."

"We're about even," Sid replied, with autumnal grace.

So—the neutrality of Dodie's eyes; the art book room; the feeling of defeat; the feeling of victory. Reverse the order, scramble the order, but add to these ingredients the one other of a silent, empty house—which I did not mind. I'm far from being a loner. I think if I were absolutely certain that the island of my imaginary shipwreck would never contain another human being, I would find the courage to drown myself. But I don't mind short periods of solitude. Even frequent periods, but short. The sure knowledge of its termination is all the flavor of isolation to me.

I showered. I gathered the scattered sections of *The New York Times.* Then I went to the bedroom and stretched out comfortably on my bed. I began to read and very soon sleep gathered behind my eyes in a soft gray wave. Then—the dream:

It began in a house in which I had never been but had seen in Depression movies of fabulous wealth. There was a spacious foyer with a broad staircase to the right curving upward to the landing above. The man who approached me was not familiar, but I knew with a sudden sinking that his expression of sad concern was intended for me. The hand he put on my shoulder was a summons, and apprehension seized my heart. Without a word, we began to ascend the stately staircase. He kept his hand on my shoulder as we climbed the stairs, and despite the breadth of the staircase we crowded each other as he began to murmur consolatory words to me. Then we were in front of a door, a large door sectioned with lacunae. The doorknob was also large and deep and intricate in its chasing. I saw it so clearly. Still holding one hand on my shoulder (which, oddly, I saw rather than felt) and still murmuring consolatory words, the man reached for the doorknob and opened the door just sufficiently for me to see the scene that had been set.

Inside the room was a canopied bed. On the bed was Dodie, naked, knees drawn up and apart, receiving with dreaming ecstasy the energetic thrusts of the stranger who covered her. A dream cry clogged my throat, and I struggled in the dream against the dream, knowing in the dream that it was only a dream and that there would be an awakening. Dodie and the stranger heard my unuttered cry, and they both turned toward me, halting but still joined in their pleasure. Dodie's eyes were pitying, asking silently that the man beside me lead me away from the terrible sight. The naked man covering Dodie showed compassion, too, motioning me away from the door. This solicitude for my feeling was at once grotesque and moving. It was as if they were telling me that the horror of their act was not mine alone; they shared it with me. But that didn't end it. Dodie's partner resumed his fierce, concentrated pumping, and the man with his hand on my shoulder began to shut the door. The thought of having the scene closed off from me administered a jolt of dread worse than anything I had witnessed. I struggled toward a wakefulness that would rid me of

32

that anguish, still knowing it was only a dream, but still unable to relieve the pressure crushing my heart. Then all the tormenting scenery of the dream vanished and I was left blackly alone in a spaceless, timeless void whose eternal meaning was the scene I had just looked upon. I struggled upward suffocatingly, until with a hoarse cry that I could hear in the borderland between sleeping and waking, I awoke . . . gasping for air like a man who had in truth almost drowned.

With tremendous relief, yet still carrying shreds of that nightmare, I reconstituted the evidences of my life. There was my dresser; there Dodie's. There was the mirror before which Dodie applied her creams and cosmetics. There the silk-screened abstraction of the Japanese artist, the valet chair, the electric clock that informed me that I had been asleep for less than fifteen minutes. The sight of these things mixed with the air of consciousness, and I breathed it in like a solvent, washing it against the memory of that dream, crumbling the dream, dissolving the dream in reality.

I picked up the newspaper and tried to read again, but the shock of the dream had so quickened the pulse of my body that I couldn't give myself to the sense of the words. Even though I was steeped in the relief of knowing that the dream had been only a dream, a dog's snout of curiosity began to sniff back to the nightmare. With fear and fascination, I began to assemble the fragments: Dodie seen with a voyeur's eyes in the act of love; that strange aura of woe and venery; the tender regard for my feelings displayed by the dream cast that had occupied the underworld of my mind; and Dodie—Dodie—legs drawn up and apart—that entranced look—and shamefully, perversely, I began to feel the slow crawl of my own lust.

Disgusted, I threw the newspaper aside and got out of bed. I put on my robe and went downstairs to the kitchen. I looked into the refrigerator. There was half a meat loaf left over from last night's dinner. I made a sandwich and ate it standing, my butt against the pantry shelf, enveloped by the varied qualities of silence coming from each room of the empty house.

The space created as I dispelled the dream was filled with remorse. It was not yet three o'clock. There wasn't a prayer of seeing Dodie before five—more likely six. The hours stretched before
me like a desert. Never, not even in those aching weeks before
we became lovers, before I knew we would be husband and wife,
did I so long to see her. The dregs of that dream had produced a
contrition in me that I wanted to make known to her, because it
was every bit as true of me—more true!—than all the resentments
and recriminations that had come to encrust our lives.

But Dodie wouldn't be around for hours. Life and its lousy
logistics. The objects of our finest feelings are never around to
receive the benefits. If I had the car I would have gone driving
for a couple of hours. But I didn't have the car. Dodie had it.
What I needed was some unimportant, brainless activity that would
keep me occupied until she returned. So I set to work on a faulty
floor lamp, replaced and rewired the light bulb socket, and it
worked fine. I am not unhandy. I will let things go for months,
but then I will be seized by a domestic fever and I do not stop
until every shelf is steadied, every fixture fixed. But it was still
only four o'clock. Eons to go. I looked out the living room window and saw across the street a pyramid of brown leaves. Yes.
That. I would rake the leaves on my lawns, front and back, every
last one.

I went to the garage and found the rusty rake I had bought so
many years ago when Dodie and I had moved into our somewhat
old-fashioned but very nice Tudor-type, half-timber house, and I
had tended the lawns and shrubs and gutters and walks with a
city boy's rootless love of property. I have lost that love of property, but I still enjoy the house, the trees, the lawns. . . .

I began to rake the leaves on the front lawn. The fine day had
become overcast, and the leaves announced their death more
brownly than they had done in sunlight. I raked, beginning at the
edges and working in toward the center. When I had collected a
mound on the front lawn, I walked around to the back and began
there. It was my thought to transport the front lawn heap to the
back, and there I would ignite a smoky offering to the season. I

34

remembered reading somewhere that there was a city ordinance forbidding such fires. Or was that only at certain times? In certain places? Dodie would know. Dodie knew about such things. But hadn't I seen white columns of smoke rising that day? The hell with it. I would do it anyway, ordinance or no ordinance.

When I had finished raking the back, I went to the garage again and got the bushel basket. I filled it with leaves from the front lawn and carried it to the back, showering the contents over the mound I had collected there. All dry, these leaves. They would burn. I struck a match and started the fire. Then I returned to the front to collect the rest of the leaves—and there was Dodie standing on the front steps of the house, looking quite perfect in her white turtleneck sweater and tweed suit. I half-raised my arm in greeting, while my heart performed a surprised genuflection at the sight of her.

"I'm burning leaves," I said.

"I don't think you're supposed to," she said.

"I wondered about that," I said. "I'll take the chance. I like the smell."

"So do I," said Dodie.

"And how was Matisse?" I asked.

Dodie smiled, and again I was given to see the art book room, which was now corrected in memory to the right of the entrance. I saw the racks on which were displayed the buff-colored, gold-embossed books. I also saw—as though my previous visions had been only an untenanted set waiting for the performers who would animate it and give it meaning—the busy movements of people wandering among the racks, glancing up and down, and with a catch of recognition I understood that I was somehow involved in the scene, had probably arranged to meet Dodie there . . . and the Gersons? Or was it just Arthur Gerson? For it was he alone that I saw standing there, waiting. Of course I can't reconstruct the exact order of my vision, but I was certain that all of this was due to some previous arrangement, and even as my mind began fingering those fine adjustments of memory that would bring this time and these circumstances into focus, Dodie said, "It was

35

lovely!"—her voice soft with reverence—and then it came to me that I had never had a meeting with Arthur Gerson in that museum, or in any museum. This image, while mine, was not of my memory. And then I knew that Arthur Gerson was Dodie's lover, and that it was Dodie herself who had given me the information.

I did nothing. Oh, there was no question of what I had seen, what I knew, but I continued to smile at Dodie, a part of me still celebrating her sudden presence on the steps of our house. I knew that my dream had been more than a portent and that my life was changed, but I kept sealed off that nerve of acknowledgment for just a few more heartbeats, and then I looked down at the green grass combed ragged from my rake.

"And how is Arthur?" I asked.

Dodie had turned to the door and was reaching for the knob when I asked my question. A drop of my soul's gathering acid must have seeped into the scene, for I see Dodie's form and colors permanently etched into that soft gray dimensionless day.

5.

I awake to the odor of frying eggs. I get out of bed, put on my bathrobe, and then go to the window, peering between the lattices. The Palisades are a slag heap beneath a flannel sky.

"Good morning," I say.

"Good morning," says Kathy.

She is wearing a maroon shift of a style I believe is called Empire. Her hair is in its free-fall arrangement along the sides of her broad, healthy face, curving inward at the neck, curving again to the symmetry of her shoulders. I know that Kathy took with her from Vermont one average-size suitcase and a small kit, a vanity case of some kind. I don't recall her returning to the apartment with boxes and bags from the department stores. Yet I have seen her in so many different dresses, sweaters, skirts, blouses, handbags, shoes, belts, scarves, and what-not. All out of one suitcase? I do believe it. I believe that she, unlike me, has lived up to and into the moment she knew from birth could call for these mutabilities and economies. She is, all twenty-two years of her, a mystery as ancient as the temples of Sumer.

"Gee, these eggs are lousy," she says as we eat. "Cold storage. Don't they taste awful to you?"

"I guess I'm used to them," I say. "Were the eggs better at school?"

"You bet!"

"At home?"

"Mm-hm."

"I'll try another market," I say. Then: "Kathy, we must have a serious talk." I turn around and take a pack of cigarettes from an end table.

"You're not going to smoke, are you?" she asks, making a face.

"Do you mind?"

"I simply can't stand smoke when I'm eating. I'm sorry. Why do you smoke anyway? It's stupid. You know what it'll do to you. Don't you believe the stuff coming out of—you know—health agencies and places?"

"But smoking is my thing, Kathy. Isn't everybody supposed to do his thing? Don't you smoke pot?"

"Not anymore."

"Kathy, do you keep those things with you? Do you have them in your bag?"

"No, for God's sake. Do you want some? I can get you some."

"Kathy, we must have a serious talk. I won't smoke. You're of age, and therefore my responsibility concerning your actions is limited to conscience. I want to know one thing: are your parents looking for you?"

"Why should they be looking for me?" she retorts. "They know where I am. I told them I'm in New York. I told them I'm staying with a friend. They have an address where they can reach me."

"But money, Kathy?"

"I have."

"How much?"

"Plenty. Enough. Five hundred dollars."

"That's a lot of money. You shouldn't—"

"Traveler's checks," she says.

"What are you planning to do in New York, Kathy? Get a job?"

"Are you trying to tell me something?" she asks.

"No, I'm trying to get you to tell *me* something. Do you have any idea how long you'll be staying in New York?"

"No."

"Do you plan to finish your education?"

38

"Why all the questions?"

"Don't you think I should ask?" I ask.

"No," Kathy replies. "If you're feeling so paternal, you shouldn't have shacked up with me."

"Why did you shack up with me?"

She shrugs. "You had the place," she says. "I like you. I mean, I was feeling very passionate that night, coming into New York and everything. It was all very exciting, and when I get excited I like to finish in bed. What's the matter, are you trying to get rid of me?"

"You lied about your great-aunt, didn't you?" I say. "Saying that she was expecting you?"

"No, I didn't lie. Not exactly. She's always expecting me, more or less."

"Won't your father or mother be coming from St. Paul to check on you?"

Kathy sits in her enviable posture and regards me with unconcealed impatience. I find it extraordinary that this girl should have carried with her from Minnesota to Vermont, with God knows what experiments en route, this superbly wrought structure of muscle and bone. There's an incongruity here I can't quite fathom. I mean her good body, her physical principles, like a sacrament in a pagan festival. Sex and pot and lies and crazy involvements (me!) and safeguarding throughout the icon of her body. Well, what's wrong with that? I don't know. I guess there's nothing wrong with that, but to me it's strange. Health and discipline should go with socially approved habits—but whose society? whose approval? She blurs my distinctions. Where is she with her youth and the mysteries of her time? Where am I with the experience of mine? I look at her clean, dead-center line of scalp from which flows on either side her soft brown resilient hair. It frames her face like a narrow stage wherein her large eyes regard me with a selfhood so complete that I feel excised, as if by bloodless surgery, the soft tumor of sympathy that was waiting to grow. I am prepared to give my own problems absolute precedence. A rare thing!

39

She says, "I swear I don't know what it is with people like you, Dave. This concern about my parents. I'm an adult, for Christ sake! Don't Jews ever let their children go? Please don't get the wrong idea, that I'm taking after my father or anything, but I've noticed that my Jewish friends, their parents, it's like they never want their kids to come of *age!*" She shakes her head slowly. "My father and mother are not going to come running after me. My father is too busy, and my mother is too scared."

"Well, yours isn't a universal condition, Kathy," I point out to her. "Although I will admit that Jews are very reluctant to grant maturity to their children."

"Why is that?" Kathy asks.

"I'm not sure. A cultural pattern. How should I know? Well, as a matter of fact, I do know. Or think I know. I think the idea of independence was dangerous for so long that Jews got in the habit of denying it to their children."

"You're going to have a hell of a time denying it to Lenny," Kathy says.

"I have no intention of denying it to him," I say. "Has he ever said anything about that to you?"

She shakes her head.

"Do you know Lenny well?"

"I wouldn't say *well*. We're friends."

"I gathered that, but—well, never mind—listen, Kathy, I asked you something last night—you were on the point of falling asleep —look, would you really mind so much if I smoked?—tell you what, I'll sit over here, on the sofa, and you stay where you are— okay? . . . Now, I said last night, and you were probably asleep when I said it, that I would appreciate it if you would tell me exactly what you were thinking from time to time—"

"But I *do* tell you. I know you think I'm lying all the time—"

"No, Kathy, I don't. Things have happened to me—I won't go into them—but as a result of these things I've become very curious to find out if it's possible for two people to be together and reveal exactly what's on their minds."

"I always say what's on my mind," Kathy asserts.

40

"Oh, come on, Kathy, nobody does. Not always—and not *exactly*. What a person says is at best a compromise between what he's actually thinking and what he thinks it would be polite—or safe —to say."

Kathy, finished with her breakfast, abandons her perfect posture. She moves her chair a little distance from the table and sits crouched forward, her fingers interlaced just below her knees. She begins to perform what looks like a three-phase exercise with her shoulders—one hitch forward, two back. The stage of her hair has narrowed even further. I no longer have a full view of her eyes.

In an assumed voice she says, "Is that supposed to be a recondite idea?"

"Recondite?"

"Mr. Finlay," she says. "Comparative Lit: 'Is that supposed to be a recondite idea, Miss Willens?'"

"I see," I say. "No, it's not supposed to be a recondite idea— but an idea. Is that some sort of yogi thing you're doing?"

"An exercise," she says.

"Would you rather not discuss this with me?" I ask her.

"To tell you the truth, Dave, I don't know what you're getting at."

"Would you rather I didn't go on?"

"No, no—please do."

"Do you think it's funny?"

"A little."

"Why?"

"Because you're doing exactly what you were just saying. You're thinking one thing and saying another."

"What do you think I'm thinking?"

"You're probably thinking about Lenny. You're probably trying to find out something about him through me."

"And if I were? Would you tell me?"

"That depends."

"Kathy," I ask her, "why are you staying here?"

"I like you."

41

"You're lying. That's not why you're staying here."

"I *do* like you!"

"Maybe, but that's not why you're staying here. Why don't you stay with your boyfriend?"

"I can't. He's with two other boys. There isn't the room. . . . All right, Dave, I'm sorry. I was being smartass. Tell me what you want."

I hesitate. I think seriously of making her find other quarters. No doubt she thinks I'm a fool, a middle-aged fool, and while I may be, I won't have her using me for her purpose, whatever it is. But even as I think this, I lose the will to enforce it. My mind is too occupied with other things.

"All right," I say, "it's this: I thought that since you and I have nothing better to do at the moment, we might attempt this thing I'm talking about—that is, you telling me exactly what's on your mind from time to time. But there must be no resentment. . . . Tell you what, we'll make it a practical arrangement. I'll let you stay here. I'll even give you some spending money. It can't be a lot. Twenty dollars a week? Lunches, carfare, incidentals. Eventually, you'll have to find a job. I'm not a rich man. But while you're here, and in return for these favors, I'd like you to tell me what you're truly thinking when I ask."

"How will you know I'm not lying?" she asks.

"Well, I won't, of course. But why should you lie? Why should you *want* to lie?"

"All right," she says.

"You'll do it?"

"I'll try. Why do you want it, Dave?"

"I have no objection to telling you, but I'm afraid if I did tell you it would make you self-conscious to the point of invalidating the whole thing. I promise to tell you in time, but not now. All right?"

"All right."

6.

Kathy left the apartment that morning wearing her Eskimo-hooded coat. I didn't ask her how she intended to spend the long cold day. I'm not indifferent to her welfare, but, as I've said, my own concerns take precedence these days. By ten thirty I was in the subway, heading downtown.

This is not "my" city anymore. I've felt this for years, although I've prowled through streets hoping that some unconsumed enthusiasm would ignite at the sight of a recent change or an old recognition. As I ride in the subway this morning, I realize that the fault is at least as much mine as the city's. I haven't the room to take in the city as I once used to. I'm too full of myself. I'm as crowded as the city. We've dispossessed each other.

I should be concentrating on my visit to Rich—my business partner—former partner—former business—but I can't. Perhaps my father was right. Perhaps I shouldn't have sold out to Rich—Ted Buchholz, rather. Routine activity, responsibility, engagement. Perhaps. But did I have a choice? *I,* that is, not another man, but David Lang? I'm not superstitious, but I've always deferred to destiny when it took on the look of a well-organized, dynamic campaign. As it certainly did a month ago. I don't think it was a case of Rich wanting to push me out, or my finding Rich's ambitions wrong or sinister, but quite simply and inexorably the two parts coming together to form a critical mass.

Rich had been campaigning—I guess it must be almost a year now—first offhandedly and then with increasing point and pressure —to convert our business of supplying schools with educational film into something else. We had the facilities, and he wanted to go into TV commercials. He had used the company facilities to make a few such films for Ted Buchholz, whom I knew to be an account executive for some advertising agency. There was nothing underhanded about it. The firm was paid for the films. I had no doubt there'd be more money in commercial film, but the prospect didn't appeal to me at all. I knew I'd be no damn good at it. Rich would. He has the flair. And he was much hungrier for money than I was. I suppose I've known for a long time that Rich wasn't content with the natural limits of our business. He had hoped for much more when we both left our jobs at the magazine and set up in educational film.

It seems like another epoch when Rich worked as a staff photographer and I as a staff writer. It *was* another epoch. And now this epoch, the epoch of our twelve years together, reached its natural end on the Monday after the Sunday of the silent explosion on the lawn. When I arrived at the office the next day, Rich was waiting, his campaign turned up another notch. Then I knew I had to let go. With both hands. Everything. I offered my half of the business for sale. To Rich, if he wanted it, had the money. Or to anyone Rich would want for a partner. Ted Buchholz was waiting. He wanted, and could get the money. Rich tried to dissuade me from selling when he learned my reason, and he still tries to dissuade me, but the gesture is only a formality. Rich, too, has a proper respect for the critical mass.

This will be the first time in two weeks that I've been to the office. The last time was to meet with Ted Buchholz and Rich to "firm up the deal." I didn't think then and I don't think now that I could have taken daily doses of Ted Buchholz.

The building is a solid fifteen-story structure made to accommodate heavy equipment. There are several printing plants here, and companies that deal in industrial equipment. The vestibule is a sooty marble cavern, fumed for decades by tobacco and the no-nonsense talk of no-nonsense men. Beefy entrepreneurs and skilled workmen making high union wages. In one corner is a cigar stand—newspapers, candy, tobacco—the longtime location and live-lihood of Abe Brenner. Abe wears a tan workcoat in all seasons. In weather like this he wears a khaki-colored sweater beneath the workcoat and a khaki-colored forage cap on his bald head. He is lumpy, mustached, neither cheerful nor morose. He says good morning to his regulars, but he never smiles. Only nods. I know two things about Abe: many years ago he made a fortune running booze out of Canada, and then he lost the fortune staying out of jail after he was caught; now he is rapidly dying of cancer.

"Good morning, Mr. Lang," he greets me.

"Good morning, Abe."

He motions with his hand, and I approach. His blue, humid eyes reveal no more than they have ever revealed.

"I hear you're no more in the business," he says.

"That's right."

"I'm very sorry to hear that," he says. "You were always a gen-tleman to me."

"Thank you, Abe."

"I hope whatever you do, you have success."

"That's very nice of you. Thank you."

He looks away momentarily, at the yellowish marble of the hall, then back to me.

"So what are you going to do?"

I'm taken aback by the question, but then I realize why he has asked. Having none of his own, he wants a glimpse of another man's future.

"I don't know," I say. "I haven't decided yet."

He nods. "Well, good luck," he says.

"Good luck to you, Abe."

This should give me some perspective, but it doesn't. I'm sorry for Abe, but the termination of his days has no effect on mine. . . . *You should be glad you're not dying of cancer!* . . . Well, I am, I am glad—from Abe's stand to the elevator.

45

Like an extinguished light fading on the retina of my nerves, the paler tragedy of Mary, the stout switchboard girl, greets me as I enter my former place of business. She sees me come in, and all the life that has been unjustly imprisoned by the gross tyranny of her body condenses in her eyes. Naturally she knows something, and has guessed a great deal more, and her trained heart bays at the scent she catches from me.

"Oh, Mr. Lang—"

"Hello, Mary. Is Mr. Richards in?"

"Yes . . . I have some letters that came in just this morning for you."

"Thank you," I say, taking them and putting them in my pocket.

"We miss you so much," Mary laments, letting me know by her voice that I have upset the latest in the long series of her surrogate affairs.

"Well, thank you, Mary."

She bows her head. We understand each other. Then she signals Rich. "Mr. Lang is here," she mourns into the mouthpiece—and Rich is out of his office striding through the corridor, his glasses flashing a welcome. He is a master of so much, is Rich, that it shouldn't surprise me if he has miraculously found the perfect expression to greet my complex state. And indeed he has found it—a fine balance of fraternal good will and tolerant worldliness—and it does surprise me. Except for Rich—and one or two others I have known—I would have been prepared to make it my philosophy that life and the conditions on earth were hopelessly antagonistic. But Rich is proof to the contrary. He is, I think, happy. I'm looking at his clothes, however. I always take a quick inventory of Rich's ensemble at every meeting. It is part of his life-style to wear whatever takes his colorful, highly imaginative fancy. Not like me, who has learned to like the compromise in every well-seasoned fashion. Today Rich is wearing a pale green corduroy jacket, fawn-colored trousers, and a fawn-colored suede vest.

46

"Dave," he says, gripping my hand and drawing me toward his office.

"How are you, Rich?"

I have been to the office only twice since the silent explosion. I must have been in a state of shock that first time. No doubt about it—I was. I feel differently today. I feel as though I have suffered an illness which has impaired my faculties. I don't quite know how to regard these familiar carpets, walls, prints, doors, furniture, windows. . . .

"Just a minute," I say as we pass my office—former office. "Be with you in a minute."

"Sure."

I walk into my office. Nothing has changed. Why should it have? The "deal" hasn't been completed yet. Things might have reversed their course. I walk to the window and gaze out. There it is, my view of the river, the docks, the ships. I've had good thoughts at this window. Not the reeling ecstasies of youth but good thoughts of a milder kind—Dodie, Lenny, work, a space of years to do the things for which I had developed a preference rather than repeat the customs of outworn habit and pretense. I think I am feeling what Mary must have felt when she saw me come in a few minutes ago—betrayal. I walk out of the office and join Rich. We go to his office and sit down. His black eyes behind their heavy lenses examine me with medical care.

"Ted Buchholz isn't here," he says.

"Oh? All right. I wasn't really expecting him."

"Do you trust me?" Rich asks.

"You know the answer to that," I say, understanding that he is asking me to understand everything at once—the reason for his talking business first; the need for trust; the things that remain the same; the things that have changed.

"Fifty thousand," Rich says.

"That was the price agreed on," I say. "That is, Buchholz—"

"In cash," says Rich.

"I'll take a check," I say, as sober as Rich.

"Now," says Rich, "the whole deal almost fell through on the

47

next item. Ted's got some relative putting up half the dough. I don't know who this relative is—I don't want to know—that's strictly Ted's business—but whoever the sonofabitch is he balked —Ted balked—at the fifteen per cent. We said fifteen per cent, right?"

"That's what we said."

"That's what it's going to be," Rich asserts. "Fifteen per cent of earnings over the next three years."

"That's fine," I say, hoping that that will end the business talk.

But Rich is very eager for me to know the whole story. He says, "Ted said did I realize how much fifteen per cent could come to if this business grows the way he anticipates it will grow. I told him that's what he was paying for, the potential. I told him fifty thousand was *bubkiss,* and he knew it. We've got fifty thousand right on the books. I told him you were selling your *interest* in the business, not your investment. I told him it was fifteen per cent for three years, or he could forget it. I heard from him last night. He phoned me at home. It's a deal. Anytime you're ready, we can go over to Temko's office and sign the papers."

"Fine, Rich. That sounds eminently fair."

Rich leans toward me and puts his hand on my knee. I look at his wonderful ring, the one he bought in Rome. Also, I am stunned by the brilliance and fidelity of the image that slides into my mind: that October morning a month ago; the sun streaming through the window igniting Dodie's hair; my hand on Dodie's thigh. . . . *Was it only a month ago! That thigh and that woman I possessed so completely!—thought I did—flown out of my life, circling in another universe for all I know!* . . .

"Dave," Rich says to me, "I want it from you straight now— straight and for all time—is this deal satisfactory?"

"Yes, Rich."

"Do you want to go through with it?"

"Yes, Rich."

"There'll be no regrets?"

"None."

"Because it can still be called off," he persists. "We can still settle the future of this business between ourselves. Ted Buchholz means nothing to me. You and I are friends, and I pray God will remain so."

"Rich," I say, "you've done all that a friend can. More than I had a right to expect. You've helped me through this period, and I shall never be able to tell you how grateful I am. This thing you've arranged for me answers the need of my life. I want you to know that."

"All right," Rich says, leaning back in his chair. "Then it's settled." He draws in an audible breath and nods at me. He is now prepared for other matters. "What are you doing?" he asks.

"Doing?"

"With your days and nights?"

"Oh—nothing much. Sitting around in Ralph's place. Listening to music through a pair of five-hundred-dollar speakers. That's just the speakers. I have no idea how much the whole—"

"Have you been in touch with Dodie?"

"Why—no."

"Dodie with you?"

"No."

Naturally Rich was bound to ask about Dodie, but the sound of her name coming from my partner and friend—more friend now than partner—prods me in the way Abe's cancer must prod him from time to time with its reminding finger. Rich was the first person to hear it from me the first day after the silent explosion. He has the external picture of me that day. Mine is internal, fragmentary. I trust Rich completely in the matter of this sale, but I'm not so completely sure he knows how to guard the heap of shards I deposited that day in his strong, hairy, artist's hands. It makes me, for the first time in all the years I've known him, a little afraid of him.

"Have you talked to Gerson?" he asks.

That's what I mean, you see! He shouldn't have asked me that! He hasn't the right instincts about what not to say! The name "Gerson" is hot lead injected into a vein and sent boiling to the tiniest capillary!

49

I shall have to develop a system of defense.

"I haven't talked to him," I reply. "Do you think I should have?"

Rich shrugs.

"Visited him with a knife and drunk a beaker of his blood?"

"You're not a blood drinker," Rich says, quite rightly, lacing his fingers over his fawn-colored vest.

I look at his ring again, the one he bought in a Roman shop about five years ago. It's a heavy gold ring with a bas-relief of Perseus holding up the head of Medusa.

"No," I admit. "I'm not a blood drinker."

"Well, then, what's going to happen?" he asks. "Are you going to spend your time listening to music? Are you and Dodie going to get a divorce? . . . Look, my friend, I would advise you not to be a horse's ass. What's happened has happened. There may have been reasons. Maybe even you don't know."

"No doubt," I say. "But you're singing a different tune."

"I don't want you to make a bad mistake," Rich says.

"Everybody's marriage looks right until it blows apart," I say.

"That's a fact," he agrees.

"Besides," I say, beginning to feel sticky with holding the shitty end of the stick, "a little compensation has come my way. A big one, I should say."

Rich looks at me.

I'm immediately sorry I started it, but now I must go on. "An odd story," I say. "I won't go into it now. You know I went up to see Lenny a couple of weeks ago. I had company on my way back. We stayed at a hotel that night. The next day I phoned Ralph Friedman, and he let me have the key to his apartment. She's been with me since."

Rich rests his elbows on the arms of his chair. He doesn't speak, doesn't smile, just cocks his head skeptically.

"Well?" he finally says.

"Twenty-two years old and absolutely no argument with nature's promptings," I say, with a joylessness Rich could never guess.

"What's her name?" Rich asks.

50

"Kathy."

Now Rich smiles. He swivels back and forth a few times. "So what's she going to do, just live with you?"

"That seems to be the plan for the present."

"Mother? Father? School? Job? What?"

"They're mysterious, Rich, this younger generation. I can't fathom what she wants beyond food, shelter, and the doubtful benefits of my poor powers."

"Maybe you've underestimated your powers."

"Maybe I have."

He goes on regarding me from that new angle of appraisal. This was not at all what he expected. *"You're* singing a different tune," he says.

"Actually I had very little to do with it."

"You could have said no," he points out. "You ought to be careful."

"Of what?"

"Legal manholes."

"I never thought of that," I say. "But now that I am thinking of it, I couldn't care less."

"Then how about bringing your chick over one evening?" Rich suggests.

"Over where?"

"My place."

"Your place? Wouldn't Vanessa—?"

"Vanessa wouldn't," he says.

I look at my partner of more than a dozen years, this swarthy, fertile man whose sandstone "Christ" won first prize in a sculpture exhibit, and I sense for the first time the true Renaissance murmurs and movements behind his stylish façade. Neither of our lives are as we thought them to be.

"All right," I say.

"Shall we make it definite?"

"I'll be in touch," I say. "In a week or so . . . You'll let me know when we're to meet at Temko's office?"

51

"Goodbye, Mr. Lang." Mary waves from a small window in the massive fortress of her sorrow.

"Good luck, Mr. Lang," Abe calls from the sepulcher of his future.

Their lives are exactly what I think them to be.

I walk out into the street, and I am immediately set upon by a bruised, bristling, bloodshot disaster: "Hey—hey, mister—cudja spare—"

I have to take off a glove and unbutton my overcoat and search in my pockets. When I find no coins on my right side, I must take off my left glove and search on the left. I hear Dodie say, "Bums take one look at David, and they know they've got the right man." I find a quarter and give it to the man, because not to do so would be too cheap a gesture of defiance at Dodie. It was she who said that people were much more likely to give in absentmindedness than in compassion. Her analysis—and the bum's instincts—were right. I guess I've shelled out more often than most in an absentminded wish for privacy. The quickest way is to pay. But the quarter I parted with bought me no privileges. It brought me, for some reason, the full sulfurous flavor that followed the silent explosion on the lawn.

7.

I must go back to that fading afternoon when Dodie stood on the front doorsteps, her hand reaching for the doorknob. . . .

I don't know how much time elapsed between my question about Arthur Gerson and Dodie's opening of the door and entering the house. The scene doesn't so much slow down as play itself over and over, as though pleading a mechanical fault whose easy adjustment would undo a month of consequences. But I knew then as I know now that there would never be any adjusting. I have never confused men and machines. . . . A minute? No, far too long. Probably no more than five seconds. She looked at me, and on her face was a reflection of the contrition I had wished to make known to her an hour or so before. She looked at me and said nothing. She looked at me, and I saw her eyes grow large with the unknown thing looming before her. Then she went into the house.

I carried the basket and rake into the garage. From there I walked through the back garage door that connects to the kitchen. Why do these kids go for drugs the way they do? I offer my own life as evidence that the ordinary chances provide more than enough rare sensation. I couldn't hope to convey what I was feeling as I entered the dining room and saw Dodie there, arms folded, leaning against the embrasure of the window, looking out. Is it possible to feel stomach-sick and soul-excited? I was. I was quivering with the excitement of the abyss. Even one's first sexual experience is a series of movements, though the act has burned in the mind for years as a magical achievement. I knew what I knew, that sundering was possible, but I also knew that it would come about as sexual union had come about between Dodie and me—a step at a time. Whatever was to be, I knew I was entering on the first step, and there was such dreadful excitement in this that I gave no thought to the means of my discovery.

I say Dodie's arms were folded and that she leaned against the embrasure, looking out, or down, I'm not sure now, but intently— so intently that it seemed to me she was waiting for some oracular sign to appear. She was profile to me, but I could make out from the set of her face a state that was neither fear nor defiance but a regret so encompassing as to nullify all the lives around her, and most particularly her own. She didn't turn when she spoke. She wanted to know how I knew, and for some reason I asked her about Jean, Jean Ferguson, her museum companion, because I had in my head a picture of Jean Ferguson leaning into my car and smiling her pretty, too-ready smile. But that wasn't Jean leaning into my car, that was *me,* leaning into Sid's car. Jean had never leaned into my car and smiled at me that way. There had never been anything in our silly banter to account for that smile. My brain had heated up. Terminals of memory were fusing in that heat.

Dodie said, "It's not what you think."

"What do I think?" I asked.

"What I suppose you have a right to think," she replied, still not turning. "David, we've been apart for so long. We haven't been able to talk. Arthur is an intelligent and understanding man. You know that."

Blood rushed to my head and sprayed red horror behind my eyes, around the inside of my skull. *Was it possible! Had Dodie said what she said! Could this howling platitude be happening to both of us!*

"Who knows that!" I roared, voice cracking. "My God! My

God, my God! That you could be capable of mouthing such sickening shit! *Understanding!* That cold-blooded bastard!"

"Stop it, David!"

"Yes. You're right. I'm sorry. There's no reason for that."

"Who told you?" she asked again.

"Told me what?"

"About Arthur."

"I thought you were going to the museum with Jean Ferguson."

"I did," Dodie said, glancing at me. "Did she tell you?"

"How could you think so? If she was so likely to betray you, why would you have trusted her?"

"Oh, David, *trusted!* Then who?"

"Is it so important to know?"

"Wouldn't you be curious?" she asked.

"Are you asking me how I'd feel if the situation were reversed?"

"Why won't you tell me?"

"But what's the difference, Dodie? I mean, if you were only meeting Arthur because we haven't been able to talk—because he is such an intelligent and understanding man?"

Poor Dodie! It had only been a reflex of defense, an arm thrown up against the heavy, implacable thing coming at her. I saw the wrecking ball of my knowledge pass through all her hasty constructions, sending frail lies spinning in slow-motion devastation. What could she say but that my dark source had already documented its falsehood? How could she qualify her museum meetings—museum meetings?—and other meetings?—where?—when?—that she didn't know, of course, at what other incriminating times and places the treacherous ghost might have been present.

"David—" she said in a low voice, and everything was confessed, everything was known.

Did I then turn around and walk out of the house? Did I then go to Dodie and strike the face that had lied to me God knows how many times?—that had smiled a different greeting to another man? No, I didn't leave. I didn't strike. I remained where I was—a distance of fifteen feet, I would judge—and watched myself being slowly incinerated.

55

I said, "Am I supposed to ask you if you're in love with Arthur?"

"You know yourself that love—" she began.

"—is not a simple thing," I finished for her. "Yes, I know."

I was more than a little afraid of what she might say. I knew what I could endure, and I was afraid that Dodie's words in their incaution might detonate another horrible explosion. I walked into the living room and opened the cigarette box on the table. There was one cigarette, stale, it crepitated between my fingers, but I lighted it. It burned my tongue. My hands were freezing, and long shivers coursed through my bowels. This house, *my* house, *our* house, had become invested with a new significance. Dodie—*my* Dodie!—had walked from room to room saying nothing or discussing household matters while thinking and remembering other things. Secret head! Capacious head! And my life, which only yesterday had seemed so completely spoken for, had drawn up before a black blankness making all that was past changed and all that was future unpredictable. And even in this there was excitement, although I knew I was sentenced to be hammered by one iron truth.

While all of this was happening to me—the excitement, the reality, the unreality—it came to me that this was the sort of thing that had happened to so many people, people that I knew, a commonplace of the age, and therefore I must bring to it reason as well as feeling. I must be intelligent (like Arthur?) and behave in a way that would not damage my claim to being civilized. After all, we do not own each other.

Did I believe that? Yes, I did . . . *but I was in hellfire! Fuck your civilization!*

"How could you do this to me, Dodie!"

There was blood in that cry. A hemorrhage. This woman had lived with me for more than two decades. The reflexes of concern continue. She turned at last, but her gesture stopped short of approaching me. Her limbs were as unpracticed as mine in the motions of crisis.

But those were the limbs that had wrapped themselves around

Arthur Gerson! Willingly! Receivingly! In unknown and forever
unknowable accommodations of passion!

I swallowed fire.

"Do you love Arthur?" I asked, coming back to the question
I had leaped away from, terrified of it, yet more terrified of the
shapes it would take if left to gestate in the dark.

Dodie again folded her arms and resumed her position at the
window. "Do you think I could have done something like this without feeling?" she replied.

"Shall I take that as meaning you are in love with him?"

"One gets involved."

"Dodie, for the sake of my sanity, I beg you please not to use
words like *one* and *involved*. You're having an affair with Arthur,
right?"

"Yes."

"Do you love him?"

"I don't know."

"You don't know? You went to bed with the man not knowing
whether you were in love with him or not?"

She raised her eyes from the sill and looked desperately out
the window. "David," she said, "I know how you feel, but I'm not
going to submit to an inquisition. I respect your feeling. Please
respect mine."

"Respect, Dodie? *Respect!*"

"Please don't yell. You know what I mean."

"How long, Dodie? How long? When did it begin?"

"Oh, David, how do I know? How is it possible to know when
something like that began?"

Indeed it is not possible to know when something like that
began. Have I not myself looked at other women whom I found
attractive and in a few seconds projected an affair down to the
last disintegrating meeting at some bar or restaurant where, all
considered, the grief, the guilt, the secret knowledge that the zest
of difference had become the disappointment of routine, I would
decide, between one remark and the next, that it must end, that it
must never begin? There could have been beginnings for me, but

there never were. Nor did I detect at the time any beginning in the scene that suddenly opened up in my mind, breathtakingly vivid in detail:

. . . A theater lobby. An overhanging cloud of cigarette smoke caught in the draft created by the opened doors and swept back into the theater. I am standing with Rita Gerson and—two others —Rich and Vanessa, of course. And there, standing apart, are Dodie and Arthur. The tide of people coming out of the theater during intermission had broken Dodie and Arthur away from the rest of us. I see Arthur raising his hand in mock surrender. People do get separated in theater lobbies—and make their way back if they are so minded—or stay separated if that suits them. . . .

This scene had never come to me before. Never. Oh, it had been *witnessed,* all right—I had been there—but this particular scene had never nudged at my mind, begging recognition. But now that it had come to me, I recall the population of heads between me and them, myself catching glimpses of Dodie and Arthur intermittently as people shifted about. I remember now how I was drawn to Arthur's face continually, heeding for the first time those qualities in him which might be attractive to a woman. And I remember now how I wondered then why it was that I had never paused to consider what men in general, or man in particular, my Dodie might find attractive. And I remember now dismissing that wonder, because for all our fights and for all our differences I couldn't conceive of another man as a possible alternative. My arrangement with fate didn't include that eventuality. Failure, yes; even death; but not that common rejection . . . And this theater scene, when was that? Two years ago? No, that was only last year, last winter. . . .

"A year, Dodie?" I asked.

That brought her around to me again. "What do you mean?"

I said nothing. I could see the puzzlement in her eyes. It was last year, of course. She knew exactly when it began, or why would that lobby scene have come to her? And from her to me? . . . *Was that what was happening?*

"David—"

"Yes?"

"Why don't you answer me?"

"I'm sorry. What did you ask me?"

"I asked you what made you say a year?"

"Nothing *made* me say it. I picked a figure out of the air. Do I happen to be right?"

"I told you I don't know."

"Yes, that's what you told me."

"Don't you believe me?"

I turned away from her and sat down on the sofa. No, I didn't believe her, but I also wished not to continue this futility. I wished, in fact, to be away from Dodie, in another room, out of the house, so that I could better assess what was happening. It occurred to me for the first time that I might be going out of my mind. The onset of madness doesn't announce itself in obvious ways. But if mad, then perhaps none of this was happening. Perhaps there would still be an awakening. But no, neither dreams nor madness would allow for the terribly clear perspectives in my head. The twenty-three years of my life with Dodie were with me. My futureless future was with me. These are the props of awareness and sanity.

Somehow the evening passed. I think I sat on the sofa for three hours, tranced, a throw pillow in my hands, staring across the room at the bookshelves. I would single out a book—*Anna Karenina,* I recall, for nice coincidence, and what I remembered, of all things was that Anna's husband's ears stuck out. Dodie prepared a dinner which neither of us ate.

"Is this what it's going to be?" she asked. "The silent treatment?"

"No," I said. "I just can't manage words right now. I hope you can understand that."

"What will you do?" she asked.

"What will *you* do?" I asked.

"I don't know," she said.

"Neither do I."

Later Dodie went upstairs. I could hear the rush of water in the tub. I wondered if—if today—if I could, would, spend my days construing horror in every action.

59

8.

Think of all the medallions and statuettes carried in American cars. And the number of people who believe in the stars. An acquaintance of mine, the president of a small college, confessed to me a belief in transmigration. I suppose no one is completely free of superstition. What I thought was my enlightenment only drove my fears underground. I rejected ladders, broken mirrors, cards, and the zodiac, but I fully expect misfortune to come orchestrated in symphonic form, three movements usually, an interrelation of themes, a coda, a conclusion. Good fortune is less formalized, but when I sense ascendency I look forward to all letters, telegrams, telephone calls, and knocks on the door. I distrusted, ultimately, my fate as a businessman, but when Rich appeared in my life I immediately saw in him a factor powerful enough to cancel my negative factor while constantly increasing the value of his positive one. I have always been contemptuous of the cruder forms of magic, but miracle I regard as a necessary human agency—the parting of the seas; the burning bush; visions; the prophetic element in dreams.

The art book room that appeared so vividly to me when Dodie spoke the word "museum" was not in itself remarkable. My mind has a tendency to store wayward emblems. "Theater," for example, is neither play, stage, nor playhouse, but a roast chestnut stand between Broadway and Eighth, the vendor shifting from foot to

60

foot, breathing warmth into his coal-blackened hands. "Football" is the Spuyten Duyvil Bridge as seen from Baker Field, where Princeton eternally beats Columbia by the score of 27–14. That is why I didn't regard it as sinister or weird when the image of the art book room leapt so immediately to mind. Nor was I made suspicious by the reappearance of that image throughout the day.

The dream? The dream was a dream. I have had many frightening dreams in my life, and the one of Dodie in sexual embrace with a stranger (another stranger's hand upon my shoulder) had the right retributive touch for sacking out in the middle of the day. My daylight dreams have always been populated by demons. I suppose another of my underground fears is that it is sinful to sleep when the sun is out. And that Sunday had in it a melancholy to match the melancholy that had come into our lives, Dodie's and mine, part of which was the growing irregularity of sex; that is, the slow, steady encroachment of reasons not to have sex—disinclination; a fight; a general malaise; the precurse blues. After all, there are only four weeks in the month. Cancel one and work the syndrome of indisposition on either side of that week, and you find celibacy becoming a habit.

Fool! Idiot! Couldn't I have guessed!

No, not even now, with everything black on white, do I feel myself guilty of willful blindness. The wind simply didn't blow from that quarter. I had thought that Dodie was waiting for a return of better conditions. I had thought that her energies were being drained in the struggle to find a different purchase in our marriage. I had thought *she* was trying to work her way to a new regard. I had thought—no, I hadn't thought that day—my thinking had been done previously. That day had begun color-cured against decay by the seasonal flame, and I had succumbed to my usual infatuation. Dodie with a glowing aureole around her head, the art book room, tennis, my dream, the lawn . . .

If you have ever experienced a revelation for which your entire past has left you unprepared, you will know what I mean. You cannot believe that the reasonable fate that has guarded you all the years could have failed to drop some clue in the second before

61

zero. You scour the ground for evidence of a device that triggered the explosion. A wire, a fragment . . . I go back to the sun streaming through the dining room window. Dodie announcing her intended visit to the museum with Jean Ferguson as companion. Did she tell me that? Yes, she told me that. That is, on Sunday she told me that, but I must take her word for it that she had announced it earlier in the week. I don't remember. Not with Arthur Gerson—that name wasn't mentioned—with Jean Ferguson . . . *"And how was Matisse?"* . . . *"It was lovely!"* . . . On the doorstep, her hand reaching for the doorknob, Dodie had said, "It was lovely!"—and when she had said that, looking quite perfect in her white turtleneck sweater and tweed suit, I saw Arthur Gerson standing beside one of those display racks in the art book room. He was smiling a smile I may or may not have seen on his face before. I'm not sure about that. I couldn't swear to that. But I could swear that if it had been *I,* not Dodie, who was walking toward him, hand outstretched, a smile of mild surprise on *my* face, then that particular smile would never have been on *his* face. No, if I had been walking toward Arthur Gerson, the angle of his smile would have altered a degree or two to express the somewhat qualified, the somewhat sardonic friendliness that marked his relations with David Lang.

So it seemed to me that it was not the Arthur Gerson of my experience or memory who stood in the art book room, waiting. Whose, then? There was that day only Dodie standing on the steps of the house . . . *"And how was Matisse?"* . . . *"It was lovely!"* . . . hand reaching for the doorknob, looking at me when I asked the question that came naturally to a mind which was drawing its last free breath before giving over to the invader who had been advancing, out of sight and out of hearing, through the concealing terrain of an autumn day, to encamp, all points taken, in the center of my life.

9.

What we did, Dodie and I, was to "give it a chance." She said that since neither of us knew what to do, why didn't we leave things as they were and wait to see what we felt like when the shock wore off. I agreed to that because, to be sickeningly truthful about it, I couldn't bear the thought of Dodie being free, of her *freedom,* a fiery pit into which my imagination would fall, naked and alive.

I continued to stay, in Lenny's room. His room was exactly as he had left it when he went off to school in September. Amid encyclopedias and blow-ups of the mythic dead (W. C. Fields gimlet-eyed over a scallop of cards; Marilyn Monroe offering sex and innocence in one moist dream; Malcolm X looking like a new age of prophecy), I learned insomnia. I had acted on the assumption that desire for Dodie would be dead. The past, the present, the sorrow, the stress—sure depressants. That I could have believed such lunacy! A room away, her movements in my ears, her betrayal became a conflagration in my blood. Dodie with her fright and remorse inflamed old lusts. She was still Dodie (more so since another man had possessed her)—green-eyed, heavy-lipped, long and leggy. I thought of her thinking her thoughts, and I nearly went mad knowing they were not of me. I constructed scenes of a meeting (the voyeur again!) between Dodie and Arthur, and while my soul perished, my sex led an insane life of its own. I lay in my son's bed and thought of the life that Dodie and I had created, a life that even now, I felt sure, would exact from us a priority above all others. That was special torment, thoughts of Lenny. A deeper outrage smoldered in me when I thought that the body I had seeded with our one child had sought pleasure with another man. It went through me like a sword. Pathetic? Medieval? Go back much further. Something ancient and Hebraic rose up in me, and the landscape of my life was dense with the smoke of great abjurings. I wore myself out with visions—thoughts upon thoughts upon thoughts.

During that first week, I found sleep by clawing at the fabric of my mind until I had worn a hole in it and could stare at a black, starless infinity of indifference.

We settled into old routines. What other routines did we know? Had I belted Dodie in the jaw, ran roaring from the house to seek out my enemy and destroy him, ended Dodie's life and my own with two bullets at close range, done anything that a different instinct would have compelled, I would have wrenched my fate out of one domination and into another. I see now that the great attraction of violence is the speed with which it effects a change of state. Obviously you've got to feel the need for that kind of speed. Obviously I didn't. And there was still that other thing demanding explanation. We fell into old routines, but each contact was a set piece framed in a pulsing, bruise-lavender fluorescence.

"I leave that to you," I said to Dodie, referring to the form request for funds from a political action group we had contributed to in the past.

"Why leave it to me?" she said, patiently, cautiously, tiredly. "If you don't want to support it, we'll drop it."

"It doesn't have to be my contribution," I pointed out. "If you want to support it, support it."

"But it *is* a matter of money," she said.

"Principle, I thought."

64

"Well, principle *and* money. That's exactly what I mean. If it were a matter of necessity, like buying a new car—"

"Do we need a new car?"

"No, we don't need a new car, David. Don't deliberately misunderstand me. I wish you would tell me what it is you object to."

"I don't *object*. I just don't give a damn one way or the other."

"In that case—" she said.

"You won't?"

"Certainly not, if you don't give a damn. Is it true that you don't give a damn?"

"Is it true that you do?" I asked her.

She looked at me in the scared, uncertain, scrutinizing way she had developed in the past week, and as she looked at me I looked elsewhere: I looked at that different time, that other place, that suddenly remembered occasion which assembled itself before me so sharply and securely that I had no fear of losing a detail of it even as we spoke. . . .

"Why do you ask me that?" Dodie asked, turning her eyes from me, looking down at the table.

"No reason. I just wonder—"

. . . Tough scrubby vegetation growing out of the soft gray sand, a surprising stretch of it extending across a desertlike trough that rose immediately to another row of dunes in the distance. Beyond that, hidden from view, the ocean . . .

"If you're going to question my sincerity in everything—" Dodie said.

. . . An overcast day. Gray light, gray sand, somber purity of vision. The Cape. The second summer with the Gersons. We had driven to Provincetown—Dodie, me, Arthur, and Rita—and had bought Portuguese bread and small tins of imported tuna and ham and cheese for just such a poetic picnic on these elegiac dunes . . .

"You haven't always been so committed," I said to Dodie.

"I'm not *so* committed now," Dodie returned. "If you remember, it was originally your idea, sending a check."

"Yes," I admitted. "Originally it was my idea—"

65

. . . The dunes were situated a little south of Provincetown as one drove on the main road. Arthur sat cross-legged, a position he could manage with his boyish slenderness, his rubbery loose-jointedness. We discovered we had brought no knife, and we had to manage by breaking open chunks of bread and stuffing the ham, the cheese, the tuna, into the dough. How clear it was! Like one of those foreign films—French or Swedish—where drama is grained into the very texture of the scene . . .

"—but as I remember," I went on to Dodie, "you didn't even know at the time of my original contribution what the initials of the organization stood for, much less their program."

. . . The riots that summer, that's what started it. We'd heard reports on the radio. Of course it was understandable, overdue, but what good would it all do? Doomed to failure. Terribly sad. But Arthur didn't think so. He said that naturally nobody wanted a slaughter of the innocents, but in history's eyes every dead Negro was worth a decade of sentimental garbage. That shocked me, hearing Arthur express so cold-blooded a view; and even while I prepared to oppose it, arranging in my mind an order of argument I had used once against the ugly rationale of trading lives for historical advantage, I noticed Dodie's eyes and the ghost of a smile, a smile that at first I seemed to recognize as her gesture of resignation in the face of one of those lead-heavy, masculine arguments, but which dawned on me a little later as a smile of familiarity, of complicity, a greeting to something she had heard before, at another time, under other circumstances. . . .

"At the time I probably didn't know what the initials stood for," Dodie said.

"But since then," I said, "you've seen a light. A gray, Cape Cod light."

We had been sitting at the dining room table, our traditional corner for household matters. Dodie got up from her chair and went into the kitchen. I could see her from where I sat, her back to me, her hands resting on the edge of the sink. Then she turned around and faced me. Wretchedness had scooped dark hollows

66

beneath her eyes, but her pale jade irises glowed with an undersea light.

"What did I say?" she asked, her voice slurring.

"Say?"

"Just now, David. In these last few seconds."

"You said that sending a check was originally—"

"Did I mention Cape Cod?"

"No."

Now her voice rose, fracturing in flight: *"David, did you hear me say anything about Cape Cod?"*

"No."

"Then why did you say that just now? Why did you bring up Cape Cod? Did I say anything, David?"

"About Cape Cod? No."

"Are you lying to me? Am I saying things I don't realize?"

"Dodie, I don't know what you think you're saying. I only know what you say."

"Why did you mention Cape Cod?"

"It came to mind."

"Why?"

"We were there this summer."

"I haven't seen or spoken to Arthur this week," Dodie said. "Do you believe that?"

"Yes."

"Then why are you tormenting me? We agreed to try."

"I am trying."

"What's happening, David?" she cried, coming toward me from the kitchen. "If you want to give this a fair chance, then please stop what you're doing."

Then stop thinking! I wanted to thunder at her—but didn't.

I knew I had to get out.

10.

I did. Get out. I bought a secondhand sport car. Swedish. Red. I bought it, I think, because it was the last thing in the world those who knew me would expect of me. And I drove toward Vermont and my son.

There was a look of snow in the thick overcast. Despite everything, I was conscious of the novelty of my ecclesiastical little Volvo, all red and black. The sticks, the pedals, the clock-faced indicators. I understood with freshness of insight why youngsters so preferred the sport car. That appetite for exclusiveness (*my* friend, *my* dog, *my* car) is better satisfied in such compact seclusion.

I like to drive. I don't mean just the business of holding a wheel in my hands and pressing the accelerator under my foot. I mean the sense of suspension it gives me. Particularly when there are hours involved. Although I wasn't able to suspend my thoughts on that trip, I did manage to relax my spirits a bit. In my untypical sport car, I was able to get out of the centrifuge which held me pressed against the wall of my whirling life. The first thing I saw was that once out I would never get back in. The second thing I saw was where I was. I was a man in his late forties whose marriage and life had just exploded. That sounds dramatic, and if one were writing a play I suppose there'd be the necessity of finding lines that would reverberate with the explosion. That's what I was doing in my little foreign car—trying to find lines that would echo with all the things that had happened to me. But I couldn't find such lines, because the only thing that saved the hallucinated history of the past two weeks from total disbelief was the fact of its happening. I had it all securely locked in my head—from the art book room to this northbound view on the Thruway—but that gave me no clue. I was not the man I thought I was, nor was I yet the man I would eventually become. I was simply the man to whom it had all happened, scene by scene, including those scenes that were not my own.

It actually did begin to snow when I reached the Vermont line. It began so abruptly that it seemed as though it were being offered like a local product along with the maple syrup and the cheese. I drove more slowly. The windshield wipers packed spongy ice in the outside quadrant of their sweep. More than once I felt a treacherous sideslip, even with snow tires. Impatient motorists, probably more used to these conditions than I, gunned past, spitting a contemptuous swath on my windshield. Suddenly the deluge ceased. There was a premonitory brightness, then another plunge of darkness, and then the sun clashed like cymbals on the white landscape.

I arrived in the college town in sunlight, drove through it and beyond to the motel at which Dodie and I had stayed when we visited Lenny in his freshman year. He was a junior now. I found the motel and checked in. The man remembered me.

"You musta hit that storm," he said.

"Sure did."

"There'll be another."

"Oh?"

"Yessir. Wind's still from the south. Gonna do some skiing?"

"No. I've come to visit my son."

"Ah-ha. Wife with you?"

"No—she's recovering from a minor operation."

"Eh-heh. That's too bad. Hope she's all right. Then you'll be wanting a single room?"

69

"Yes. Single will do fine."

As soon as I was in my room, I phoned Lenny. He was living in a private boardinghouse, sharing a room with another student. Miraculously, he was in.

"How are you, Lenny?"

"Dad? I'm fine. How are you? How's Mom?"

"We're both fine."

"Are you calling from your office?"

"No."

"You home?"

"No."

Lenny's hesitation came through from the other end. Members of the same family calculate in terms of experience rather than logic. Two such "no's" from his father narrowed a world of possibilities to remarkably few alternatives for Leonard Lang.

"Where are you?" he asked, his attention drawing in several hundred miles.

"The Clear Acres Motel."

"What Clear Acres Motel?"

"The one about three miles from where you are."

More calculation. His voice was unhurried. "Mom with you?" he asked.

"No, she isn't."

"Anything the matter?" he asked.

"Nothing's the matter. I had to see a client in Albany, and I decided to keep going. Is this inconvenient? I know you had exams coming up."

"Of course it isn't inconvenient," Lenny said. "Why didn't Mom come with you?"

"How could she come with me if I didn't know I was coming myself?"

"Oh . . . yes . . . well, why did you go to a motel? You could have come straight here."

"I wanted a place to sleep, in case I stayed overnight," I explained.

70

"For crying out loud, Dad, were you planning to go *back* tonight?"

"I wasn't planning anything, Lenny."

"Well, you could sleep here, in my room."

"But you have that boy rooming with you—what's his name?—Bob—"

"Rohrmoser."

"Rohrmoser."

"Bob can sack in anywhere. You know that."

"I didn't know that," I said. "What's the difference, Lenny? Are we going to talk accommodations all day? I wish you would tell me if this is all a nuisance."

"I'm glad you're here, Dad," Lenny said. "You just took me by surprise, that's all. I don't understand why you went to a motel if you're by yourself. But okay. Do you want me to come over there, or do you want to come over here?"

"I'll come over there. And you're quite sure I'm not lousing up any plans?"

"Cut it out," Lenny said, with that terrible patience he can sometimes get into his voice.

"All right," I said. "Expect me in a half-hour."

I love my son. I realize it would be impossible for anyone to believe in my objectivity, but for what it's worth I offer my conviction that Lenny is a very admirable young man. He is physically attractive, and he has a good mind. In recent years, I have come to discern the outlines of his personality. It's a strong one. It surprises me how strong it is. And cool. Different from my own, I must confess. And while I'm confessing, let me say that in the process of getting to love my son I was able to make out, at not too great a distance, those junctures where the process might have failed. If the process might have failed with me, I'm certain it did fail with others. Other fathers, I mean. I'm a man much inclined to love his son. It will shock no one these days to suggest that there are men who aren't.

In my drive from the motel to the college, I tried to reach back

71

and find significant stages of that love. Dodie claims she can remember just how Lenny looked, talked, acted, dressed, at all ages. I wonder if that can be so. If it is, then her mind is indeed different from my own. Frankly, I don't see how it's possible. Oh, I too can pick out scenes here and here—winter scenes, summer scenes—Lenny in a swimsuit, Lenny in a snowsuit—but these scenes are flat and distant. They are not sensible to my mind's touch. I recall that each time I tried to recall, my memory was overpowered by the latest Lenny, whenever that was. Five years obliterated infancy; ten obliterated five; and twenty with its height, hair, acne (disappearing), and above all its sudden, absolute, accumulated *privacy* stands a six-foot-one witness against these tender incarnations. Yet I am left with two decades' worth of loving. I cannot recall the stages, but I am left with the accumulation.

Lenny is, as I've said, tall. I don't know why I never expected to be overtopped by my son, considering Dodie's height as well as my own, but the fact is that I didn't. Since late high school, whenever I would try to engage his eyes with my own, he would look away. I don't mind his being taller than me, but sometimes I think he thinks he's done a disrespectful thing. Perhaps that's what's behind it. I'm not sure. He's tall, and he has shoulders from here to there, and he has just enough meat to cover that large, lateral bonework, not a milligram more. His hair is brown, abundant, with glints of copper, a gift from his mother. He has also had for some time two rosebuds of acne in the hollow of each cheek. From a distance, it looks like a blush. Two years ago, it was much more extensive. It's disappearing, thank goodness. There's a concavity to Lenny, and a downward directed attention, as though he were only partially committed to human exchanges—or perhaps exchanges just with me. But he listens, and there's nothing sloppy or pretentious about his mind. He will tell whatever it is I wish to know, but little else, and rarely does he tell me anything without being asked. I don't know why this should be so. I have treated him with love and intelligence—qualities, I had always assumed, that made for openness.

How wrong the theories are.

72

Lenny

11.

Lenny Lang stood at the window of his room and looked out at the school library situated at the other end of the campus area. Light from within the library defined the alternate sections of stone and glass. He visualized the students cramming away in there, each one a huddle of limbs and books. The seasonal agony. He thought of his own upcoming exams, and he felt secure.

It had snowed intermittently during the morning, then cleared in the afternoon. Now, late afternoon, it was snowing again. The very weather he had hoped for. The white fall covered the dead grass and concrete walks—and would be adding to the depth on the slopes, where there'd be no skiing for him this weekend, Lenny definitely concluded. Which was a disappointment. He'd been looking forward to skiing this weekend, but with his father on the way over . . .

The phone call had scared him, coming as it did from the Clear Acres Motel, that sometimes shack haven for college couples. What the hell was his father doing there anyway? That was the place his mother and father had stayed when they visited him during his freshman year. It wasn't like his father to come this way. It would have been much more like his father to have phoned from Albany to announce his coming. Not that David Lang opposed surprises—at times he was full of them—but not the kind that might turn out to be an imposition.

"I hate the kind of pest who just drops in!"

No, it would have been much more like his father to have phoned first. Unless something was wrong. *Was* something wrong? Someone sick? Dead? One of his grandparents? But a phone call from home would have taken care of that. His mother? Something insidious and creeping they had held off telling him about, until it was no longer possible to keep it from the only child of a dying woman? . . . *Cancer?*

Lenny turned quickly away from the window. He listened inwardly to the sound of his father's voice as it came to him over the phone a little while ago, and he knew that his mother was all right. Whatever it was, it was not that. He had interpreted too many vibrations in his father's voice not to be able to define limits. He could never be sure exactly what those vibrations meant, but he could be pretty sure what they did *not* mean.

He glanced at his watch. If his father came soon, they could get away to dinner before Bob came banging in. The combination of David Lang and Bob Rohrmoser made Lenny uneasy. Not that his father was embarrassing out of his age group. On the contrary, he was *too* good. David Lang gave out with a special obligingness and a special wit in the presence of his son's friends. There was, however, just one thing wrong with that father-of-the-year act: it was an *act*. His friends laughed, thought Mr. Lang very amusing, but always there was the slightly sour aftertaste, the lingering sense of phoniness. His father came on strong with his friends, but Lenny knew that that spontaneity was for his sake, for the sake of the son of David Lang, and not for the sake of David Lang's irrepressible self. David Lang was not a natural clown or a born character. That was the sad thing.

Lenny heard the door signal clatter below. He strode quickly out of the room, took the stairs two at a time, and swung open the heavy door with the lace curtain.

"Hi."

"Hello," said his father.

"Come on in."

76

His father scraped his shoes on the mat, looking at what Lenny knew he would look at, in the way Lenny had anticipated he would look at it.

"So," said his father, "you had to have your share of hair."

Lenny smiled. He just managed not to put his fingers to his mustache, but he was very conscious of it, silky, new-fledged. He was proud of the character it had taken, a distinctive Stephen Crane drape at the ends. It was ragged without being raunchy.

"My room's up here," Lenny said.

They mounted the steps, Lenny in front, his father behind. Lenny carried with him the image of his father as he had appeared in the doorway, and his sense of the particular increased. David Lang looked very much himself with his customary Harris tweed and his haggard-healthy look. That look always made it difficult for Lenny to tell when and how much trouble might be oppressing his father. Right now, Lenny guessed at trouble of some sort. Not the eyes but the mouth, whose smile hadn't quite surfaced to gladness.

The door to Lenny's room stood ajar, and Lenny motioned his father in. This was the first time his father would be seeing the new place. Lenny had lived in the dorm as freshman and sophomore. Now, a junior, he had put in with Bob Rohrmoser in this private house. It was a big, old-fashioned room with a high ceiling, hardwood floor, and a big silver radiator sizzling in one corner. Mrs. Martin, a divorced woman with two grown children living in other cities, managed a scrupulously clean house, four boarders, and a long affair with a member of the German department with no sense of discrepancy. Discreet herself, she asked no less of the college men under her roof. What the boys did was all right with her providing they kept it their business, not hers, and not the town's. But the clean chenille covers, the two maple dressers, the two small writing tables, the leather armchair, everything, in short, contributed to an atmosphere of traditional New England propriety.

"Very nice," David said. "Are you comfortable here?"

"Sure."

"Do you get along with this Bob Rohrmoser?"

"Oh, sure. He's okay. You'll probably meet him. I think you'll like him. Why don't you take that armchair, Dad. I'll hang your coat away."

"And when did you grow that thing?" his father asked.

"Began in September, when I got here," Lenny replied. "Does it bother you?"

"No, it doesn't bother me at all," David said, with a little smile. "It's fine. If you like it. Do you?"

"Yes."

"Why?"

Lenny shrugged. "I don't know," he said. "It's natural. Hair grows on your face, you let it grow."

"Then why not a beard?"

"Maybe I'll grow that, too . . . no, I won't grow a beard. I don't know. You sort of experiment with things."

"Masculinity?" asked David.

"Maybe," said Lenny.

"All right," the father sighed. "It's good to see you anyway. You've got exams coming up, haven't you?"

"Yes."

"Prepared?"

"I think so."

David nodded, looking round the room, his gaze coming to rest on the photograph on Lenny's dresser. Lenny followed his father's gaze and joined him in looking at the color photograph, the one taken on the front lawn of the house, with his father standing hands in pockets, and his mother reaching out toward a blaze of pink azaleas.

"How's Mom?" Lenny asked.

"She's fine."

"How come she didn't come with you?"

His father turned his eyes back to him. "That's about the third time you've asked me that, Lenny. I told you I was seeing someone in Albany. How could she come with me if I didn't know I was coming myself?"

78

"Oh, yes. I forgot."

"Have you been doing much skiing?"

"Just started, really," Lenny answered. "There hasn't been much on the slopes till recently."

"I hope you're being careful."

"Yes, indeed . . . Who'd you see in Albany?"

"Someone on the school board," David answered, looking toward the window. Lenny, sitting on the edge of Bob's bed, thought he caught in his father's manner the flat quality that marked certain moods, moods that had their roots in ground other than the one he seemed to be treading with such patience. "Incidentally," David went on, "I'm selling out my half of the business to Rich"—David broke off and grimaced—"I don't know why I keep saying Rich—not Rich, actually—a fellow by the name of Buchholz—Ted Buchholz."

"Selling out?" Lenny said with surprise, grasping that *this* was the matter, or part of it. "No kidding? Why'd you do that for?"

"Conflict of interest," his father answered promptly. "Not that Rich and I weren't getting along. He saw an opportunity to convert the business into something more profitable, and he was quite right. It's just that it wouldn't have been right for me. At any rate, I don't want you worrying. I get a sizable amount of money on the sale, and more to come over the next few years. So all foreseeable needs will be taken care of."

Lenny nodded slowly. "I'm not worried," he said, and wasn't, not about family funds. But selling out? What would his father do? Go back to the magazines? Write another novel? "You got some other business in mind?" Lenny asked. His father shook his head, saying, "No, not at this time," and Lenny knew that selling out was indeed only part of it, because his father had proclaimed more times than he probably remembered that God, before His abdication, had performed one last minor miracle in providing for David Lang. That business, with Rich as partner. A perfect life solution. For reasons too far off for instant recognition, Lenny's attentiveness sharpened.

"Is that why you came up here?" he asked.

79

"Is what why I came up here?"

"To tell me that?"

"Not exactly. But it is of family interest, isn't it?"

"Yes, it is," Lenny said. "Then why'd you have to see a client in Albany if you've sold out?"

Lenny watched the faint, prideful smile come over his father's face. Jesus! Would he ever get over the amazement that his own flesh and blood had a brain? Five years ago, he could take his father in chess, but the elder Lang still went on celebrating symptoms of intelligence in his son. And it wasn't only the intelligence that floored his father, but the different *kind* of intelligence. As though he couldn't believe that he had contributed to nature's variety.

"My selling out didn't relieve me of all—" began David, stopping at the crash below.

"Bob—" Lenny said, as thunder rolled up the stairs, and in another second Bob had flung open the door like some goddam character in a biblical play. Job or somebody, all whiskers and doom.

"That prick! That infinite prick of infinite misery!"

"Bob—" Lenny said, indicating.

Bob looked, and saw, but he was too far gone in his rush for any checks.

"Donovan!" he croaked. "Five fucking essay-type questions on a fucking one-hour exam! I *mean!* Explain Skinner's *Behaviorism* briefly—*briefly!*"

"This is my father, Bob," Lenny said.

"Pleased to meetcha," Bob said, shaking hands. "Sorry about the language. We just got butchered in psych."

David nodded, smiled. "I'm sorry to hear that," he said. "But I'm sure you passed."

"Thanks. I hope so. If I don't get my average up, I'll be ass-deep in the rice paddies of Vietnam."

Bob and his dramatics. Lenny could see that his father had already taken to Bob. Everybody took to Bob. You couldn't attribute any of the really depressing aspects of life to such a face.

80

Round, a nubby nose, nubby cheeks, and a coppery outcropping of beard that looked ready to give off sparks.

"Say, you know," Bob suddenly burst out, "I read your novel, Mr. Lang. The one about the war. *Another Sky,* wasn't that the name? I really liked it. I mean, you know, given the time and the subject and everything. The part that knocked me out was that bit about the Canadian Air Force girl—"

"Oh, God!" Lenny murmured.

"—telling the guy she charged for a shack job."

"Why don't you sit down?" Lenny suggested. "Or fall down. Or something."

Bob grinned. He was wearing old-fashioned galoshes, open, and the tops flowered like great black petals. "Do you mind my saying that?" he asked.

"No, I don't mind," David said.

"I'm impetuous," explained Bob. "Ask Lenny."

"Ask me," Lenny confirmed sorrowfully.

"Anyway, it was a good job, that book."

"Thank you," said David.

Bob turned to Lenny. "Hey, how come you didn't tell me your father was coming?"

"This was a surprise visit," David explained.

"Well, great," Bob said. "You can stay here, Mr. Lang. I can sack in with somebody else."

"That won't be necessary," David said. "Look, Lenny, why don't you get some of your friends together, and we'll all go to dinner. This will be my party. Bob? You'll join us, won't you? And anyone else you'd like to have along. Girls, if they're available. I wouldn't in the least mind the company of girls."

"You sure you want to do that?" Lenny asked, skeptical of the time and the occasion. "Aren't you tired?"

"Not a bit," his father replied.

"Hey, great!" Bob encouraged. "We can ask Mike."

"Who's Mike?" David asked.

"Mike Talbot," Lenny said. "A friend."

"Mike is welcome."

81

"Vera?" Bob offered again.

Lenny shrugged.

"Is Vera your girlfriend?" David asked Bob.

"Sort of . . . How about Kathy?"

Lenny was waiting for it, and there it was, that careful indifference, that pussyfooting, nonprying, mouse-trapping *casualness*.

"Is Kathy *your* girlfriend?" his father asked.

"No, Kathy is not my girlfriend," Lenny replied. "She's just a friend."

"Well, Kathy is welcome, whoever she is."

"That's five," said Lenny. "That's plenty. Dad, are you sure you want to take that many people to dinner?"

"Positive."

12.

The car gave another turn to Lenny's attention. It was parked at the curb in front of the house when he, his father, and Bob came out into the cold, snow-cushioned night. Lenny glanced at it impersonally, not connecting it with his father at all, a nice red foreign job with a powdering of snow on the roof and hood. Desire gave Lenny's heart a little pat. Behind it, lights on, wipers swinging, was Vera's fat old Buick.

"How do you like it?" came unexpectedly from his father.

"Like what?" Lenny asked.

"The car," his father said, pointing.

"That? Is that yours?"

His father said that it was, that it was his not by rental but by purchase, and Lenny felt the same nameless discomfort and guilt that always came over him whenever his father would reach out and cup the back of his neck in his hand, bringing his reluctant head against the fatherly shoulder.

As they walked to Vera's car (David had warned that they all couldn't go in his car, that it was too small, and Lenny had previsioned some skimpy orphan of the rental lots, pale coffee in color, unbeauteous in every detail, not because his father had no taste but because it had always been his father's attitude to be contemptuous of style in cars), Lenny knew that there must be circumstances to explain that car; some recent spasm of elation or despair. That was not David Lang's car. Not naturally. David Lang was a swinger in principle, but in practice he was as conservative as a clock.

Mike Talbot was already waiting for them in the back seat. The girls had picked him up on the way over. Lenny and Bob got in beside Mike, leaving David to share the front seat with the girls. Introductions were made in the car. The girls said how nice it was of Mr. Lang to invite them to dinner, they did appreciate it, and David Lang allowed that the pleasure was his, and Lenny's senses puzzled over the mingled perfumes, his father, the visit, the car, heading out to dinner with such unaccountable elements.

"Anybody know where we're going?" Vera asked as she moved the car away from the curb.

"How about the inn?" suggested Kathy.

"Hell, no," said Bob. "They start zapping you with the Vermont death-ray look at nine thirty over there."

"How about The Powder Horn?" Mike suggested.

"Isn't that kind of expensive?" Kathy said.

David spoke up: "My son probably kept from you the fact that his father is a very rich man. I've recently sold my oil holdings, so The Powder Horn doesn't frighten me in the least."

The girls laughed. Lenny looked at the back of his father's head, pleased with the way he'd handled that. That was good Lang vintage. That's the way it usually began. The beginnings were always best, because they had the benefit of surprise and David Lang's curious half-British, half-New York accent. Lenny wondered for the thousandth time where his father had ever picked it up.

"Ear! If you have an ear you don't have to carry around dialects the whole of your life."

Maybe—but then you were stuck with whatever you made for yourself, and what his father had made for himself was distinctive all right, and hard to locate, and just because of that it had a faint taint of the fake. Like one of those old Shakespearian actors. Voice training.

Lenny made a sharp inward turn away from his own critical thoughts, and the instant reaction was a flood of feeling tasting of

84

the ocean bed of his life. He turned away from that too, and listened to Bob's cantering account of a student committee session with the vice-chancellor in charge of admissions. The vice-chancellor had agreed to the committee's program for black student recruitment, pending, of course, approval of the Board. "Big deal," Mike remarked, undisguised in his scorn. Lenny hoped that Mike wouldn't come down too hard on Bob. Mike had no use for the committee, considered it a collection of hand-picked finks. Not that Bob was a fink, but he just didn't see that all the talking had changed nothing and *would* change nothing. In a way, Bob was like his father: he believed in the mystical value of talk. If you went on talking long enough, you would wake up one morning with all necessary changes accomplished and all differences reconciled. Which was strictly bullshit. Real changes made people uncomfortable, and as long as people remained comfortable you could be sure there were no important changes coming about.

Brought back to his father, Lenny again experienced that familiar time-brewed taste of his own beginning. He didn't know why, but every time he was drawn back his mind touched in passing that green wool sweater his mother had knit for him when he was five or six. She had knit many sweaters for him, but that's the one that had trapped in its weave the flavor of the past. And with the sweater would always come the memory of snow and a sled and his father pulling him along over a dazzle of white, the sun a bright somnolence in his eyes. Just that—sweater, sled, snow, sun—and he was one million golden years into prehistory.

He had revealed to no one his earliest memories, not even to Marie, to whom he loved to bring favors of reminiscence because her eyes ate them like candy. It was neither vagueness nor embarrassment that prevented him from sharing these secrets, but a feeling of sacred privacy that exposure would profane. Like the push-pedal fire engine he had wanted so badly and which had appeared one morning in a splash of holy light on the living room floor. Paintings of the Christ child with their radiant centers subsequently reminded him of that miraculous morning. And the countless mornings and afternoons riding the car seat beside his mother. The smell of her, the intense smell and feel of her as she had lifted him in and lifted him out, had saddled him into the shopping carts and rode him through the cookie canyons. Was there enough silt in the years ahead to cover *that?* The hills of home had bright green and red labels, and the floor of earth was loomed of nylon twist.

Whenever he made that brief inward trip (something in the nature of the journey always assured its brevity), he would come away with a consciousness encircled by two equators. His mother and his father. The radiation from each was the same, although one was a steady emanation and the other pulsed in irregular flares. He was loved, all right. Memory went back through geological layers of it, and if it went back far enough the two equators merged into one band of brightness.

It was when he moved up that the separation occurred. It was when he moved up still further that his love-heated planet cooled and the crust formed and the features showed. It was a teeming world of school and seashore summers and indoor winters and Scrooge and *The Nutcracker Suite* and Macy's and Thanksgiving and the amazing city that bedecked itself once a year. They had stored this inventory in order to give him the universe a piece at a time. And they, too, were having it again by having it with him. Of course he had never made that distinction at the time, but later he knew it to be true.

It seemed as though it would never end, but it did. Abruptly. Not that there were no more things, but it was no longer they who could give them to him. Suddenly he didn't want it from them. Suddenly the value of a thing, anything, consisted solely in discovering it for himself. Or with a friend. In one way or another, each in his own way, they gave him his freedom in a way that was not freedom. They wanted to *share* his discoveries, his freedom, to talk about the music and the hair and the heroes—and it was all so hopeless, because it was only information to them, and for him it was the beginning of history.

He had learned how to protect himself from love.

86

The Powder Horn was five miles out of town on a snowy road. Vera drove sanely for a change, skidding only once. The rear end of the car slewed around to the right, but Vera drove on without touching the brake. No comment. From anyone. The headlights carved a tunnel of light into the darkness. Snowflakes rushed at the windshield. The wipers brushed them away with metronomic patience. Twenty-five years ago the restaurant probably had an authentic flavor. Now it looked as if some interior decorator had tracked down in the shops of New York just the right artifacts for a rural restaurant. Early American, every stick. Crossed sabers and rotting flintlocks on the wall. They checked their coats. Lenny noticed his father survey the amplitude of thigh exposed by Kathy and Vera in the miniskirts. A black bow tie found them a table.

David Lang asked his young companions what they would like to drink, and Mike was the first to inform him that he would have nothing, thank you, because he had no intention of going through the Vermont nonsense of producing his ID card. "*Streng verboten* in Vermont, Mr. Lang, under twenty-one."

"Well, in that case I don't have to have liquor either," David said.

"That's ridiculous," Kathy protested. "You had a long drive from New York. I don't see why you should be deprived."

"And you?" David asked her. "Are you also below the drinking age?"

Kathy leaned toward him confidentially. She said, "Just between us, I'm trying to keep my status with the younger set."

The rest were under twenty-one. David yielded and ordered a scotch and soda. The others ordered soft drinks, except Mike, who ordered nothing. When the drinks were brought, David lifted his glass and proposed a toast to all their futures. It wasn't exactly a silly thing to do, but Lenny felt embarrassed. He glanced at Mike, who was showing his teeth in an amused grin.

Mike wore metal-frame eyeglasses and wrested "A's" in almost all his courses with fang and claw. He went to this "dumb little middle-class seminary" because it was the first one to come through with a full tuition scholarship. Mike not only needed but insisted on every gratuity the world had going. A matter of principle. Mike Talbot was clever and caustic and uncompromising to the point of lunacy, and there were plenty who hated him for it. Bob Rohrmoser made it a masochistic point of honor to let himself be tormented by Mike. Lenny Lang made it an intellectual point of honor to befriend and defend Mike's abrasiveness.

But Mike's smile had made Lenny apprehensive.

The girls kept up the small chatter needful to the occasion. Conversation was naturally limited when a parent was present. So Vera asked Mr. Lang where he had gone to college, and did he find schools very much different these days? Mr. Lang replied that he really didn't know if colleges were different these days. He assumed they were from what he read, but that visiting schools, for him, was a matter of walking round and round the ivied walls, peering into halls and rooms, but knowing no more about the spirit within than an Australian bushman.

A waitress came to take their orders. Then Kathy remarked how envious she was of the Langs, living right *in* New York. "Not *in* New York," David corrected her. "Long Island." Kathy said that was close enough. She was mad about New York, had an aunt living there, would be going there shortly for the Christmas holiday, was looking forward to *that*.

"Don't you love it, Mr. Lang?"

"I don't know," David confessed. "I do and I don't. Certainly I did love it at one time, but it's changed so much. I've tried to accustom myself to the changes, but I don't think I've been successful."

"Don't you like changes, Mr. Lang?" Mike Talbot asked.

"Yes, I like changes," David answered pleasantly. "I like changes that bring about an improvement, changes that make things better."

"What's 'better'?" Mike asked.

"Oh, I don't know. Don't you think the great majority of people would agree on what's better? Clean streets are better than dirty streets, wouldn't you say?"

88

"Maybe," Mike said, "as a matter of hygiene. But as a step in the leveling process, it might be better to have all the streets crapped up for a change."

Lenny observed the change of expression on his father's face as his father became aware of Mike Talbot. David Lang did not like Mike Talbot, as, Lenny now realized, it was inevitable that he should not. For Mike was one of those chrome-plated, surgical personalities that the father of Lenny Lang so despised. There was a covert little flush of satisfaction in this for Lenny, because he had never been a match for his father's verbal quickness, and Mike was. That was the advantage that had compelled so many silences in Lenny where his father was concerned—that quick and easy assembly of words. And even that wouldn't have bothered Lenny so much if his father hadn't used the facility to demonstrate that the old man wasn't going to be so easy to put down. A game. Scoring points. And after the points were scored, his father would try to get at what was really on his mind, and that was when Lenny was least inclined to tell him.

His eyes fixed on the Coke glass before him, Lenny heard his father say, "I can't see that that's a particularly useful symbol. I'd much rather have the bad areas improved—as I'm sure the people living in the bad areas would too."

"Well, Mr. Lang," Mike said, glints of debating fire showing in his white teeth, his glasses, "I'm *not* so sure."

Lenny felt a tentative touch on the toe of his shoe. Another. He glanced up. Kathy was looking at him, her wide eyes pantomiming alarm at what looked to be an impending Talbot bombing raid. Lenny dropped his gaze.

"Really?" said his father. "How so?"

Another two taps on Lenny's shoe, signaling stand-by alert. He was both grateful and annoyed—grateful that the rescue operation was on hand if needed, annoyed at Kathy's continued mothering since their period in the sack had ended. That was almost six months ago, for Christ sake! He wished she'd forget it. She owed him nothing.

"Well, look at it this way, Mr. Lang," Mike said. "When you've got an infection, you don't want to keep putting on local dressings forever. You want it out. You want the thing lanced and the pus running."

"Mike," Kathy put in, "you are the absolute world's winner when it comes to pleasant table talk. Do you think we could change the subject?"

"Sure," Mike said cheerfully. "How about homes and gardens?"

Lenny glanced at his father and saw scorings in the pale flesh that neither Mike Talbot nor mere time could have put there. With a shock, Lenny saw the deepness of his father's nervous exhaustion, and he was confirmed at last in his suspicion of some profound change. He reached out with his mind, but he couldn't as yet make out the dimensions of the sudden recess he had discovered in the retaining wall of his life.

13.

They drove to the ski area the next morning. Lenny proposed it—for the ride, the scenery—and his father agreed. This was after breakfast, after his father had driven over from the Clear Acres Motel. Despite Bob Rohrmoser's repeated offers to "sack in elsewhere," his father had insisted on returning to his motel after dinner. Lenny was aware how badly his father wanted and needed privacy. Fatigue had eaten into his face like chemicals on film. After that exchange with Mike, his father had kept up conversation with obvious effort, nodding, smiling, putting in a question now and then, but in no way his usual self. This was David Lang in withdrawal, beat.

Although he did look somewhat better as they had breakfast in the drugstore, at the counter. His face was shaved, composed, redolent of his customary after-shave lotion, but the eyes were still punishingly marked, and from time to time he would narrow his lids, as if even these anemic fluorescents were inadmissibly bright.

"You feeling okay?" Lenny had asked.

"Oh, yes," his father had replied. "A little tired, perhaps. These last few months have been hectic. But I'm fine."

Lenny didn't believe he was fine at all. He was convinced now that his father was never further from fine, and that the trouble was located where he first suspected it to be located. The domestic scene. Mother and father. The long murmurs behind closed doors. Silences whose bulk and weight he could calculate with the expertness of an old postal clerk. Talk that was set down word by word, like bricks, until the two of them were effectually sealed off from each other. All that hiding and decorum for his sake, of course. Everything was for the best in the best of all possible etceteras. Therefore he never knew what was really bothering them. Sex? No love? Boredom?

Lenny mused on these things as he turned his father's astonishingly unlikely little foreign job into the road leading to the ski slopes. "How come such an un-Langish job?" he had asked when his father had handed him the keys and said, "You drive." His father had replied, "Maybe you're out of touch with what's Langish these days."

Maybe. Very possible. The truth, the sad truth, was that he wasn't very interested. Whose fault? His? Theirs? No one's, of course. He loved them, all right. They were the single band of brightness and the double equator of his beginning. And they loved him! But despite the love, he had only to turn his thoughts in their direction to feel his arms pinioned and his lungs taking in the narcotic air of that tranced world where people sat around and talked while Lee Harvey Oswald's bullet passed right through them and left them still talking about plays and books and art and progress and *The New York Times*. His mother and father were part of that world, and to understand them he would have to understand that world, and he couldn't because he just couldn't stay with it long enough to get interested, and whatever lack of love or trouble with sex they might be having, that trouble was somehow rooted in that tranced world.

As they passed beneath a rust-colored, jagged cliff of granite, his father said, "Do you like this boy, Mike Talbot?"

"Yes," Lenny replied, "I like him. He goes too far sometimes, but he's sharp."

"Yes, he is," said his father. "Cuttingly."

"He's not your type, is he?" Lenny said.

"No," his father admitted. "I've known such boys at one time

92

or another in my life, and I must admit I've never liked them. We used to play a game called 'King of the Hill.' The idea was to push off all comers and hold the top at whatever cost. A hot and pointless game. It seems to me your friend, Mike, plays king of the intellectual ice hill. His game is cold and pointless."

"Mike does have that effect on people," Lenny said.

"Then why doesn't he have that effect on you?"

"Because I don't think his game is pointless."

"I see. Well, perhaps you're right."

Lenny was about to say something else, but his father had turned away and was gazing out the car window. They came to that sudden retreat in the hills, and the sun blazed on a meadow of new snow. Lenny glanced and saw his father shade his eyes with his hand. His father had no sunglasses. He was wearing a business suit and his raglan overcoat, and Lenny with his down jacket and ski goggles felt remorse lodge in his throat like a bone.

"What's the matter, Dad?" he asked.

His father turned his head, looking straight ahead, narrowing his eyes.

"Things haven't been going well between Mother and me."

A flat truck piled hugely with sawn logs swayed toward them on the narrow road. Lenny jockeyed the little car along the far right edge of the road. He wished this moment of reprieve would last indefinitely. He felt an old familiar guilt and resentment. It was comparable to the feeling he experienced when some teacher announced a surprise quiz. . . . "The material has been covered." . . . The material, indeed, had been covered.

"I know," he said.

"You do?"

"I know there's no great happiness."

"You're not the first to tell me that," his father said. "Apparently there are none so blind. But I am surprised. I didn't think that the absence of great happiness could be taken as the presence of great unhappiness."

"It wasn't that," Lenny said.

"What was it, then?"

Lenny didn't know what it was. How could you process ten thousand seconds and drop an answer in one?

"I don't know, Dad."

Out of the corner of his eye, Lenny caught his father's slow nod, which he took to be a sign of the father's acknowledgment of the son's latest defection. A voice spoke to Lenny: *"Give, give endlessly, but for God's sake don't ask for five cents' worth of recompense, because when you do you'll be told, 'I don't know.'"*

His stomach tightened. He said, "You lived such separate lives."

"Separate?"

"I mean, you walked around in the same house, you talked, you ate at the same table, but you never seemed to be sharing anything."

Again Lenny spied the nod.

"And did we share anything with you?" his father asked.

"Aw, come on, Dad—"

"No, no wait," his father interrupted him. "Since you've brought up this subject of sharing, let's talk about it. I know how popular it is with your set to think of its parents as having lived in a perpetual night of noncommunication, but that's crap, Lenny. We shared, all right, at least as much as children are willing to share with their parents. Let me tell you something—"

What David Lang wished to tell, Lenny Lang already knew. "Your invisible room . . ." his father said. How he had stored everything away in his invisible room. All the distinctions and judgments and likes and dislikes of his developing life . . . "It was *you* who walked through the rooms of your house," his father accused him. "*You* who opened the refrigerator, watched TV, said good morning and good night, discussed finances, and were terribly shocked—I remember this well—you were terribly shocked when President Kennedy was murdered, but of what you were really feeling you said nothing. And there was no lack of interest, Lenny. You were asked. God knows how many times you were asked, but all I or your mother ever got was a shrug, or a mumble, or a sigh of impatience. And you make accusations about communication! I remember that time you came home puking sick from that nice suburban boys and girls party. We took a drive the next day, if you remember. . . ."

Oh, he did remember! He remembered that drive very well! The god-awful make-believe of his father talking to him about sex. It was as if his father had taken him into his bedroom and opened drawers in which were collected old condoms, pro kits, and dirty pictures. It wasn't supposed to be that way. It was straight and se- rious and—God knows!—well-intentioned, but that's the way it came out. Maybe it was because it was too late. Maybe it was be- cause he knew all these things. Maybe it was because his father had come on too strong about being a father and not strong enough about being a man. And so he had sat in the old station wagon on that rainy day listening to his father go on about sex and drugs while the insistent rain was slashed left and right by the insistent wipers, remembering the plastic odor he had breathed perma- nently into his blood stream that first time when the car was new and he had been sandwiched between his mother and father as they drove somewhere upstate in autumn to buy bittersweet and preserves and a pumpkin, which of course he had selected.

"I remember," he murmured.

"Yes, I'm sure you do," said his father. "I don't know, Lenny. Perhaps you were too young. Perhaps I was saying the wrong things, but I have tried, many times, to have that talk with you. After all, I'm not my father. I'm not Grandpa Sam. I've read widely. I've even written, as you know. I've left myself open to ideas. I thought surely we would sit down one day and have that talk, you and I, but it hasn't happened. There's no getting away from the fact that it hasn't happened. Never once did you tell me why you made the choices that you did, what it was you loved and what it was you hated. Perhaps you told your mother, but not me."

"I couldn't," Lenny said. "Neither you nor Mom."

"And *why,* may I ask? Is it that you found us so stupid, so narrow?"

Lenny shook his head. He wished his father would drop these

95

stale hypocrisies. This endless digging for praise and validation. Both of them—his mother as well. No, they weren't stupid or narrow, and they knew it. They were clever and sophisticated. And he wished now that he had given sympathy—and no more! Just said how sorry he was and let it go at that. Because he did feel sorry, and sympathetic. There was a great ball of it in him. Then why was he also angry? Here, for the first time in his life, his father was making a direct plea for his sympathy, his understanding, and he felt *angry!* Why?

"Did you ever tell me?" he asked.

"Tell you what?"

"About *your* invisible room. About what you loved and hated. You told me things you thought it would be good for me to know. The truth I had to find out for myself."

"What truth?"

"Well, for one thing, the truth of what a lousy marriage you and Mom had."

"And when did you discover that?"

"I don't know. A long time ago, I guess. Look, Dad, I'm awfully sorry about what's happened. Really I am."

"But I'd like to know when you made that discovery," his father insisted. "Or if not when, then how."

"I wouldn't know how to explain it," Lenny said.

"Try. You do quite well on explanations when you put your mind to it."

"That deadness," Lenny said.

"Deadness?"

"I mean that deadness between you and Mom. *That's* been going on for a long time."

"I must take your word for that, Lenny. I wouldn't have thought so. God knows things weren't perfect between us, but I never would have described the situation as dead . . . *deadness!*"

"Well, okay—you're probably right about that," Lenny said quickly, thinking he saw a way to extricate himself. "My choice in words is never the best."

It was awful. Everything he said came back to him with a cold,

uncaring ring. And he didn't feel that way. He didn't! He wanted
to give his father the truth, because this was one time he felt sure
that the truth was exactly what his father craved; but each time
he touched what he thought was the truth it fragmented, fell into
pieces. What he should do was shut up. Cut his losses. Right now.
But he knew he couldn't shut up, and he knew why. His father
was asking for a very small payment on a very large bill.

He said, "You say I never told you what I loved and what I
hated. Do you realize that I couldn't? I never learned *how* to from
you—or Mom. Things weren't to be loved or hated, that's the impression I got all my life. You didn't love or hate, you just understood, and that's bullshit, Dad. The world is full of things to be
loved and hated, but I could never find out from you or Mom
what those things were. There was always this side and that side
to everything. I never really found out what you felt, and so I
never could get to know you as people. As parents, yes, but not
as people. And that's why I don't know how to feel about what
you've told me. I don't know who to blame and who to feel sorry
for."

"Good God, Lenny, I didn't tell you this for the sake of partiality! I don't want you taking sides! What surprises me, what
hurts me, is that you seem to feel nothing."

"But that's not so," Lenny returned. "I feel rotten! I know that
if anything happens—a separation, a divorce—I know how lonely
you'll both be. Do you think that makes no difference to me?"

And somehow that too was not the right thing to say. Lenny
could see from his father's profile that he still hadn't said the right
thing. He was indeed sorry, but it was not the intimate family
sorrow his father had been looking for. Nor had he explained
the other thing well at all. The trouble was that he couldn't use
the words he would have to use to tell the truth as he saw the
truth. Such words would sound stupid and pretentious, and worst
of all they'd be pointlessly hurtful. He couldn't use that one encompassing word—*passion*. He couldn't say—what a hell of a thing
it would be for him to say!—that he'd found no passion in their
lives. Not against injustice, not for a better world, not for each
other—but only for him—only for him!—*only for him!*

97

14.

The ski lodge was crowded. Several rows of chairs faced the picture window which gave out on the final run where all the slopes converged. Lenny would have liked his father to sit there and see the action, but all the seats were taken. They went to the cafeteria for coffee, and when they returned to the main room there were a couple of vacant seats. They watched the skiers.

"Is it difficult?" David asked.

"Not very," Lenny replied. "No more difficult than ice skating. Easier, I think. You'd have no trouble with it. You've got good reflexes, and you're in good shape."

"For my age?" David asked, smiling.

"For any age."

"Somehow I don't think I'd survive," David said. "What's the essential trick?"

"Balance," Lenny informed his father.

He went on to explain the skills and joys of skiing. He realized his father had shifted their talk to other grounds because the first had been so full of land mines. Lenny would have liked to retract it all, to wipe out that half-hour from both their minds and give his father what he had come to Vermont to find.

Even as he talked about skiing, another part of his mind went over their conversation in the car, testing to see if it was perhaps less fearsomely frank than he thought. It began with Mike. He had said that he didn't find Mike's game so pointless, whatever that meant, and then his father had told him about things at home, and then came the invisible rooms, and then the love and the hate business, and then the lousy marriage. Eeee! He had said "lousy marriage"! To his father! And *deadness!* Dear God, take it away! Make it not be! No, he had said it, and it couldn't be unsaid, and there wasn't a dab of balm to be had from the whole raw mess!

So Lenny played on skiing as though it were an opera, he taking all the parts, putting into it lyricism and love. . . . *See, Dad, I can share things with you. My invisible room has twenty inches of snow, and this is what I do and how I feel about it. Welcome to it. I have profound respect for you—and love—and whatever a son is supposed to have—I do—*

"—and as you get more and more confidence," Lenny said, "you get to shift your weight from ski to ski, and that's the whole trick. What's so nice about it—"

"Why didn't you bring your equipment?" his father broke in.

"Why should I have? What would you do, sit here and watch me ski?"

"I wouldn't mind that in the least. Can you rent the equipment?"

"Sure you can, but—"

"Then do. Even if for only an hour."

"No."

"Lenny, don't be ridiculous. How much does it cost to rent the stuff?"

"I don't know—about six, seven dollars."

"Then do. I'll pay for it."

"Dad, I don't want to."

"Yes, you do, and I want you to. I want to see how well you ski."

They fenced in that silly way for a few more minutes, and the elder Lang finally prevailed. Lenny went to rent the equipment. He put on the boots, then walked outside on the terrace and showed himself to his father on the other side of the window. His father nodded and smiled.

Riding the chair up to the top, Lenny told himself that he could easily have forestalled anything like this from happening had he not worn his down jacket and corduroy pants. You couldn't very well go skiing in a pair of slacks, shirt, tie, etcetera. So there must have been a little ember of unquenched hope smoldering away. Why was it that parents did so much for their kids, always putting themselves second? Would he be subject to the same unimaginable change? It didn't seem possible. Although he'd heard from others about parents who lived their lives as though having children were of no more consequence than a case of measles—a period of quarantine and then everybody goes his own way. Kathy, for one, who'd made so complete a break with her parents that it was doubtful she'd ever go home. At least that's what she said. She was going to New York, to join Brian Miller, of all the dumb things! That shit, Brian Miller!

Lenny experienced a twinge of sex revulsion in his thoughts of Kathy. It was really strange how turned off you could get about a girl. Sexually, that is. He liked Kathy. She was honest. But in the sack she took over like a professional bronco rider looking for prize money. Once she got going all contact was between the legs. Feeling and fucking were one, and she was always out to establish records. That could be fun for a while, but then something happened. What had happened to him was a sort of cunt hostility. Actually. The whole nerve complex that was his sex response tightened up like a sphincter at the thought of Kathy. It was a good thing she had become interested in Brian when she did. And he in Marie.

Lenny's thoughts switched to Marie as he neared the top. This was the high point of the lift. A skier shot beneath him, plowing deep into powder. Lenny knew the path. There was one bad spot. You had to turn quickly if you didn't want to wrap yourself around a tree. He decided he'd take that path, even though he was a little afraid of it. Too bad his father couldn't see him on the really difficult part of the run.

Lenny stood up from the chair and skied down the decline away from the lift. He inserted his gloved hands through the loops of the poles. . . . *And how he wished Marie were here! Not in Cleveland bridesmaiding some damn cousin's wedding, but here!* . . . He skated on his skis over the level ground, coming to the first hill, which he took without a turn; and then the next, steeper hill, on which he had to turn often to avoid moguls; and then he came to the split in the path, taking the one to the left, the less used one, where the powder was deep, and he picked up speed, riding back on his skis to keep from nosing too deeply into the snow. When speed threatened to overwhelm his control, he turned, slowing, scraping up a flurry. Several times he fell, ass over tip, feeling the always surprising coldness of the snow on his face, down his neck. Then the trickiest part of it was over, and Lenny skied with speed, turning well but not with the marvelous ease of the naturals who became one swiveled synchronization of skis, knees, hips, and shoulders. He'd never be champ, but he was good enough to make the wind whistle and to feel his body do its best in balance and reflex, and by all this speed and whip and sweet presence of body to be lifted unreachably above all intimations of decay and death—and to come, at the bottom, to a right-angle stop, arching a wave of white before him.

He looked toward the lodge and saw his father standing at the window, one arm raised in a salute to his performance. Lenny motioned that he would take another run, and his father nodded assent. He took two more runs in all, then he turned in the equipment and joined his father in the lodge.

The sky had again turned overcast, and it looked like more snow.

"I think," said his father, "that I'll start for home right now."

101

15.

It was on the ride back that it sank in—sank not into any late-formed discriminations but way back into his cosmic beginning. Lenny felt the kind of shake that topples buildings. He wanted to run, but his hands were gripping the steering wheel of a car. His mother and father! The solid earth of home and love, school and city, past and present, all points fixed, all points known! That shake would change the contour of everything, and there would be fissures ten miles deep. He would have to map out a new terrain. And what would *they* do? A fierce resentment took hold of him. What right had they? After all the years, they surely could live the balance with whatever was bothering them! No, that was ridiculous. They weren't that old, and if they were unhappy together why then of course they'd have to split. It happens every day. How many of his friends' parents were divorced? His mind played with it reasonably for a full minute, and then he felt another temblor, and again he wanted to run. In fear and resentment, he spoke:

"It would have been different if you and Mom were *engaged* in something—you know, where there would have been a clash of interests or careers—"

His father made an explosive little noise which Lenny took for one awful second to be the onset of tears. He had never seen his father cry. But his father wasn't crying. He was smiling and shaking his head.

"You'd be surprised how engaged I am," his father said.

"Yes?" Lenny said, intending no irony. "In what?"

"Oh—in living."

Lenny tested the remark for facetiousness and found none. He turned his eyes back to the road, touching for the first time the periphery of David Lang's life—not his father's life, but David Lang's. It was a new sensation.

They were silent for several seconds, then his father said, "You know, Lenny, even if something were to happen, something definite, a break, it wouldn't be the end of the world."

"Nothing is the end of the world," Lenny said.

"True," said his father. "As far as you're concerned, there's no distinction to be made between your mother and me. You are cared for. By both. You do know that, don't you?"

"I know that."

He knew that—and that was about the extent of knowledge they'd given him about their lives. Maybe it had to be that way. Maybe it was best that way. What would he do with all the information if they started to unload on him now? . . . Lenny braked the car as they came to a narrow bridge. The stream that ran in the gulley to the right curved and flowed under the bridge. There was snow on the banks, and a short shelf of ice grew from the banks above the flow of the stream. He would live someplace not too far from scenes like this. Maybe he would work in a city, but he would make it his life's business to be near something like this. . . . On the other side of the bridge, a dumb collie darted out, stopped, crouched in fear, and Lenny had to swing sharply to the left. His father lurched against him. The contact seemed to jostle their thoughts into alignment. A moment later his father said, "I was surprised to learn that Bob Rohrmoser had read my book. I didn't know you kept a copy with you."

"Why shouldn't I?" Lenny said.

"There's no reason you shouldn't. Of course. Perhaps my surprise was due to the fact that I never really knew if *you* had read it."

"Now why would you think something like that?" Lenny returned. "Why wouldn't I have read my own father's novel? As a matter of fact, I've read it several times. I don't even remember when the first time was, but I do remember not understanding it at all. Then I read it again about five years ago. It meant a little more to me then. Last year—no, it was this year, about in March, I read it again."

"Well, I didn't know that, you see," said his father. "We've never discussed it."

No, they hadn't discussed it, and Lenny's thoughts suddenly darted as the collie had darted, and stopped, and crouched, wondering which way to go. Here was his opportunity to make up for the "lousy marriage" and the "deadness."

It was a great book, Dad. I mean, you know, not up there with the giants or anything, but a damn fine book!

"It was kind of awkward," he said.

"To discuss it?"

"Well—yes."

"Why so?"

"Because you've never discussed that part of your life with me. What I mean is that—I didn't know what was biographical and what was made up. Do you know what I mean?"

Lenny saw his father lower his head and smile. "I know what you mean," his father said. "I am a little surprised. I wouldn't have thought that would make a difference."

"It doesn't, really. Not to me. But I wasn't sure whether it would to you or not. But I can tell you one thing—I wouldn't be passing that book around to my friends if I didn't respect it myself."

"I'm sure," said his father. "Does 'respect' mean you liked it?"

"Yes, Dad, that's just what it means," Lenny said. "I thought it was a very well-written book. I got the feeling it was a very *personal* book."

"Is that good or bad?"

"Aren't personal books supposed to be good?"

104

"That depends on whether you like personal books," his father retorted. "Do you?"

"Yes, I like personal books. I wouldn't say it's my *favorite* type of reading. I really don't consider myself a good judge of fiction anymore."

"Really? Why not? You're an English major, aren't you? I seem to recall that you were interested in writing yourself at one time. Have you given that up?"

"Oh, God, yes!" Lenny exclaimed. "I'm no writer. I found that out quickly enough. I wrote a few short stories in my freshman year. They were awful. And besides, why would anybody want to *add* to everything that's been written!"

"I quite agree," his father murmured.

Utterly hopeless! Why couldn't he say the right things? Why, when he knew so fucking well what his father wanted to hear, couldn't he say the right things? Could it be that he *wanted* to hurt? No, he didn't want to hurt. He didn't! But every time he opened his mouth something took hold of him that he couldn't control. His life, was all! The life he had to rescue, or for all their intelligence and enlightenment and good will, they would pull him out of his orbit and into the great, selfless, gravitational drag of theirs! It came to Lenny in a sudden sunburst of understanding:

They clung to their lives no less desperately than he clung to his! That made it fair! He didn't have to struggle so with his conscience, feel so goddam guilty about the words that came to him naturally and honestly! It was all fair!

They arrived at the highway, and in turning onto it Lenny gunned the car in tribute to the thing he had discovered.

"How do you like the way it handles?" asked his father.

"Beautiful," he said.

"It's yours," his father said.

"What!"

"Yes. I see now that you need a car here. Of course I'll need it to get back to the city, but when you come home for the holidays you can take the car back with you."

"Wow!" Lenny breathed. "Too much! What are the right words for that?"

"I'll leave you to struggle with that," said his father.

"How about thanks?"

"That'll do."

Lenny felt the pull, the great, selfless pull, but he remained steady, thinking: *It's fair, it's fair, it's all fair!*

Lenny drove his father directly to the motel. He helped him pack his things and then carried the suitcase out and put it in the trunk of the car while his father went to the office to check out. He waited so long for his father that he was on the point of investigating the delay when his father finally came out of the office. Lenny had seated himself in the companion seat. His father got behind the wheel.

"I'll drive you over to your place now," his father said, "and then I'll take off." After a few seconds, he added, "There was a message for me in the office."

"Oh?"

"Yes. It was from Kathy Willens."

"Kathy Willens!"

"Yes. She left a number to call, and I did. She asked if I would give her a lift to New York when I returned. Do you know of any reason why I shouldn't?"

"Me? No. Hell, no. I mean, you know, if you've got the room, and you don't mind."

"I don't mind. She asked that I meet her at a gas station just outside the south exit. Do you know where that is?"

"Yes. It's about a half-mile down the road. I'll show you."

When they came to the boardinghouse, his father drew up along the curb, letting the motor run. He said, "I can't predict what will happen, Lenny, but whatever does happen I want you to know there'll be no havoc about it. It's difficult to know what is the right thing to do. Perhaps I shouldn't have said anything at all, but sooner or later you would have to know, and it seemed to me

106

that this is the best place for you to sort out your feelings. I hope I was right."

"You were right," Lenny said.

"Ski," his father advised. "Do whatever occupies you most pleasantly, even if you can't be completely happy."

Lenny nodded. Then he got out of the car and walked around to his father's side. He gave his father the directions to get where Kathy Willens would be waiting for him. He put his hand out, and his father took it. His father said:

"Whenever you feel like it, for whatever reason, phone me, phone your mother. And if you do talk to Mother, I think it would be foolish to pretend that nothing had been said between us. Do you understand?"

Lenny nodded, his gaze fixed on the library across the campus. He thought of Kathy accompanying his father, and a sudden fantasy flowered up in his mind. He killed it. There was a limit to absurdity.

"Anyway, I'll see you in a few weeks," he said.

"Right," said his father. "Take care"—and drove away.

David

16.

"Dave?"

"Hello, Stan."

Stan is my brother, five years my junior. I loved him, too, when we were both younger, but I haven't understood him for so many years that my feelings toward him have become very confused. He has, incidentally, a deep, rich voice, bass-baritone, and I'm sure that this accidental asset has done much to shape his life. This is the first time I've heard from him since that late afternoon on the lawn.

"How are you feeling?" he asks.

"Fine."

"I knew about it two weeks ago," he tells me, "but I didn't think you'd want to discuss it with me. I thought if you wanted to discuss it with me you'd call me. But you didn't call me, so I'm calling you."

"Well, thank you, Stan," I say, "but may I ask what happened to make you think I'd want to discuss it with you now?"

"If you'd rather not—"

"I didn't say that. I said that—"

"Mom is worried," he says.

"I see."

"Dave, I'm sorry, deeply sorry, but I can't say I'm surprised."

"Oh, really? Why not?"

"Well—" His deprecating baritone with a dying fall, which I understand to mean that I *should* understand what he means, but I don't. Truly I don't.

"Tell me," I say.

Stan has kinky hair and the kind of face which at all times has mysteriously revealed what he looked like as a child and what he will look like as an old man.

"Come on, Dave."

"Come on *what,* Stan?"

"You and Dodie," he says. "You've never really connected."

"Is that a fact? How would you know?"

"Look, Dave," my brother says hastily, placatingly, "the last thing in the world I want is to get into an argument with you. You *did* connect. All right? I'm calling you right now simply to say that I'm sorry—and to ask if I can be of any help. I know how hurt you must be. But you know, Dave, there's no point in taking it out on Mom."

"We won't argue," I say to him. "Perhaps you know something I should know. Please believe me when I say that I'm in the dark. How would you know that Dodie and I didn't connect? Did she tell you that?"

"Tell me that? No, of course not, Dave."

"Then how do you know?"

"How does one know something like that," Stan says in that tone which has regrettably set us apart since my discovery of its permanence. It took some years. I was at least thirty before I accepted the reality of my younger brother's nimbus-shaped election. One must go back to old religious paintings to find the like. That divine assurance. He goes on with his analysis: "You and Dodie operated on different levels, that's all."

"Me?"

"Both of you. You and Dodie. This is not a moral judgment, Dave. There's no right or wrong. It's just a fact."

"And this is something you've been able to determine in the three or four times we see each other in a year? Does Ilse concur in this, incidentally?"

112

Ilse is Stan's wife. She's a handsome efficient woman who retains the high flush of her origin. German. Ilse runs her home like a modern business with separate departments for education, hygiene, entertainment, community affairs, and so on. With the exception of a single area, I haven't the faintest idea what their married life is like. I wonder why Stan has ideas about mine.

"I don't need Ilse's concurrence," he says. "It happens that she does, but—"

"Stan, what the hell do you mean by 'operated on different levels?' That doesn't mean a goddam thing to me. It's just gibberish. If I'm on the first floor and you're on the second, then I can understand what you mean when you say we operate on different levels. Otherwise it's just words."

"You've got your back up," Stan says. "I don't blame you. You've been hurt."

"My back is where it always is," I say. "Try to explain it to me."

Stan's career, to my mind, has always been at strange odds with his gifts. For reasons I could never fathom, he became a junior sales executive in an insurance company on graduating college. In five years, he was top producer, specializing in estate planning. He made over forty thousand in one year. It was no miracle. Or if miracle, it had the right provenance for miracle. He carried the message of insurance like early Christians carried the faith. Clients were drawn into his charismatic field, resolving the mortal condition with premiums. They became his personal friends. Then, all of a sudden, he gave up insurance, became an enthusiast in the new wave of movies, took all his money and invested it along with two others in a string of art movie houses. In the suburbs. He's thriving. I guess you have to admire him.

"Look, Dave," he says, "there's nothing mysterious about it. You and Dodie are incompatible. Always have been. Good Lord, man, you know that!"

"Good Lord, man, I don't know that," I say. "I *didn't* know that. How are we incompatible?"

His words come in a mild, measured way. He doesn't want to hurt. He's applying healing truth like a poultice. "You and Dodie,

113

as people, you simply didn't respond to the same things in the same way. Your reactions were always at a different intensity."

"And," I return, "do you know of any two people in your wide circle of acquaintances who react to everything with identical intensities? Do you and Ilse, for example?"

"There's a critical point," he says.

(Which is true.)

"Did she tell you this?" I ask.

"Who?"

"Dodie."

"Me? No."

"What do you mean 'me no'? Did she say anything to Ilse?"

"What's the difference, Dave?"

"You called me up," I say, spacing my words with as much care as Stan. "This is a sympathy call. You understand that I've been hurt. If you want to do me a kindness, Stan, then do it in my way."

"All right," he says. "Dodie did say something of the sort. Naturally we've been in touch."

"Who's been in touch? You with Dodie, or Dodie with you?"

"Dave, what difference—"

"It makes a difference, goddamit! To me it makes a difference!"

"All right. Calm down. Dodie got in touch with Ilse."

"She did? For what? To tell her that? To tell her that shit about intensities?"

"Calm down, Dave."

"I'm calm. Tell me."

"You're being silly," he says. "Why would a woman like Dodie get in touch with her sister-in-law? She's hurt, too. Hurt and lonely and scared."

I'm about to say something, but I desist. Thank God, I desist. What good would it do now to bring up the fact that my wife has always disliked my brother's wife; always, from their first encounter, Dodie disliked Ilse with the unremitting aversion of one woman whose every sense was offended by the *intensities* of another. And yet it is just possible that Dodie would have phoned

114

Ilse to tell her this very thing. Self-justification knows where it will find the warmest welcome: not where it has reason to hope for the greatest understanding but the greatest forgiveness.

"What about Mom?" I ask.

"She says you haven't been in touch with her."

"Not true. I've been in touch with her."

"You haven't been to the house."

"That's true."

"Why punish her?"

"Was that her word—'punish'?"

"Don't be paranoid, Dave."

"I'll try not to be. My love to Ilse. I'll be in touch with Mom. Thanks for calling—"

"Dave—"

"Yes?"

"What's with the hideout?" he asks. "How long do you intend to stay out of touch?"

"I'm not out of touch, Stan. Here we are talking, are we not? Dad has been over to the apartment. I've talked to Mom on the phone several times. Surely you can tell from talking to me that there's nothing seriously wrong with me. We'll get together and talk, as soon as I'm in the mood. Frankly, Stan, I'm depending on your understanding and forbearance. Yours particularly. I'm doing whatever is needful to my days right now, to my condition, and my condition changes from day to day. You and Ilse apparently knew things that I didn't know. You must have been right. Events have proved you right. But, you see, what I've got to do is train myself to receive the truth of all of this. It isn't easy. My old ego is a little too battered to handle the situation. Somehow I've got to work a new one into existence out of the acceptances I can make. Do you see what I mean, Stan?"

"Absolutely, Dave," Stan says. "Absolutely."

I'm glad he does, because I don't. I had no idea what I was going to say when I began that terribly sincere speech. I just wanted to terminate this talk without closing off this avenue of communication.

"All right, then," I say.

"If you need anything—" he says.

"Thanks, Stan."

"Take it easy."

"You bet."

I could have told him to go to hell, but that isn't the way I speak to my brother. But I do want him off my back at present. That's why I handed him that bouquet of paper flowers. Ego and acceptances. Dependency and forbearance. Stan loves words like that. He and Ilse. That's the one thing I know about them, that passionate hobby of "studying" and "understanding" people. Stan doesn't allow it to interfere with his sound business sense, nor does Ilse allow it to disturb the efficient running of her home, but after a day of profit and order they love to relax over cocktails and psychology. They'll be talking about my surprising access of self-knowledge tonight. They'll be happy about it. I don't know why I'm going on in this way. They're not nearly as bad as I'm making out.

Five years separate Stan and me, but occasionally when some incident, odor, or pattern of clouds moves me to early tenderness, I am likely to confuse my brother with my son, saying one's name when I mean the other. I can't bring myself to react to Stan purely on the basis of what he has become. I feel like it sometimes, seeing that selfhood, hearing that voice, but the past is too full of shades to allow for a final attitude. It will always be like that, I guess.

116

17.

I must visit my parents. To delay any longer will change my mother's smoldering sense of exclusion to fright and self-pity, and I don't think I could deal with that right now. As Stan said, why take it out on her? I don't want to take it out on her. Truthfully, I don't want to take it out on anyone, and I know I must get rid of some of this venom if I am to go on living.

I drive into Queens at about six in the evening. The traffic is heavy but not impossible. This is the first time I will be visiting Forest Hills in my new condition, and I realize that the reason I haven't done so before is not so much the ordeal of facing Lily Lang but the fear of establishing a new routine. Regular visits. Once or twice a week for dinner. After all, why not? Lily is a superb cook. And where else could I get such partisanship? One hundred per cent! Which is precisely what I don't want. Venom is what I must get rid of, and partisanship is the mud puddle into which I mustn't sink.

Although it was never likely that I would feel at home in the Forest Hills apartment. That apartment marks the postwar life of my parents, and that life no longer included me. Stan, yes, for a few more years, but I had flown the coop. Acts of God and wars are acceptable riders in the everlasting Jewish contract.

The Forest Hills apartment is serene and full of the somber glints of polished mahogany. The upholstery bellies in smooth

117

permanent pregnancy. There are no rough boys to disturb the medium-priced, Regency order fashioned out of Lily's dream of style.

But there were other rooms. There were rooms in Harlem that I barely remember. We lived in a brownstone near Mount Morris Park. Lower-middle-class class. The city's ethnic trek was just about to begin. Even then, Sam Lang was able to keep his family well above the marginal line. It's strange. Despite his perpetual cry—"*I only have two hands!*"—he was always able to meet his wife's minimum requirements (which were never at the level of self-denial) and send two sons to college and maintain a gradual but constantly ascending life-style. He is a master craftsman, and that gets around after years of plying the needle, and there are always men willing to pay fancy prices to smooth out the sags and slants of their bodies. I shouldn't be surprised if Sam has socked away a nice figure against that dreaded day of retirement. By his own standards, he is a success.

I was about seven or eight when we moved away from Harlem. What I took with me was the tower which stands atop a hill in Mount Morris Park. I'm quite sure I couldn't have conceived this notion while we still lived in view of the tower, but the sights, smells, and sounds of genesis were with me at that time, and such sensations need a symbol. Mine was the tower. It was later in life that I painted the tower gold. My notion was that if I ever climbed its metal staircase to the top, I would be able to see my future by gazing out on the wide street that debouched on another, nameless park that rolled on to a point in time and space whose juncture took the form of my destiny. And just by turning around in the tower and looking the other way, I could look into the dark mystery of time before memory, the primal dust of all beginning.

The tower—and the horrible opened-up man. I had nightmares. I think of them as nightmares, but more likely I couldn't sleep, thinking of that cardboard display propped up in the window of a drugstore, the figure of a man opened up in a glossy, multicolored display of veins and arteries, liver and lungs, heart and entrails. All packed like the innards of a chicken that my mother would

118

scoop out after splitting open one of the creatures. Red, brown, blue, and green. How could I be contained in—or contain—crayon colors and mere *meat!* I cried and babbled about the man in the drugstore, and often at the dinner table (I've been told) I would stare at the chicken meat or lamb chop, gagging, until I had to be taken away to the bathroom.

Spirit and body. Everybody finds his symbols. I had mine.

We moved north, scarcely two miles, but to me it was over the Himalayas, to the other side of the world. We moved to another apartment on another street, this one even more quiet. On the other side of the street was a cemetery. On the corner of the street was a slate-colored church full of spires and pigeon droppings. I hadn't a friend in the world. It took me months to find one, and all through childhood, right into high school, into college, I've never had much more than one at a time. I can't blame Lily and Sam. It was not that generation's concern to case a neighborhood for their children's social life. Survival beat too closely at their backs for such considerations.

We lived on that wide, quiet street with the church on the corner, the Hudson River at its foot, and the Indian Museum midway between, until I went to college. I took my younger brother to that museum. We examined kayaks and tepees and breathed in the cloistered air. That was my odor of sanctity. I took my younger brother by the hand and we walked to Broadway for the Sunday paper. I played ball with him on the wide street beside the museum. I didn't think of myself as being lonely; I thought that all people must make it in solitude until the time they found their ideal companion.

That enforced sense of ideality took root early and grew like a tree—one solid, sequoia-high tree on an empty plain. Occasionally I would find in school or on the streets one whom I hoped would be the ideal friend. I wanted to do everything with that friend. I wanted that friend to do nothing without me. I have no doubt that it was suffocating to be my friend. I learned in time that others had not cultivated the same sense of ideality that I

119

had. Somewhere in the process of learning this, I turned to books.

I was a reader. I had found my vocation, my infinitely docile, infinitely varied friend. What I discovered in books was that my condition was not unique. What I also discovered was that there were injustices in the world. I embraced that discovery like a lover. It was the explanation of my life and its direction. *There was injustice in the world!* I didn't want to march with anybody or put out a flag; I wanted to read more books.

In college, I found friends. Others who had a similar view of the world's injustices. I was made to understand that injustice was not just a reflection of my life's solitude but gaunt starvation and bloody murder. I joined parties. It was the time of the united front. I was in the world.

But if the truth be known—and it had better be!—the world had merely taken knowable dimensions, and I was still looking for myself, self-revealed, on the other side.

"One thing I don't understand," says my father.

"What's that?" I ask.

"Sam," my mother interrupts him, "I thought you were going to bring in the ice cubes. I thought you were going to make David a drink."

"I wish," my father says, "you wouldn't try to shut me up."

We are sitting in the living room of the apartment in Forest Hills. Lily is sitting in her armchair. Sam is sitting in his Barcalounger. Just sitting. His wife, my mother, doesn't like my father to make full use of the Barcalounger in company. Even partial use. My father had had no passions in his life, but he has had some unshakable convictions. One is in the honesty and efficacy of all patent medicines. He is the man for whom advertising claims are written. Another—late—conviction is in the life-giving properties of the Barcalounger.

"What don't you understand?" I ask my father.

"I don't understand—what happened. With you and Duddy."

My mother looks at me darkly. This is as she had anticipated, and she blames me for having encouraged him. Her look tells me that this would be the inevitable outcome of allowing Sam Lang to ask questions.

"What happened?" I say. "I told you what happened."

"But I don't understand," he insists.

My mother half-raises out of her chair. "I'll get the ice cubes," she declares.

"Sit," my father says, slapping the arms of the Barcalounger. "I'll get them."

He gets out of the chair and goes to the kitchen. My mother looks at me and shakes her head. "David, David," she whispers.

Now that my father is out of the Barcalounger, I realize what a freak that thing is in Lily Lang's living room. Among the tables and lamps and chairs and bric-a-brac—a delicately carved and formal sea—my father's Barcalounger breaks the surface like the hump of a rising hippo. A misplaced monster. It is a tribute to the years that my mother has finally yielded and allows it to wallow there. She believes monarchically in female dominance in the home, but age and death are assaulting; it is time to make concessions.

"Have you heard anything?" asks my mother.

"From Dodie? No."

She nods, sighs. She has grown old, the indomitable Lily. She has defeated everything but time. Each time I see her of late, I become more aware of this shrinkage, like an apple withering, but after a few minutes in her company my mind supplants the woman before me with another, one caught in ripe perfection— Lily at her best. But I suppose that image too will fade when I have seen her long enough in her withering.

My father, coming in with a bucket of ice cubes, says, "You want a scotch and soda?"

"You sit down, Pa. I'll make it."

My father resumes the Barcalounger and begins to tip back. To the degree that my father moves backward in his chair, my mother moves forward in *hers*.

"Are you getting ready to lay there the whole evening?" she asks.

"Recline," my father corrects, from the brochure that accompanied the Barcalounger.

"Well, it's not *pleasant* to talk to a person who looks like he's waiting for an operation."

"Mom, stop it, will you?" I say. "Let him relax. It's only me in the house."

My father tips back in unexpected victory. "She doesn't let you live," he says.

I go to the table containing the bottles and mix a drink for myself. "I don't understand what happened either," I say, turning around and looking at my mother. "Perhaps you can tell me."

Lily's face sags in sourness, but her eyes ignite in cold fire. "You're finally asking?" she says. "Yes, I can tell you a few things."

"What can you tell me?"

"I can tell you I'm not surprised," my mother says.

"You're not the first not to be surprised," I say. "Why aren't you surprised?"

"Because if a person hasn't got a heart, then you can expect anything. That girl never had a heart!"

That isn't true, of course. Lily is not going to be a reliable witness, but then neither was I. It's interesting to me, however, in just what way my mother is not going to be reliable.

"What do you mean she never had a heart?" I say. "It seems to me she was always nice to you—to both of you."

My father tips forward a little. "This is not me talking," he makes clear. "This is your mother talking, not me."

My mother looks at my father, looks at him reclining, all ease, while she sits forward in her chair rubbed raw with family misfortune. Lily has always been a master at creating these quick allegories. But I notice for the first time there's a routine quality to the scene. A thousand such scenes dwindle recessively in my mind. Something has happened to my parents. It seems to me the hope of changing Sam has gone out of Lily, and the chafe of fearing Lily has gone out of Sam. They have changed to accommodate

122

each other, not out of human will but like rock and running water. Lily turns back to me.

"It's not a mother's place to open her mouth, so I kept my mouth shut," says Lily. "But now I can tell you. This girl never liked your family. Not us, not cousins, nobody. A snob! Is that plain enough? And *nasty!* Do you remember when I refurnished about eight years ago, she bought me a present? A painting? You remember? Are you going to tell me that she didn't know I wouldn't put such a hideous thing on my wall? That it wasn't *deliberate?* And the cousins' club? How many times I pleaded with that girl, please, Dodie, what would it harm? No! Never!"

"I had something to say about that," I remind my mother.

Lily shakes her head. "No, David, if a woman wants to preserve family, she'll do it. She had absolutely no feeling for your family!"

"Now listen—" says my father.

"Yes?" I say.

Sam raises himself upright.

"—I want you to know one thing," he says. "I don't care what anybody says. I like Duddy. I always liked Duddy. Every year, without fail, on my birthday, Duddy called me up at my place of business to wish me a happy birthday. Heh? You didn't know that! I'm telling you now you say she's got no family feeling. I don't say what she did was right, but don't tell me no family feeling. Who else called me up at my place of business to wish me a happy birthday? Who?"

My mother and I look at Sam Lang, silent in the image of Dodie's surprising communion with Sam Lang.

Driving back to my apartment, I catch a glimpse of myself and Dodie in the long concealment of our marriage. She never told me about phoning my father on his birthday. That was her own thing. Why did she do it? What turn of compassion or conscience made her do it? I see Dodie shaking her head over some of my father's peculiar densities. I didn't think she thought of him much at all; or if she did, then as an odd, stubborn life form, like lichen or desert plants. But obviously she did think of him—perhaps even found affinities I could never imagine.

And that print she bought for my mother eight years ago, was that deliberate or not? I don't know. It could very well have been. They didn't love each other, Dodie and Lily. They were women of strong preferences who let their preferences show. But I knew all that. My God, there was so much I knew and didn't know in our marriage!

I told Lily that I had heard nothing from Dodie, and that is true. Dodie is drawing away from me, assuming different proportions in my mind. I haven't heard her voice since that day almost three weeks ago when I phoned her to say I wouldn't be coming home, that I had been in touch with Ralph Friedman and that I would be staying at his apartment. I had just returned from Vermont.

"What about Lenny?" she wanted to know.

"I told him things were difficult between us, that's all."

"When is he coming home?" she asked.

"Holidays."

"What am I supposed to do?"

"I don't know, Dodie. Whatever you want."

"Can you give me an idea what your plans are?" she asked.

"No, I can't, I'm afraid. I have no plans."

"It's all up to me, is that it?"

"I wouldn't say that," I said. "It's up to me, too. That's why I'm staying away. We weren't getting anywhere."

"David—"

"Yes?"

"I'm seeing someone," she said.

"Besides Arthur?"

"A doctor. An analyst."

"Oh? Why?"

"Why do you think?"

I was silent.

She went on: "You know very well what you were doing. I won't be driven off the deep end, David. I'm not the type."

124

"Don't talk nonsense."

"All right," she said. "I'll need money."

"You have the passbook," I told her. "It's a joint account. Take whatever you need."

"I want you to know. It's your money. I want your permission."

"Oh, for God's sake! You have it."

"Thank you."

"Take care of yourself, Dodie."

She didn't reply to that. I think she was crying. She hung up.

Dodie was never much for tears, but just then I think she was crying. And when I questioned her during that ghastly period when we were both stretched on the give-it-a-chance rack. And once before that I clearly remember—when we first made love. That rounds it off neatly. No doubt there've been other times, but these are the occasions which come to mind. I've thought several times before to talk of our meeting, our courtship, but I couldn't. I think I can now.

18.

How we met? Is it at all important how a man and woman meet? We met. The first time at a house party given in honor of a Greek poet who had recently come to this country to do the lecture circuit. My novel had already been accepted for publication; therefore I was on the fringes of the literary crowd. I was invited. I took the tall, slow-moving girl to be the mistress of the Greek poet. She seemed the one most solicitous of him. Several weeks later, by pure coincidence, I met the tall, slow-moving girl at a wedding in Manhattan—she a friend of the bride, I a friend of the groom. I told her what my imagination had made of her and the Greek poet—discreetly, of course. She laughed. She told me she worked for a man, Bernard Reinitz, who made his living importing European notables and booking tours for them. Her job was just about everything—secretary, hostess, tour director, and amateur therapist in easing poets, musicians, writers, and I-was-there survivors out of a decade of nightmare. Other aspects of the job I learned later.

Dodie with her tallness, her languor (which I thought at the time affected; it wasn't, isn't), her interesting green eyes, her thickish nose (which even then I didn't find unattractive)—all of the Dodie I held in my arms as we danced at the wedding of friends (it was June) was so devoid of the meaning it would have an hour hence, and for more than twenty years thereafter, that

126

I find in my memory of that distant Dodie the power of myth, which when touched restores to my senses the full flavor of the world and my life at that time.

We danced. I held the flat of my hand against her back. She was very pliant, accommodating the movements of her body to the less than instinctive rhythms of my dancing style. She wore a perfume which lingers in my memory as fox-fur brown. I remember the imperturbability of her pale jade eyes, which I took to be a pose. I became curious about the pose, and because I became curious about the pose, and because of the long loose lines of her body, and because of the fragrance in my nostrils, my senses gave a turn and I was suddenly and completely open to this girl's attractions.

I accompanied Dodie to where she was then living with her parents on the West Side of Manhattan. I asked if we could see a play, a movie, a concert, whatever she liked. She liked all those things, but she couldn't that week. Perhaps next? Yes, next. And then there were many concerts and plays and movies.

All considered, it was a rotten courtship, if joy is any measure. There *was* no joy. It started with Dodie's famous confession that she had been in love—recently—perhaps was still in love, to be *honest*. Which didn't surprise me. She was twenty-three at the time. Girls of that age who hadn't been in love at least once would be suspect. But the complication was that the man she had been in love with—was possibly still in love with—was the man she worked for. Ah! That was not so good. There's nothing in human experience to indicate that the difficulties of courtship necessarily adumbrate the difficulties of marriage, but there, if I wanted a sign, was one. What was past could easily have been buried, but it was my fate to wrestle each day with a ghost that had had a good night's rest; a freshly shaven, vigorous, charming ghost. Bernard Reinitz. A male surely designed for conquest. Custom-cut hair with the right amount of gray in the right places, blue eyes, a virile face, German accent sautéed in British overtones. Herr Reinitz took the heart out of me by being, to top it all off, the genuine article. He spoke four languages. Everything about him gave evidence that his rescue of European talent was not just a business but a cause. He went out to me with a warmth and friendship that all but demolished any hope of competition. But Bernard was married. He would never, he had made clear, divorce his wife. He was the one to end the affair with Dodie. He was honorable to boot.

"Why do you go on working there?" I had asked Dodie.

"Why not?" she had replied. "I couldn't hope to find a more interesting job. Besides, he's away much of the time. He travels to Europe quite often. I'm left alone, which I prefer to a place full of people I don't care for."

I could have quit then—perhaps should have. I had been given an early and unmistakable option to do so. And perhaps if I were at that point helplessly in love with Dodie, I might have done so. But I had the idea that it was still in my power to help myself. I lingered. There were the imperturbable jade eyes, the fox-fur brown scent, all the charms which kept guard over the isolated Princess spinning gold in the tower or cellar of her interior castle. Of course I didn't tell her that. It sounded ridiculous even to me, the fantasy I had woven about her, but in a rational part of my mind I had the feeling that it was true, or at least partially true. What was equally true and ridiculous were all the affinities I was fabricating between myself and the hidden Dodie. The tempo of our going together increased. I hadn't begun to work on that second, failed, novel. I had taken a job with a national magazine, and I could afford all those plays and concerts and dinners and my own apartment, to which we went, often, for me to suffer the brutality of limited lovemaking. She wouldn't, she said, until she was sure.

It was June when we met. Months later, on a day when a warm sun cracked the husk of winter in the city, we were together on one of our frequent lunch dates. Passing a department store, Dodie was reminded that she needed a new lipstick. We stepped inside, went to the cosmetic counter, where Dodie bought her lipstick. There was a mirror on the counter, one of those ruthless mirrors women can tolerate only when they're alone and dealing with their face a feature at a time. I observed Dodie staring at her reflection, and I too moved so that I could see her in the mirror, see what she saw, the thick volutes of her nose, the fullness of her mouth, and the eyes which gazed on these imperfections with such inveterate hatred that I felt a rent like the tearing of tissue. Then I found myself through the wall of Dodie's castle and into the room where she spun not gold but grief.

"You're a handsome woman," I said to her.

"Men are supposed to be handsome," she said, turning and walking toward the exit.

I followed, saying, "Would you rather I had said pretty? You're not pretty. Pretty doesn't suit you at all. You're handsome. You're all of a piece. You have your own style, and it's a very attractive style."

"I wanted to be beautiful," she said, with ancient antagonism.

"I wanted to be a genius," I said.

I had trained myself in hidden affinities, and when they revealed themselves I had the right words. We walked out of the department store and into sunshine that glinted blindingly off windows and metal trim.

We had dinner that evening, and then went to my apartment. When I touched her, she began to cry. Whatever I had guessed about her, I had never imagined such a storm of tears. Her body shook, and though I comforted her I was not in turn comforted with the knowledge that tears were to be her signal of surrender. But it no longer mattered. Between the afternoon and the evening of that day, I had fallen in love. She occupied me as completely as a victorious army. I made love to Dodie with the odor of her tears in my nostrils, with the salt of them on my tongue.

We too were married in June.

129

19.

Our marriage. Almost twenty-three years. What did we do? I think now that I sold out to Ted Buchholz so that I could be free to ask myself this. I've applied myself to this question most of the minutes of my freedom, but for some reason my mind has refused to handle it, has skittered here and there, disorganized, among a few hasty recollections, and like a confused dog has flopped flat, muzzle between paws, eyes closed.

Do I really not remember? No, I do remember. With diligence, I can reconstruct everything.

We lived in the Chelsea section of the city. Dodie's father, whose law practice was heavily in real estate, used his influence to find us an apartment when apartments were very scarce. The room I had been living in was very nice for a bachelor, but it was scarcely adequate for a married couple.

Dodie continued to work, not for Bernard Reinitz—I wouldn't have that, naturally—but for some medical research bureau. I had quit the magazine to begin work on that second book. We had calculated our resources to give me a year. I wrote in a room with a window which afforded me a view of a comically tiny park surrounded on all sides by a brutal flow of traffic.

I began this account with the statement that I was alone for the first time in my life. Well, I was alone then too, but now that I have both rooms in mind—this one and that other distant one—

I see the difference even more clearly. Never was Dodie more intensely with me as in those hours I spent alone in our first apartment. It was when we were apart that I most felt the newness and weight of her presence.

I loved Dodie. Feared her, too, a little. I feared her past, so dense and unknown to me with a recent lover and old ambitions. But I was confident. I would become well known. I would make money. Out there in time, not too impossibly far, was a point where everything would converge. I would work very hard and become the best that I could be. Dodie and I would move out of our separate histories into the one we would create together. And we would have a fine time in the creating. We had the means and the taste to enjoy this overloaded city. I thought we were lucky.

We had honeymooned on Cape Ann because Dodie had been there before and had loved it. We stayed there for a week, grew bored, then drifted over to Cape Cod. I have color transparencies of those few weeks. They're in the house in which I no longer live. I remember one particularly, a photo of Dodie standing before a fabulous junkyard operated by some bearded character who wore a green visor, dungarees, and who sat in a rocking chair amid his psychedelic rubbish. I remember a flamingo-colored commode, a pastel-blue automobile tire. . . .

We lived in the Chelsea apartment for four years. Lenny was still an infant when we bought the house in Long Island and moved away from the city. What did we do in those four years? I wrote that first year, did not like what I had written, gave it up and went back to work for the magazine. Was it really as easy as that? Was there no bitterness, no hurtful sense of loss in giving up an ambition? I don't know. At the time, I would have said no. Regret, surely, but not the acid defeat which might have corroded the next twenty years. That second book seemed like such an immense amount of work to say such a small thing. I knew then—as I know now—that real dedication survives the most meager returns, or no returns at all. But if I didn't have the dedication, I wasn't going to pump it into myself. Also, I was a little afraid of the kind of

131

life that committed itself to goals it couldn't reach. I think I was afraid of being nailed to that cross.

But I didn't know all this in the beginning of that first year. I had worked assuredly on that second book through the molten end of summer, the freshness of fall, the first phlegms of winter. Dodie continued in her job.

"Do you mind this?" I asked.

"What?"

"This setup. Your working, my staying at home."

"Not at all. Don't make it sound as though you're lazy or un-employed. You are working, you know."

"Yes, I know, but still you don't have to do it. There's enough money. You can quit."

"What would I do?" she asked.

"Whatever you wished. You have the city of dreams at your disposal."

"What are you saying, David? What city of dreams? Daylight dreams? Would you want me hanging around while you work?"

"I wouldn't mind."

"I would," she said. "And you would, too."

Of course she was right. We both would have minded. Con-science prompted those remarks. The man sitting at home, the woman leaving each morning. Some scared little immigrant ethic sat in a corner of my brain and looked at me moodily.

But what I did I did because I liked doing it, not because of a bad conscience. Often I phoned Dodie during the day and ar-ranged to take her to lunch. Often I would meet her at a bar near her office, and we would have a cocktail, and then dinner, and then a movie, or a play, or visit friends, or just to walk around a selected corner of the city and accumulate the odd purchases of pleasure that could be had from the sheer surfeit of places and people. We were living the New York life, Dodie and I, and I thought we loved it. I did. I thought Dodie did. I thought Dodie loved what I loved.

Now that I'm reconstructing so well, I remember something else. It's very strange that this shouldn't have come to me before, considering the origin of all these musings. . . . It was winter, near Christmas, as I recall. I guess I must have phoned Dodie and arranged to meet her at the museum—*the* museum—the one in my daymare. I set out from the apartment sometime in the late morning. Snowflakes had already begun to fall when I entered the subway on Twenty-third Street. When I emerged in the Fifties, it was a blizzard. Wind-driven snow whipped at my eyes as I came up the stairs, and I walked the short distance from the subway to the museum bent into the wind, looking up obliquely from time to time to place my progress and avoid crashing into some other blinded pedestrian. Judging myself to be near my destination, I looked up once more and saw Dodie looking at me from behind a plate glass window.

It was the museum. She was waiting for me there, behind the window. I smiled, or waved, some sign to mark the comedy of my standing in a blizzard, while she, a foot away, stood dry, warm, and contemplative. She was that, all right—contemplative. She looked straight at me without a glimmer of recognition. We had lived together for half a year, had known each other a year before that, had passed hours and hours in each other's company. In all that time I had never been able to judge how near or distant she may have been from me at any given moment. I doubt that more than five seconds passed between the meeting of our eyes and her return from whatever peak or plateau her reverie had taken her. But the *distance!* That's what I remember now, the distance.

She recognized me at last, her eyes large in the wonderment of finding me all white and intrusive in the middle of her green landscape. Then she smiled and raised her eyebrows and motioned me—for God's sake!—to get in out of that polar weather. In the few steps to the museum entrance, I thought that my Dodie could get far from me, indeed. I don't recall that I was particularly alarmed by the discovery. I just remarked to myself that this was how far it was possible for Dodie to get from me; that she was in all likelihood still inhabiting the world she knew before she met me, or perhaps the world she still projected despite me. And I was so respectful of the mind's privacy that I stamped my shoes, slapped the snow from my coat, kissed my wife, and let the moment go by.

What did we do?

We went to movies and restaurants and museums and concerts and visited friends. And friends visited us. Dodie prepared fancy dishes—French, Italian, Mexican—and we drank wine and talked politics and art with our friends. Small groups because we lived in a small apartment. And after our friends were gone, we would open the windows to dispel the smoke. We cleaned the dishes and talked not of politics and art but of the lives of those friends with whom we had talked of politics and art, guessing at the degree of this or that one's unhappiness. I don't know, do other people do other things? We had survived the war, and we were celebrating that. But Dodie—Dodie and me—what was our life like? Our life was exactly as I describe it. We went to movies and plays and concerts and museums. We visited friends and friends visited us. Dodie had her job. I wrote. We made love. We agreed we didn't want a child yet.

The next summer we went to Cape Ann again, not because we had enjoyed it on our honeymoon, even in retrospect, but because not to go would have been a negative admission of some sort. We walked on the wharves, looked into the shops where all sorts of overpriced *kitsch* was sold. Dodie loved to look. I had learned that about her, she loved to look.

"Why?" I asked her.

"Don't you?" she returned.

"A little goes a long way," I said—or words to that effect.

I must have pressed the point, because I remember her conveying to me in one way or another that her fascination lay in the fact that all these things had been made by human hands. Countless millions of beautiful things fashioned by human hands. She imagined a single desire passing through generations and expressing itself in hands luckily blessed with the gift of talent. I had known before this that Dodie wished for such hands. But if she

134

had had talent it would have shown itself before this, and therefore I let the moment go by.

I didn't decide to give up my book so that I could be a partner in Dodie's longing. I knew before Cape Ann that I was through with the thing I had been working on. My assurance had faltered halfway through the year, and by the time the trees in the tiny park were in dusty leaf I was certain it wasn't going to work. But I hadn't said anything to Dodie. Who wants to announce the waste of a year? It's true I'd bought myself that year, earned it, but still . . . Another thing: I was afraid of being diminished in Dodie's eyes. I was afraid that an item in our unwritten marriage contract was the faint luster of my one accomplishment. I thought I would be removing a source of pride or replenishment from Dodie's life.

Toward the end of that vacation in Cape Ann, we sat in a restaurant and looked out over a placid inlet coppered by a lowering sun.

"I'm giving up the book," I told Dodie.

She looked at me doubtfully. "You're not," she said.

"Yes, I am. It's not worth going on with. It isn't that I haven't been able to say what I wanted to—I have—but I see now—have seen for weeks—that it's too damn small."

"Won't you let me see it first?"

"If you wish, but it won't matter."

We were silent for several moments, then Dodie asked, "What will you do?"

"Take a job. I'm pretty sure the magazine will take me back. If not that one, then another."

Dodie nodded, looked out the window, brought her green gaze back to me. "I'm sorry," she said.

She was, but I realized in that moment that she wasn't losing anything. She was sorry for *me,* but my efforts in that year had not replenished her.

Lenny was conceived a month later. We wanted it to happen, and it happened. I had no difficulty in finding a job. Without consulting each other in any deliberate way, we both knew that we had

135

entered a new phase. I thought I sensed in Dodie a willingness to let go the history she had lived before me. The weight of her pregnancy seemed to settle her. The need for the restaurants and plays and museums and friends grew less, and because it did so I was able to judge how much these entertainments had supported us.

Dodie's obstetrician sent her to a hospital on the East Side. Lenny was born with difficulty. Things did not go well. There was hemorrhaging, and the doctor told me that an operation would be necessary. He was sorry, but there was no choice. All would be well in a matter of weeks, but unfortunately there would be no more children. My wife, he told me, had already given consent. I stayed in the hospital, in the visitors' room, until a nurse came to tell me that the operation had been performed and that my wife was quite weak but that there was no great danger. She was under sedation. It would be best if I went home and got some sleep myself. So I went back to the apartment and slept for a few hours, waking at daybreak. I was certain that Dodie was dead, and the terror in me blanched the world to a bloodless white. I saw before me years of terrible alternatives, hired nurses, the strong swoop of my mother, and all that Dodie and I would never know gathered in a crushing mass of love and regret.

Unable to wait until I got to the hospital to learn all this, I phoned and was told that Mrs. Lang was resting comfortably, and yes, I could come anytime I wished.

It was May, a morning irrigated in my memory by a city sanitation truck sending up a spray of water and cigarette butts along the curb. The streets were shadow-blue beneath buildings that blocked a sun rising out of the rust and dust of Long Island City. My life had been restored. Color came back to the world. I was again confident—confident that it was not my destiny to suffer certain things.

Dodie was in her room, and I was allowed to go right in. She was combed and perfumed, worn and awake, and she held out her hand to me. I took it and pressed it and bent to kiss her lips still tainted with ether. When I moved away, I saw a look of selfhood and distance in her eyes. She had suffered her own visions. Humbled and afraid, I let the moment go by.

20.

We moved away from the city when Dodie, out with Lenny in the baby carriage one morning, saw a rat stroll along a building across the street and duck into a garage repair shop. We were going to move anyway. The city is no place to bring up a child. I know, thousands do, but either they can't help themselves, or they are even more obsessive than Dodie and me.

We bought the house, performed the usual rites of innocence with agents and banks, moved in, and shortly became involved with the rites of transfer. Was it the ancient Hebrews who took with them into exile a handful of beloved soil? Dodie and I took more than a handful. We brought the city with us. We brought whole suites from Bloomingdales, armchairs from B. Altman, lamps from Lexington Avenue, odd pieces from the Village. It seems to me now we consumed years getting settled in a house some fifteen miles from our uninhabitable Manhattan.

And we found something to talk about. My God, did we ever find an inexhaustible source of talk! Tables, chairs, rugs, bookcases, phonographs, curtains, bed covers, paint, prints, floor lamps, table lamps . . . We plotted decoration as conspirators plot revolution. Having missed out on passion thus far in our lives, we found it in purchases. A curvilinear couch (they were fashionable then) or a straight one? Dodie wanted the curvilinear. I didn't. She planned a whole room around a curvilinear couch.

"Please, David."

137

"It's only a fad, Dodie. You'll get tired of it."

"Everything's a fad."

"Six hundred bucks, Dodie!"

"Please!"

I wonder now whether I took such a hard line because I had such definite ideas, or because I was enjoying the contest. I don't wonder, I know. I was enjoying it. I think we both were. We enacted a romance in furniture. We thought about, fought about, became reconciled over furniture.

And there was Lenny. We were equally consumed with the one child we would have. I don't remember exactly when it was, but somewhere between Lenny's birth and kindergarten I decided that our one-child parenthood was a significant stroke of fate—a balance in nature to keep increase limited to existing capacities. Whatever Dodie and I had was not meant to be spread too thin.

The house and Lenny. We were occupied. The pattern of our life was set. Visiting grandparents with Lenny. Saturday trips to the city to look at something advertised in the newspaper. The Central Park Zoo. Birthday parties. Christmas. The surprises of an unfolding life. It seemed that David Lang and the nation entered a halcyon time together. Entrenchment guarded by the Eisenhower grin.

Then Rich and I were sent on that cross-country trip gathering material for a major article on the "crisis in education." Rich was then employed as one of the staff photographers on the magazine. I had worked with him before, knew him to be lively, ambitious, full of abilities. We worked well together on that trip, and we learned from educators of the need of good educational film. I had some money. So did Rich. We decided to take the risk.

But what does all this mean? What does it explain?

It explains the passage of time. I keep asking myself what happened to time. This is what happened to time. Lenny was born. Dodie and I watched him grow with the usual fascination. Rich and I formed our own business. And somewhere in those years it must have become apparent to Dodie and me that the enchantment of Lenny had ended and the relentless business of feeding his long life had begun. It would go on for years—eighteen, nineteen, twenty—who knew? We would be irretrievably middle-aged by the time the incubation period was over. There was nothing to do about that. We both loved Lenny, would sacrifice anything for him, given a crisis.

But there was no crisis. We merely lived. I was absorbed in building my new business with Rich. Dodie had grown plump, and I saw her entering a phase of matronliness. I don't remember what was the frequency of our lovemaking, or how satisfying it was. There couldn't have been anything radically wrong. If there were, the fact of it would be scored somewhere on that smooth surface of time.

Of course the wife of John F. Kennedy had nothing to do with it, but time has a way of conjoining private and public lives when memory starts groping. I never asked, "Does Jacqueline Kennedy have anything to do with this transformation?"—and so I can't be absolutely sure. I do know that Dodie was full of admiration, and that the transformation was coincident with the admiration. Dodie at least ten pounds slimmer. Dodie in new hair styles. Dodie in new dresses. Dodie appearing out of a domestic chrysalis, opening wings marked with colors I couldn't have imagined, ready to fly.

"Why don't we see people?" she asked.

"I thought we did," I said.

"Once a month, if that."

"Then let's see people."

So we began to see people again. Every Saturday night. We invited people to our house, and we were invited in return. We found a reliable baby-sitter. We went to plays. We went to art exhibits at the Metropolitan, the Modern, the Huntington Hartford, the Guggenheim, not to mention the private galleries as plentiful as candied fruit in the enormous art-cake offered by the city.

Desire breeds companions. Women, it seems to me, can do this better than men—find friends to meet the needs of their lives. Or is it just me who still clings to some idea of perfection in friendship? Left to myself, I doubt I could have gathered the circle of people Dodie did. She never hesitated to invite some interesting man, woman, or married couple we might meet for the first time at somebody's Saturday night party. At times I was annoyed.

"But we don't know them," I would complain.

"What do you mean 'don't know them'? We talked for hours at the Engles'."

"I know, but isn't that a sort of secondhand acquaintance? I mean, how do you know they'll like us?"

Dodie had—*has*—why should I assume she's changed?—has a way of slowing up in conflict. Her speech begins to drawl. She picks her words more carefully. Even her body slouches more than usual, and sitting (she was usually sitting when we argued) she would become annoyingly languid.

"I *don't* know," she answered. "But if they'd rather not know us, they can always say no."

"Yes, I suppose so, but it seems kind of *eager* to be running after people that way. Why not wait? Why not have them call you first?"

"Oh, my God, David! How absurd!"

"Why? Why is it absurd?"

"Because it is. A child's ego in a man is absurd."

No doubt she was right. I can see that her way of looking at things was more mature. I guess I could see it even then, but how surprised and secretly angry I was that she didn't guess at a reluctance that had nothing to do with ego, childish or otherwise. Dodie had chosen a direction for our lives, and she hadn't consulted me at all about my willingness to go along. It's true that my interests were *more or less* in the direction Dodie was going, but there was something in that social-art frenzy that I didn't like —a kind of new idolatry; a special, New York idolatry, where the circle of devotion was so vast and varied that starting points would seem new by the time one completed the round.

But if I didn't want that, then what did I want? I don't know. I only knew what I didn't want.

I didn't want the plays. I began to hate the plays. Was there some envy in the fact that I had quit writing myself? Perhaps, a little, and that little may have deepened and accelerated my reaction, but the *plays,* not my envy, were the wormy apples of discord. How stupid they were! Oh, not all, I suppose, but certainly enough for the feeling to grow in me that I had signed on for a perpetual tour of lurid exhibitionism, the kind of exhibitionism displayed behind those plate glass-front whorehouses in old Berlin where erotic fancies paraded body-warm and dream-costumed. Devoid of meaning. Hysterical rages and perversions dressed up to pass for ideas and emotions.

I remember an evening when after one such play we had gone for a drink at some bar—another couple, Dodie, me. It was the three of them against me. They had liked the play, defended it. I hated it, execrated it. The other chap—his name was Lester, I recall—Lester Pickering—we never saw the Pickerings again after that evening—anyway, it was Lester who said he wasn't sure he had understood the play but that he didn't have to understand the play to enjoy it. I laughed and shook my head sarcastically. I said I didn't believe it. He said it was quite true; things not understood could be enjoyed. I said it was a pathetic self-deception, the very thing these frauds depended on. What was that, Lester wanted to know—what was it these frauds depended on? I said they depended on the general human knuckleheadedness that equates obscurity with meaning. Lester tipped his knuckle head, raised his eyebrows. Lester's wife looked at her watch.

Later, in the car, Dodie and I had a fight. I supposed aloud that I shouldn't have said what I said, but I couldn't see why I had to sit still for that kind of idiocy. We were both smoking, I recall. We both flicked our ashes furiously at the ashtray protruding out of the dashboard like a malicious tongue. I remember that particularly, how our arms went out, our fingers tapped, our cigarettes sparked. I said that in a very real sense Lester's remarks were just as insulting to me. It was insulting to expect me to accept his brainlessness.

"I happened to have enjoyed it, too," Dodie said, slowly, distantly.

"Oh, come off it, Dodie, you did not."

Silence.

"You feel you *should* have enjoyed it, but don't fall into the Lester Pickering trap of believing you did."

Silence.

"If you did enjoy it, then there must have been a reason. You must have understood something I didn't. Would you mind telling me what that was?"

Silence.

"Dodie, for Christ sake, don't sit there pretending that there are some things which are just beyond words, that there are some things which can't be explained to hopeless fools like me. I *understand* words, Dodie! I even *write* them! And that play was nothing but words! There was nothing going on beyond my powers of comprehension."

"Wasn't there?" Dodie said.

"No! Nothing!"

Silence.

"Explain it to me!" I challenged her.

Silence.

"Goddamit, Dodie, explain it to me if you're so fucking hip to the scene. Explain this esoteric shit to me. Don't let me flounder in ignorance my whole life!"

"David, either you stop shouting at me or stop this car and let me get out."

I wonder why I was so angry. *Why so angry?* I think I was so angry because I feared that there was indeed something I didn't understand. Not the plays. The plays were mindless. Or were they? Was it only to my mind that they seemed mindless? Is there a way of being that is completely unlike my own? Is there a world of sensibility I haven't even approached? Do things appear to other people in a different light?

Oh, I recognized what was happening, but I assumed it to be the kind of difficulty that naturally comes to people after a certain time of living together. Lenny was growing up. Dodie and I were growing older. But I still looked for convergence somewhere in time. I mean, how many things can one person be in a lifetime? How many things can one person do? When does experiment end

142

and *being* begin? I had been through a Depression and a war. I had done my share in building a business. I enjoyed good music and good books. I loved my son and my wife.

I mean I *loved* Dodie, despite the difficulty that had crept into our lives. Christ, I don't know what sex is supposed to be! What women want it to be! I hate this D. H. Lawrence crap! God made men and women as he made them, and I wasn't going to be crippled by the cult of male inadequacy.

"Is it a matter of time?" I asked Dodie.

"What do you mean?"

"That it's over too quickly, that's what I mean."

"Don't be silly."

"Then what?"

"Did I say anything was wrong?" she asked.

"Yes. Not in words. You know very well what I mean. Is it supposed to take *hours?* Do you want me to do *tricks?*"

"David, please, don't be ridiculous."

"Then what?"

"Nothing."

"Dodie, what is it?"

"It has nothing to do with our bodies," she said, softly, distantly.

I took her words to mean that I was performing well but that sex wasn't everything. Indeed not. I knew that. There was conflict. We seemed to want the same things in different ways. A question of degree, no more than that. In time there would be convergence. But it had nothing to do with our bodies. Other needs required adjustment. If there had to be a disarrangement in our lives, this was the one my pride preferred.

We had planted a Japanese cherry tree some years after we had moved into the house. It stands to the left of the garage driveway as one faces the house. In ten years it has grown almost as high as the house itself. For a few weeks in spring, it puts forth blossoms so lavishly pink that sometimes I have felt embarrassment walking out on bright mornings and seeing that naked sensu-

143

ousness sunning itself on a suburban street. And on springtime nights, when Dodie and I—or sometimes Dodie and I and Lenny (for I seem to connect the fullness of the tree with the fullness of Lenny's adolescence)—would return from a visit, the headlights of the car would flood into the blossoms and expose that palpitant color concealed in the darkness. Seeing the Japanese cherry tree during the weeks of its efflorescence clogged my throat with repletion and joy. It was my talisman. It promised me forgiveness and renewal. Sometimes, when I would walk out of the house on my way to the morning train, I would call "Hey!" to Dodie, and she would join me on the doorstep to look at the tree together for a few moments.

I think it was three years ago—yes, three—a bad time—everything and everybody had become an occasion for argument—that Dodie refused to come to the door one morning when I called her.

"The tree," I said.

"Yes, I know," she said from the house, not advancing. "It's lovely."

"Don't you want to look?" I asked.

"I'll look later," she said.

We had had people over the night before, friends gathered from the professions, business, advertising, art. There was the usual talk of politics and art, and then the small, select exchanges among those who have tested each other in areas of true interests and concerns. The women who wished to talk about their children. The men who wished to talk about new accounts and old grievances. All very familiar, very harmless, and for me, that evening, very deadly.

What happened was that it came to me (a revelation ripening for years) that I didn't love these people. But not at all. And I was sure that they didn't love me, because I was usually the odd man out when these little pairings off took place. I guess I never did have the patience, or the sympathy, to make myself a partner in these intimacies. When it happened on that night, I did what

144

I customarily did: made myself useful. I gathered the loaded ashtrays and the empty glasses and carried them to the kitchen.

There's a small radio in the kitchen, and I often turn it on in the morning to hear the latest catastrophes, or, if that is too disheartening, to listen to music. I switched on the radio that evening as I rinsed glasses. A contralto voice throbbed out the last notes of something very beautiful.

"Shit!" I whispered regretfully to myself.

"What?"

Dodie had entered the kitchen.

"I could have been listening to that," I said softly, trying to blur my meaning with a smile.

Dodie went to the cupboard and took out the coffee percolator, which she began to fill with water. When it was filled, she spoke without looking at me: "Do you know that you are your father all over again?"

"Come off it," I laughed.

"Completely and utterly your father," she emphasized, "and you don't begin to have his reasons for being that way."

The next morning she would not come to look at the blossoms —or any morning after that.

21.

Kathy wears her black dancing outfit and improvises to Berlioz'
Symphonie Fantastique. Gray imprints of dust patch her behind
and knees. I can see that she is not familiar with the music, and
her eyes have the frantic concentration of a little girl trying to
keep up in a game which is proving a little too fast and tricky for
her. The musical ideas run ahead of her. I feel as though I'm
watching a film in which the sound track is out of timing. Now she
is on the floor, one leg beneath her, the other leg stretched out,
head bowed, right hand grasping her right ankle, a pose expressing the inexpressible—a mother's grief, the sack of cities. But the
music has bounded away, and Kathy is on her feet with a jump,
a two-footed *thump* upon the floor. The people below will be up
any second crying havoc! It is muscularly clear to me that Kathy
is not ashamed of her body. I hear the voice of some other black-
garmented female saying, *"Now the first thing you must learn is
not to be ashamed of your body."* Kathy has learned the first thing
well. She strains for positions, putting her Maillol-proportioned
limbs at the service of some fugitive choreographic idea. Her face
is beaded with sweat. Her mouth is open and her nostrils flare
as she noisily sucks for air. Occasionally she breaks wind. No
matter. She is not ashamed of her body. She is dancing.

"Hah-h-h-h!" she wheezes, lying cruciform on the floor, rib
cage heaving. "Hoo-o-o-o!"

146

Berlioz is through, too.

"Will you make a career of dancing?" I ask.

"No."

"Why not?"

"I'm not good enough."

"You look good enough. You love it."

"That doesn't make me good enough," she says, getting up from the floor and going to the bathroom to shower.

She decides to shampoo while she is up and doing, and after her shampoo she spreads a towel across her shoulders and arranges her hair over the towel like fibers let to dry in some old handcraft process.

Now she sits opposite me in her Empire robe, damp and glistening, eating fried eggs and ham and canned asparagus. She sits with her usual orthopedic perfection.

"What are you thinking?" I ask.

She glances at me, shaking her head. "Nothing," she says.

"Kathy."

I can see she is remembering her promise. "What I was thinking?" she muses. "I was thinking about a boy by the name of Chris Tomlinson. A kid in school. An absolute nut. He couldn't sit still a minute. Always had his hand up. He had an opinion on everything—but *everything!* Not that he was stupid, he wasn't, but one time"—Kathy lowers her head and giggles into her hands—"I remember one time—it was in American Lit—we were discussing *The Portrait of a Lady*—by Henry James—you know?—and suddenly Chris burst out"—and here Kathy's voice goes surprisingly into a higher register—" 'The trouble with the goddam book is that it isn't only Ralph Touchett who hasn't got any goddam balls, *nobody* in the book's got any goddam balls!' "—and with the last word Kathy lifts her head, holds her hands prayer fashion in front of her, and lets herself go in the pure ringing abandon of one still near enough to childhood to retain the full virulence of laughter.

"Did you like this boy, Chris what's-his-name?" I ask.

Kathy sighs deeply, lowers her hands. "Sort of," she says. "He

147

didn't mean anything to me one way or the other, but I sort of liked him."

"Did you find him attractive?"

"God, no! He was tall and skinny. He had a face like a hatchet."

"Then you can like boys you don't find especially attractive?"

She looks at me in a dilation of wonder. "Of course I can!" she exclaims. "What do you think I am?" After a pause, she adds, "I can't imagine him in bed, though. He's a friend of Brian."

"Who's Brian?"

"Brian's the boy I told you about. The one who lives in the Village. Brian Miller. I was thinking about how Brian and Chris used to sit around on the floor in Brian's room and drink beer—"

"Where?"

"In school."

"Not you?" I ask her.

"Not me what?"

"Not you sitting on the floor and drinking beer?"

"Oh, yes. Me too. Sometimes."

"Go on."

"I was unhappy then," she says.

"Why?"

"Because I was no more to Brian than Chris was. It seemed to me he would just as soon be with Chris as with me. I always wondered why. I even thought sometimes that they might be making out, but I know there's nothing faggy about either one of them. It wasn't that Brian didn't enjoy it with me. He did. We used to fuck in his room, and it was wonderful. I mean for him too! I could tell. Chris could never do that for him. Why would he want to be with Chris as much as with me? That's why I was thinking about Chris when you asked me—and then I thought about that time in the classroom."

"Was there something in that classroom scene that made you understand Brian and Chris better?" I ask.

"Sort of," she says. "But I don't think I could explain it."

"Try."

She is silent for several seconds, her bare feet propped on the crossbar of the chair, performing a dreamy simulacrum of her three-phase exercise. She says at last, "I don't know, thinking of Chris waving his arms and stammering, I realized you couldn't make up enthusiasm you didn't feel. No matter how much you wanted to. Even if your life depended on it, I guess. Brian and Chris used to sit around and talk books until the words were like taffy in my brain. Did you ever see one of those taffy machines? You know, one of those"—she extends the forefingers of each hand and rotates them round each other in an eccentric motion—"bars that turn and turn, pulling the taffy. My father once took us to Atlantic City when he was attending a doctors' convention. That's where I saw the taffy machine."

"Yes," I say. "You were telling me about Brian and Chris."

"So what of it?" she snaps vexedly. "I mean, you said I should tell you whatever was on my mind."

"That's true," I say. "I'm sorry. Are you thinking of your father in Atlantic City right now?"

She shrugs. "Not really. I thought of him because of the taffy."

"I see," I say. "Go ahead."

She looks at me sullenly. "Go ahead where? About Brian and Chris? The taffy? My father?"

"Whatever you're thinking."

"I'm not thinking anything right now. Frankly, I think this is dumb."

"Then that's what you're thinking," I say. "Why is it dumb?"

"Because the mind doesn't stay on one thing," she answers. "The second you start talking, you begin to think of other things."

"That's quite true," I admit. "But one of those thoughts made you angry. Which one?"

"I don't know. *You* made me angry, asking all those questions. You know, you're not a psychoanalyst. . . . All right, I'm sorry, I promised. What do you want to know now?"

"Nothing except what you're thinking. Whose image do you have in mind now?"

"Brian's."

"Do you love him?"

149

"I don't know. I used to. I used to be terribly in love with him. But he won't let himself be loved."

"That's never stopped anyone from loving," I say. "How won't he let himself be loved?"

"How? You don't really expect me to answer that, do you? He just *won't,* that's all! By looking at me, that's how. By looking at me with that smile, as if he had something tremendous on his mind, and he'd just love to tell somebody about it—*but not me!*"

"Do you think you'd understand if he did tell you?" I ask.

"Oh, Christ, yes!" she cries in exasperation. "I'd understand. It isn't all that"—she compresses her lips, looks for the word, finds it—"*recondite!* In fact, I *always* understood what he and Chris were talking about. It's just that it got so *boring!* They'd go on and on about Fitzgerald and Faulkner and Hemingway and Anderson and Sartre, and I would understand every fucking word, so help me, but it got so unbearably *boring!*"

"Kathy, for God's sake, why would you want to stay if you were so bored?"

She shrugs.

"Why, Kathy?"

"Why do you think?" she replies at last. "Because of Brian."

"Because you love him? Why do you love him if he bores you?"

"He *doesn't* bore me."

"But you just said he does. He and Chris. Talking."

"The talking bores me. Brian doesn't."

"That's a very curious distinction," I say. "I don't understand it. It would seem to me that if Brian's talking bores you, then Brian bores you."

"That's how much you know."

"Tell me what you know."

"Oh, really, David, please! Don't be dense! What does one thing have to do with the other?"

I look at her, not smiling, not frowning, just waiting. Kathy broods on my density for a time. Then she begins to make the distinction for me: "He has gray hair," she says. "You know, premature gray. Not much, just a little. And sort of gray eyes. He cuts

150

his hair short. He's not a hippie, or anything. And he has the most beautiful smile I've ever seen on a man." She pauses, gazing at the topography of her love. "Perfect teeth." She plants the heels of her hands on the sides of her chair and rocks back and forth.

"Then why are you staying here?" I ask her.

"Brian shacks up with other girls," she answers promptly, her voice going flat. "I know he does. It doesn't mean anything to him, so why should it mean anything to me. There were other boys before Brian, I can assure you. I mean, I know I'm going to get married someday, and it probably won't be to Brian, and in the meantime I'm physically mature, have been for years. I know, you're shocked. I'm sorry, David, but that's your hangup, not mine. Oh, I don't go to bed with everybody I happen to like. Don't get that idea. The circumstances have to be right, and when they are—well, there's no reason not to. Besides—"

"Besides what?"

She tips her head, looks arch. "I was kind of curious about you."

"In Vermont?"

"Before that."

"Before?"

A retrospective smile touches Kathy's lips. Suddenly I am made to feel the wealth of concealment this talk, or months of talk, will never touch.

"Lenny used to be in on those book-yak sessions," she tells me. "Brian borrowed your book from Lenny. He liked it. Brian did. Maybe I shouldn't tell you this, but Brian and Lenny had a sort of argument about the book. Lenny—"

"I'm familiar with my son's views," I say quickly.

The smile remains on Kathy's lips. "Brian would like you to read his novel," she says.

I get up from the table and go into the kitchen for the coffeepot. I pour coffee into Kathy's cup, into mine, and then I sit down again.

"I'm flattered," I say, "but I don't think I'd want to pass judgment on Brian's novel."

151

She shrugs. "That's okay with me," she declares, waving one hand indifferently. "That's strictly your business."

"Yes," I say. "Tell me more about your father."

Kathy snaps her head away from the question. "I don't want to tell you more about my father, if you don't mind."

"Why not?"

"Because I'm tired, that's why," she replies, her words heavy with hostile energy. "If you want to go on with this sort of thing, you'll have to put a time limit on it."

"All right," I say. "That ends the session for today. Shall we say fifteen minutes in the future? Unless, of course, you feel like going on. I'll sit over here and have a cigarette. Do you mind if I put on some music?"

Kathy drinks her coffee. Her hair falls forward. She hooks a moist mass over each ear.

"It doesn't look to me that you have that much to do," she says.

"I don't," I readily agree. "I have literally nothing to do, except think about my life and make love to you."

"I don't see that it would be such an awful imposition," she persists.

"No imposition at all, if I wanted to. But I don't."

"Won't you even consider it?"

"I don't know, Kathy, do *you* think I should consider it? Do *you* want me to read it?"

"I think you could at least consider it," is all I can wring from her.

"All right. I'll consider it."

22.

That novel. Mine. About London in wartime. The fact is I did have in mind to say something large and permanent, but somewhere in the writing (which means somewhere in my recollection of that time, because I actually began the novel at the war's end, in Germany, while awaiting redeployment, and finished it during my first six months of civilian life) I realized that the true source of feeling was not love and the nightmare of wrecked cities but war and the fantasy of myself walking London streets in daylight or in the blue terror of searchlights. I was in love with London, and when I began to write I transposed that love into a girl by the name of Blanche—which, incidentally, was not the name of the Canadian Air Force girl mentioned by Bob Rohrmoser, or the name of the actual girl used in my story. I don't know why I feel reticent about names and identities at this point in time and distance, but I do. At any rate, the girl, the real girl, the one who became Blanche in the story, lived in a little cellar room off Baker Street. For months I paid the rent.

I was not in love with her, but I did take her places—movies, restaurants, bars, even concerts. She was a plain girl with fair, frizzy hair, and a childish inability to pronounce her "l's": "*I'm code. Please cuddoo me.*" She worked as a clerk in one of the ministries. The pay was a joke. The first time she asked me to pay the rent was when she had bought several "frocks" in order to look nice for the nice occasions when we went to movies or a restaurant. I was glad to pay the rent, because I felt so sorry for her. And I was happy that she was happy about the movies and the restaurants and the nights we spent in her icy room feeding life into the gas ring with shillings.

But, as I say, the true love was born of the fantasy of myself walking along the Serpentine, having a pint of ale at Verrey's, standing on the Strand and looking in the direction from which the old conquerors had come a thousand years ago. I drew that girl into the love, and I began to re-create it a little later with different names for the people and different directions for the love.

This is a digression, I know, but it's a needed digression. And perhaps it isn't a digression at all. At first I didn't know why I thought of war and London and the girl after the telephone call I just received, but perhaps I do now. The war, myself in London, that too was both fantastic and inevitable, given the world of those years. Similarly, I knew that the drift of these days couldn't go on indefinitely. I've been more or less waiting for the hard, eventful bend that would signify a change. And now here it was—the telephone call from Arthur Gerson.

Even as he identified himself—"Hello, David. How are you? This is Arthur"—I felt a strong need to understand certain things about myself. My mind groped for supportive memories. I thought of the war, my novel, the girl on Baker Street, all the astonishing things that had become part of my history.

I don't know if this has ever happened to you. It has to me, several times in my life. I mean the crisis occasions when the instincts choose among themselves which shall predominate—panic or calm, fear or courage, murk or lucidity. When Arthur announced himself to me, I experienced a reaction which hitherto I had thought confined solely to books: "flesh crawled" . . . "hair bristled." The sensation centered around the nape of my neck. A swarm of dormant nits seemed to have become activated by his voice.

"So there you are," I said.

"I'd like to talk to you, David," he said. "Will you let me talk to you?"

"How did you know where to find me?" I asked.

"Dodie," he said.

"Did she want you to get in touch with me, or is this your own idea?"

"I don't know," he replied. "Let me think. Does it matter? Look, David, I'm not *representing* Dodie, if that's what you're thinking. There's a lot of nonsense going on, and I do think it's time we all cut our losses. Could we meet and talk about this?"

"Talk about what?"

"I suppose you know that Lenny is not coming home the first week of Christmas?"

"Isn't he? No, I didn't know that. How the hell do you know it?"

"Dodie told me. The last time she spoke to Lenny, he told her he would stay in Vermont during the first week of his Christmas holiday. He said—"

"If you don't mind, I'd rather not discuss Lenny with you. Do you mind?"

"All right," said Arthur. "But would you want to discuss other matters over the phone, or shall we get together?"

"You would want that?" I asked. "You would want us to get together?"

"I would. I think it's time we all cut our losses."

"Yes, you said that before. Of course there've been losses before now. Considerable, from my point of view. I wonder why it is that *now* is the time for all of us to cut our losses? Has the distribution of losses shifted or something?"

A slight intake of breath at the other end. He said, "I don't think sarcasm is going to be helpful in this situation. I don't blame you for being sore, but under the circumstances sarcasm is silly and futile. Frankly, David, I didn't think that cruelty was your bag."

I spaced out the seconds before answering, fighting down what had to be fought down. "When would it be convenient for you?" I asked. "I was going to get in touch with you, if you hadn't got in

155

touch with me. I agree that it's time we all cut our losses. Would tomorrow do?"

"Well, I'm— All right, I'll make the time."

"Where?" I asked. "Your office?"

He hesitated. "Wouldn't you rather have lunch somewhere?"

"I'd just as soon meet at your office, if that's all right."

"All right. Twelve thirty? Most of the people here will be out to lunch."

"Fine. Twelve thirty. Your office."

Several days after I had returned from Vermont, I phoned Lenny to tell him that I had taken up temporary quarters away from home. I gave him the address and the telephone number. Since that time, I haven't heard from him, and for the first time in my life, or his, I did not succumb to impulse and phone again. Since he was—oh, what?—fourteen?—fifteen?—I've been saying to myself that I must take the right occasion to see if so many years of investment could produce some return. Naturally, I have no idea how many times Dodie might have phoned Lenny, or he her. Possibly there has been daily communication. Possibly Dodie has been carrying on her own negotiations at a furious rate, and Lenny has been waiting to hear what counterproposals I have to make. These are mere figures of speech, of course. Anyway, these things have been present in my mind for the past few weeks. The fact is I have no counterproposals to make. I would have waited indefinitely for Lenny to phone me, but now I must phone him. I did so. He was not in his room. I left a message with Bob Rohrmoser for Lenny to phone me at whatever hour he returned.

Kathy returns to the apartment at about ten thirty in the evening. She says hello, removes her mottled coat, hangs it away, walks directly into the kitchen and pours herself a glass of milk. She saunters back to the living room and sits down in the sling armchair. I am sitting on the chrome-and-foam sofa. God knows what she does with her time, although her large face looks ruddy enough. Has she been in touch with her parents? Her aunt? How long does she intend to go on this way? Will she go back to school after the Christmas holidays? Is she taking drugs? She looks sullen, unhappy. I know nothing about her.

"What's up, Kathy?" I ask.

She regards me with her large, hazel eyes. The sclerae have a bluish tinge. Perhaps it's her eye shadow that makes them appear that way. Health and anomie. Is it a habit of mind which makes me ask continually what is to become of her, what she intends to do with her life?

"Brian asked if he could meet you sometime," she says.

"Would you want me to meet him?" I ask.

"Why ask me?" she says, twitching one shoulder violently. "That would be something for you to decide, wouldn't it? You wouldn't be obliging *me*."

"I thought I would be," I say. "I told you before, Kathy, that I wasn't the least minded to oblige Brian. I don't know him, and I have a feeling it would be best if we left it that way."

"Then okay," she says. "Then I guess you better not."

"Then I guess I won't."

"What the hell's turned you off tonight?" she wants to know, looking at me sourly.

I regard Kathy silently, thinking of the inflated verbal currency she uses, they all use: "turned off" . . . "turned on" . . . "thing" . . . "bag." They have to shop in the same marketplace I do for the multitude of life's needs, and this vernacular play-money will never cover their expenses. New currency is printed all the time, and those left with last year's issue are pauperized. Besides, I've not been "turned off." I've been "turned on." Not in the way she means, however. My nerves are humming. By tomorrow afternoon, I may be a murderer.

"I take it you had a fight with Brian," I say.

Kathy sits down on the floor yogi-fashion, looking into the cat's-cradle formed by her legs. Her hair falls forward. All this drapery and mysticism. No, I won't be a murderer. I'm not the murdering type. But what shall I do between now and noon tomorrow? I refuse to spend all those hours devising a gesture. It's too humiliat-

157

ing. I must depend on some instinctive action when the moment arrives. But I'm not good at instinctive actions. I've always covered uncomfortable moments with smiles and patter and a vague general dismissal of the absurdity of crisis. That part of my life is over, however. I've come to understand that crisis is crisis, necessary confrontation, not to be dismissed.

Kathy peeps up at me through the foliage. She says, "Do you believe that anybody, a man, can love everybody he comes into contact with, indiscriminately, male or female, *everybody?*"

"I don't. Does Brian?"

"You should see her!" Kathy seethes. "The latest creep they've got hanging around. She looks like a pigeon with eyeglasses! I swear! A dead-white pigeon with big, pink eyeglasses! Can you picture it? She's a poet. She's had a poem published. In a real magazine. That makes her the most interesting female since—since—Jane Austen!"

"What are you thinking, Kathy?" I ask.

Again she gazes downward, the foliage falling forward. "It's confused," she says. "I was thinking that if you read Brian's book, then—"

"Yes?"

"I don't know. . . . I'd love to see his face when you tell him it stinks."

"Have you read it?" I ask.

"Parts."

"Does it stink?"

"I don't know. Sometimes I think it's good, sometimes I think it's awful."

"Depending on how you feel about him?"

"Yes," she nods, emphatically. "Yes! I'm not kidding. When I hate Brian, I hate his stupid book. I think it's stupid, pretentious, and a bore! I mean, *juvenile!*"

"And when you're loving Brian?"

"Then I love his book. Then I see it as a way of telling the truth. I—"

The phone rang.

"That could be Lenny," I say, going to the phone.

But it isn't Lenny. It's Rich.

"Where the hell are you?" he asks.

"Right here, Rich. How are you?"

"There's mail for you here," he says. "I keep telling Mary to hold on to it, expecting you from day to day. There are things I want to discuss with you. I don't like this disappearing act. I've had requests from any number of people who want you to do free-lance assignments. Are you interested?"

"No, Rich. Not now."

"Why have you disappeared?"

"I haven't disappeared, as you see, hear. I'm just doing a little hibernating. How are things going? How are you getting along with Ted?"

Rich disregards that. He says, "Dave, we're going to make a lot of money here. You shouldn't have bugged out, you shmuck. You could have been a rich man."

"It doesn't matter, Rich, but from habit I feel jealous. I'm glad it's going well."

"Listen," Rich says, "do you still have little Miss Hot-Box with you?"

"Yes."

"Why don't you bring her over to the house Saturday night? We're having some people. No one who would be embarrassing."

"Rich—"

"What?"

"I'm seeing Arthur Gerson tomorrow."

A few seconds of silent thoughtfulness. My mind does a quick sketch while I'm waiting: Arthur Gerson's bare chest with a pipette sticking out of it. Beneath is a large, gem-encrusted goblet receiving the blood.

"Where are you going to see him?" Rich finally asks.

"His office."

"Don't be an asshole," Rich warns. "Slug him in his office and you're cooked. You'll be giving Dodie all the ammunition."

"No heart's blood?" I ask.

159

"The time is long past," he correctly points out. "Dave, behave."

"You know me," I say.

"What are you seeing him for anyway?"

"He thinks we ought to cut our losses."

"Jesus! Do you want me to go with you? If I hit him, it's simple assault."

"Thank you, Rich, but I've got to know the outcome of this meeting. I think it's important to my future."

"Okay. How about Saturday?"

I put my hand over the mouthpiece. "Kathy," I say, "would you care to visit some friends with me on Saturday?"

She shakes her head. "Can't. Not Saturday."

I remove my hand. "Mind if I come alone?"

"Of course not."

Lenny's call came after midnight. I had stretched out on the sofa, a funnel of light from the pole lamp directed on last week's Sunday supplement, which lay like a large marker between consciousness and the dream that had been waiting for me on the other side of the page I had been reading. The ring of the telephone incorporated itself into the dream in a heartbreaking way that I couldn't recall.

"I have a long-distance call for David Lang."

"This is he," I say, overwhelmed by a sudden flood of love for Kathy, for Lenny, for Dodie, for myself, separated as we all were by petulance and pride.

"Hello," comes Lenny's voice—and everything is re-established, all the secrets of personal history that cannot be undone.

"Lenny. How are you?"

"Fine. Bob gave me your message—"

"Yes. I phoned. I understand you're not coming home for the holidays."

"Who said that? Just the first week. I have almost three weeks. It's the first week I won't be home."

"That's what I meant," I say. "Under the circumstances, don't you think you should come home as soon as you can?"

"If you think so."

"Don't you?"

"Mother didn't ask me to."

"Did you phone her?"

"She phoned me."

"Have *you* phoned *her* since I saw you up there?"

"But, Dad, she's called me twice."

"I see. And I didn't call you. Therefore the silence."

Silence.

"Lenny—"

"I wasn't sure you wanted me to phone you," he says.

"Oh, come off it! You'll have to think of something better than that! What manner of reasoning would make you come to such a conclusion? Have I ever not wanted you to phone me in the past?"

"Look, if you'd rather I came right home—"

"I want an answer, Lenny. I don't understand your attitude. All these advanced views you pretend to have, but when you're faced with a situation calling for a little understanding, a little maturity, you draw into yourself like a sulky animal."

"I didn't want to be a go-between," he says.

"*Go-between!* What the hell are you saying? Were you ever put in such a position before?"

"Christ, yes! Not directly, but—you know you have, Dad, in one way or another."

I know nothing of the sort, but suddenly I am cold and cautious. Apparently there's no limit to the things I don't—or didn't—know. But I have begun to learn how to hunt in this wilderness.

"What did you plan to do that week—ski?" I ask.

"Yes," he says, his voice brightening considerably. "I'm just about at that point where I can really *ski*. There's a guy up here, sort of a semipro, Lars Schreiber, and he's been giving me some pointers. If I skied steady for that week, I'd really be over the hump."

"And Mother has no objection to your staying?"

"She didn't say anything."

"Then stay."

"I got my marks," he says. "Two 'A's' and three 'B's.' "

"That's fine. How will you be coming home?"

"By bus, I guess."

"Well, if you do, phone me beforehand, let me know what time you'll be arriving. I'll pick you up at the terminal."

"Okay."

"Take care," I say.

"Right. See you, Dad."

Kathy, whom I thought asleep, is sitting up in bed, enfolding her legs with her arms. It seems to me there was a girl in my dream who had done just that very thing.

"I hope," she says in a drowsy voice, "I just hope that if I ever have kids, I'll never forget that they have eyes and ears."

23.

Morning. Another bright day. I started out much too early, telling Kathy I had business to attend to. She stood at the bathroom door combing her hair straight down on either side of a plumb-line part. I found South Sea island connotations in her hair, her nudity, her facial bone structure. Were I less preoccupied I would have asked her what she was thinking. I wondered whether we were undergoing a change through the usual operations of involvement. I could see myself taking Kathy in my arms and making a plea for understanding and forgiveness. I could see us venturing out as lovers, making an odyssey of the city, telling each other the selected fables of our lives. But I will be forty-eight not too far into the new year. I am capable of only so much self-delusion. I have embarked on a serious project. I left Kathy her weekly twenty and walked out of the apartment.

Into a crisp, clear day. It's only ten o'clock. What shall I do with the hours? I begin to walk south, toward Columbus Circle, then east along Fifty-ninth Street to Fifth Avenue, then south on Fifth Avenue, where the shops are dressed for Christmas. There was a time when I loved the shops at Christmas. Now I feel nothing. They are not vulgar, as so many claim. I think they are done in good taste, but like almost everything else these days they are in the hands of fashion. Everything is in the hands of fashion, and it strikes me that history will note this as one of the prevailing modes when something comes to an end. I don't know exactly what. Civilization? Maybe. Not the world. Lenny said that nothing is the end of the world, and he's quite right. My mood, however, is shot with lurid flashes of finality. The man I was would not have been the one for this coming interview, but the transitional man I think of myself as being as decreed that this interview shall take place. Am I kidding myself about the transitional man? But look at how unlike myself I've been. Look at all the harsh things I've done. It was I who left my—our—house. Look at the way I've handled my father, my mother, my brother, Kathy, Dodie, even Lenny. . . .

I'm as far as Rockefeller Center in my southbound stroll. I did love this city at one time. I think it's this: I think a city of this size and inhuman variety can be the metaphor of human longing while that longing is still young and undefined; but when one knows what one is, what one can do, then the city no longer substitutes for the dream. The dream is defined, and one can pass through these looming streets and never once look up from that small, personal definition.

Twenty-three years ago, almost, Dodie and I stepped through the doors of that department store across the street after I had seen the annihilating look she had given herself in the mirror of the cosmetic counter. The sun was glinting off the metal trim of windows, as it is doing now. . . . The arcade of Rockefeller Center is jubilant with white, wire-wound figures playing bent fiddles. Beyond is the resplendent Christmas tree whose dimensions would have been the pride of the city, when the city took pride in anything. Inside, the rink and the skaters. I walk inside and look at the skaters. There's an Oriental gentleman on the ice performing an excruciating ballet of wish fulfillment. He can scarcely skate, much less figureskate, but clearly his heart is full of graceful swoops and pirouettes, which he executes with his hands, his hands only, while his awkward skates wobble gracelessly here and there. Two girls on my right squeal their mirth into their covering hands: *"Look, look, he's gerna do it again! O, my God, look at that! Look at those hands! I'm gerna die! It's just too much! . . ."* It's

164

now eleven o'clock. The Oriental gentleman at last falls on his prat, his hands still performing sinuous prayers. I leave the arcade and continue my way downtown.

At Forty-second Street I turn west and start toward the Seventh Avenue leg of my journey. A crosstown wind blows into my face. Once, on the last day of a dissolving friendship, I sat in that desperate little park across the street with my friend and listened to him recite in a monotone a story of such long and bizarre strife that I had to keep reminding myself that the two people he was talking about were Phil, himself, and Amy, his wife. The nature of that strife stunned me. Nine years and three children too late, she, the wife, hungered for nighttime streets, lean young men, beginnings, Bohemia. But even more stunning was the role I had unknowingly played during all those years. His wife would have been content, my friend informed me, if he were like me. *Me!* That is what she had told him, countless times, if he were like me a little, if he had brought into their lives some air of former freedom, wit, imagination—who knows? . . . *"Anyway, Dave, that's the way it's been. I know it's not your fault, but I have to be truthful and tell you that your existence has crapped on my life. It's an accident. I admit it. Like a couple of cars skidding. But I can't be friends with the other driver who hurt me. See? Give my love to Dodie, but for Christ sake stay the hell away from me! Maybe ten years from now, but right now forget it!"*

It's been more than ten years, Phil, but I think you'd still be interested to learn what has become of wit and imagination. Ten years is too high a price to pay for a little irony, but you might like to tell Amy, if she's still your wife, that nothing works forever.

And I do remember—now that every square of paving in the city is determined to contribute its mnemonic bit—that Dodie was neither surprised nor depressed at the fate of Phil and Amy. Yes, she could see Amy's point about Phil. Phil was a bore—well, not exactly a bore, but a man who had settled like a house on its foundations, all cracks showing. Of course I couldn't see. I was Phil's friend. I didn't eat and sleep and everything with Phil. All I took from Phil in our steadily decreasing meetings was a clutch of re-

165

membered hikes across the George Washington Bridge, Boy Scout packs on our backs, to build a fire and roast hot dogs somewhere on the Jersey Palisades. . . .

It is now eleven thirty. I have been walking very slowly, stopping at the display windows of Army and Navy stores, beneath the marquees of movie houses where the faces of girls in black panties are blocked out, like secret agents who risk their lives for our security. All that walking and all that thinking, and I am no nearer the word, the gesture . . . all right, then, this is what I will *not* do: I will not shake hands with him. That civilized I am not. And I will not sit down in the brown leather chair of his. I will just stand and look at him. Not a word. He must utter the first word. . . . Down these steps—buy a token. . . . Have you got the first word, Arthur? . . . No, this will never do. I must get off the next station and phone him. I must tell him not to wait for me. I must tell him that I will not subject myself to the sight of his sickening mug. . . . I will do nothing of the sort. I will stay on this train and do what I must.

Chambers Street. I walk the few blocks to the inescapable building—and push the elevator button for the twentieth floor—(you see, Arthur, I do remember)—and I am almost there—and here is the door: "Hillsborn, Gabriel and Gerson"—and this is surely the first crisis of my new life. . . . Well, then, what? What do I truly think, and what do I truly feel? No more digressions, no more retrospections. Just what do I truly think and feel? I truly think that I must truly think of what I truly think, or I shall go down to a dreadful defeat. I truly think that Arthur Gerson has done nothing which my wife, Dodie, did not wish and bring about. I think that in this time of enlightenment and free choice, Gerson owes me nothing but a decent regret for unhappy consequences. I think I cannot hate Arthur Gerson for having done what Dodie found most acceptable. I think that now I must enter this place. . . . "That you, David? Be with you in a moment" . . . and discover that while I must not hate Arthur Gerson for what he has done, I can't help hating him for having thought what

166

he thought while he was doing it! *Yes! I can hate him for that! Thank God, I can hate him for that!*

"Well, David—" His hand out.

Fair hair. Fair skin. Shell-frame eyeglasses. A little brown mole on his right eyelid, which I had forgotten. There is no consciousness in raising my arm, but like witnessing my own dream I witness the raising of my arm, and see myself swing, and feel the full, frank, considerable impact of my hand on Arthur's face, and see the shell-frame eyeglasses fly to the wall and fall. A full heart. A full, humiliating slap. As I had intended. As I had from the first intended. And there is Arthur, who has said, "Ooo!" with his hand to the left side of his face, where I have hurt him frankly and considerably and intentionally.

I feel shriven.

24.

"Are you satisfied?" he says.

"Somewhat."

"I can crucify you."

"No witnesses."

"I don't need any."

"Yes, you do."

"Oh, shut up! I was wearing *glasses,* you fool!"

"I was aware of that."

He has the glasses now, examines them. They're not broken. Tactilely it was everything I could have wished for, but to all my other senses it was an insulated experience. The wall from which Arthur's glasses rebounded is a large slab of cork, dark as the bark of a tree. The office settee on which they fell is another foam job, covered with royal blue fabric. The carpet to which the glasses then fell is a deep pile, sort of a tweed weave. Arthur has a handkerchief to his face. He puts his eyeglasses in his breast pocket, then looks at his handkerchief after dabbing it to the corner of his left eye. No blood. The light in this anteroom is not very good, what with these handsome somber surfaces, but I think I can make out a raw pink blossoming in the pale flesh.

"Well," he says, "are you going to finish the job?"

"I'm finished," I say. "Unless you'd like to continue."

"You know, I *am* going to press charges against you," he says, his light eyes unintimidated. His eyes are tawny. So is his hair. I see that he has gone in for the long sideburns. He comes toward me, and I put up my fists, assuming a posture I have never assumed before: David Lang, boxer. But Arthur has something else in mind. He stomps past me, rips open the door of the office, charges out. My posture disintegrates. Arthur returns in less than a minute, accompanied by an alarmed-looking gentleman with a friar's tonsure and a little potbelly.

"Mr. James," Arthur says, "I want you to witness this scene. This man, David Lang, has just now struck me in the face. I was wearing my glasses. Would you please look at my face. Does it appear to you that I've just been struck?"

"I would say—" begins Mr. James, but Arthur quickly takes over again.

"Do you admit striking me in the face?" Arthur asks me.

"I admit it," I say.

"Thank you very much, Mr. James," Arthur says to his neighbor, shaking his hand.

Mr. James nods, looks at me, departs. Arthur, I observe, already has a slight swelling around the corner of his left eye. Suddenly I feel the need of legal advice.

"Can I go to jail for that?" I ask.

"You're damn right you can! And I'll see to it that you do!"

What I have in mind is to go at him with both fists, thinking of sheeps and lambs; but though I detest him no less now than I did before (more, in fact, principally for his not having lost his self-possession), I find that I have lost all desire to hit him. I wanted to satisfy myself, not destroy him, and I've done that. I'm quite satisfied with what I've done, but I don't want to go to jail for it, or even be sued and have this particular period of my life taken up with a lot of legal nonsense. I know lawyers. And accountants. And insurance men. Not only will I be asked how much all of this is worth to me, but I'll probably get caught up in trying to figure it out. I don't want to spend my time in that way.

"You had your goddam nerve, asking me up here," I say. "What do you think I'm made of?"

169

"I don't know what you're made of, and I don't give a damn," Arthur replies. "You can get the hell out of here now."

"You wanted to talk to me," I remind him.

"Are you out of your mind! You come up here and hit me in the face, and then you carry on as though nothing has happened." He regards me with genuine curiosity. He says, "I didn't know whether to believe some of the things Dodie told me about you, but I see now that she knew what she was talking about."

His mention of Dodie's name sends a needful rush of chemistry through my veins. Adrenaline. Lye. Nitroglycerin. All passages are cleared, and my mind stands ready to race off in six directions. I choose what looks like a promising one.

"Does Rita know about you and Dodie?" I ask.

Arthur finally puts away his blasted handkerchief and takes his glasses from his breast pocket. He puts them on and points to them.

"Am I safe in doing this?" he asks. "Or do you think you might have another Neanderthal fit?"

"You can drop that shit," I tell him. "I asked you a question. You don't even have to answer it. Rita doesn't know, does she? That's one of the losses we're supposed to cut. Shall we sit down?"

"Let's go in my office," Arthur says.

We do. I've been in his office before, so I know where to look for the items I'm now free to despise with all my heart. Being an activist, Arthur keeps himself surrounded with active art and memorabilia. Goya and Daumier prints, of course. Several photographs of Arthur together with big shots in labor, civil rights, etc. Damn him, anyway! He makes me distrust my own inclinations. Off to one side, Arthur has the usual leather-bound volumes on the law, but more prominently displayed are the many shelves of protest literature. Commercial books in their dust jackets. So what's wrong with that? Nothing's wrong with that. Bravo! Except that I don't like people who wear their slogans too obviously. *Keep Christ in Christmas*. As if anyone keeps anyone from keeping his personal Christ in Christmas. And who's preventing Arthur from being engaged with his engagements? My prize emetic

170

is that collage—the first thing you see on entering—the one made of newspaper clippings and a meshed set of gears in the center. I know I'm describing this in the most invidious way possible, and that's deliberate enough, but even without my special effects I believe this office carries its own distinctive cachet of offensiveness.

Dodie! This!

Arthur sits down at his desk. The lighting is better in here, and I am able to make out the pink-and-white schematic of my hand on Arthur's face.

"Are you going to remain standing?" he asks. "Sit down. No, Rita doesn't know. If you're planning to say anything to her, I wish you'd let me know."

"Why the hell should I? Did you give me any advance notice of your plans?"

"Don't be ridiculous. I didn't have any *plans*."

"Like hell you didn't."

He looks at me quizzically. Clearly Arthur has been told something. I remember the dream of that afternoon in late October. What astonishes me is not the prophetic power of the dream but the miraculous chain of events that followed. The dream, after all, told me nothing about that. The dream itself was rejected by my terrified soul as an evil visitation, not to be accepted even in the helplessness of my dream, and by now it has become a little pocket of the past, warm and familiar, while each waking moment of my life since then has danced with fantasy.

"Look," Arthur says, "I don't know what Dodie has told you—"

"That's rough," I say. "But it does make things a little more even."

"I'm going to be absolutely truthful, David."

"You'd better be, since I happen to know the truth."

Arthur shakes his head. He swivels his chair around, looking out the window to his right. Eyeglass, eye mole, my hand upon his face. Several times he has twitched his cheek. I hit him hard. The sensation of it lies curled in the palm of my hand like a bristly little animal. He's angry now. It wouldn't do to push Arthur too far. He's neither a coward nor a fool.

171

"We've known each other for over three years," he says. "Dodie and I were attracted to each other almost immediately, but we did nothing about it, for at least two years. And there was all that visiting back and forth, if you recall."

"I recall."

"This despite the fact that you and Dodie hadn't had a decent relationship in over ten years."

"Who says?"

He removes his gaze from the window and turns it to me. "Did you?"

"I'm asking the questions!"

"Who do you think says?" he replies. "Dodie."

"What did she say?"

"Don't be ridiculous. You don't really expect me to tell you, do you?"

"I do!"

"And if I won't?"

"I'll be on a phone talking to Rita within five minutes."

Arthur swivels to the front of the desk. He slaps his hands down on the desk. "You can do as you goddam please!" he says, looking me straight in the eye. "I've had it with you." He points. "There's the door. Get out!"

He begins to get up. I begin to get up, too. Maybe he's not entirely wrong in his interpretation of my movement. He seizes a triangular brass ruler on his desk.

"You come near me, you sonofabitch, and I'll split your skull!" he says, and I think means.

"Sit down," I say.

"Get out!" he yells.

I sit down. "Arthur, sit down," I say, my voice quiet, controlled. "Why shouldn't you want to tell me?"

"Because it's none of your business," he says, sitting down and chucking the ruler on the desk.

"Whose business is it but mine?"

"Don't pretend that you don't know," he says. "People generally know that much about their lives."

172

"I *don't* know," I insist. "It's not true that we didn't have a decent relationship. I don't think it's true. But if Dodie said so, then I must know her reasons for saying it."

"Why don't you ask her?"

"We're not in touch, as you very well know. Besides, I don't think she'd tell me."

"Well, that would be her prerogative," Arthur says, sensing the shift in power.

"Whatever she said," I ask, "did you believe it? Really?"

"Of course."

"Then tell me."

"Why should I?"

"Because I loved Dodie very much, and when I found out about you and her I suffered the very old death of having rocks piled on me until I was crushed. You say that people know that much about their lives, whether they had a decent relationship or not—and maybe you're right—but the fact is that I thought Dodie and I did. If we did not, did not to the extent that all this would seem to indicate, did not for as long as you, or Dodie, say we didn't, then I must be told the truth."

"Why did you hit me?" Arthur asks.

"Because of the things you thought when you were making love to my wife," I tell him promptly.

"How would you know what I thought?"

"Because I'm human."

"I didn't think of you at all."

"If you didn't know me, I'd believe that," I say. "But you did know me, and you thought of me, and you pitied me, and you rationalized me, and you derived an added spice because of all of it, and I would ask you as one who has been hurt considerably more than you to please drop this now and tell me what Dodie told you about our relationship."

Oh, he is going to tell me the truth now! The decks of his realistic conscience have been cleared, and he is going to let me have it broadside!

"Well," he begins, "if you insist on knowing, Dodie told me that

173

you deliberately and systematically undermined her individuality, her quality as a woman, a human being. You weren't crude or obvious, but over the years you took away everything that gave her pleasure. By a long, subtle system of disparagement, you destroyed everything she wanted or enjoyed."

"Why are you telling me this, you lying bastard!" I shout, utterly astonished.

"Because you asked."

"I thought you would tell me the truth!"

"I am telling you the truth."

"No, you're not! You're making this up! Dodie couldn't have told you any such thing! There isn't a word of truth in any of it."

"Oh, is there not? Naturally, you would think it's a lie. I didn't imagine it was possible, but I guess you haven't the slightest conception what you were doing all those years."

"Is this Dodie's way of getting back?" I ask.

"Back for what?" Arthur asks, watching me closely.

"Never mind. Tell me—what long, subtle system of disparagement? Was she by any chance explicit?"

"The art lessons," he says.

"What about them?"

"You made her give them up."

"Then it's simply a matter of lies," I sigh. "Ordinary, garden-variety lies."

"Are you denying that you said to her that the world is full of mediocrities?"

"Did I say that? Yes, I said that. After she herself admitted that—she said that she realized—the context in which—"

"And the courses at N.Y.U.?"

"She was *bored!* Did she not tell you, as she told me on countless occasions, that she was *bored?*"

"You mocked her friends."

"What friends? Her friends were my friends. *You,* for dirty, treacherous example!"

"Books," he says.

"Books?"

174

"You always made snide comments about her reading detective stories."

"Snide comments! I simply said—when she asked—"

"And you refused to share her enthusiasms. That kind of childish perversity. Just because she would like a thing, you wouldn't."

"Oh, you couldn't have made this up!"

"And you were selfish."

"Selfish? How?"

"I can better tell you where."

"Where?"

"In bed."

I am on my feet, and Arthur is on his feet, and he has the brass ruler in his hand again, but I have no intention of attacking him. This interview is over.

"Put your mind at ease," I say to him. "You've cut your losses."

I walk out—out—and go down twenty floors—and walk out—out into the bright day.

25.

This city! It's unbelievable! Savages! Cannibals! The first two telephone booths had "Out of Service" labels pasted across the coin slots. The next one had the phone hanging at the end of the cord like a lynched rat. The next one had the coin box gutted and the dial mechanism twisted off. I could go to my old office, Rich's new enterprise, which isn't far, but I'd rather not. I don't want to talk to anyone but the one I want to talk to. There. There's another booth. Five will get you ten—ten?—a hundred!—a thousand!—sure enough!—look at that!—mouthpiece gone, earpiece gone! I tell you, I was in London during the war, the world was coming to an end in thunder and flame—Armageddon!—and the phone booths in the streets were in working order. I tell you, I don't remember a single one marked with the lyrics of a sex maniac's lullaby, much less this naked evidence of mechanical rape. This, mind you, in a city at war, blacked out, bombed nightly . . . Sid Simon isn't far from here. Sid Simon, my tennis partner, the odd extra, the figure who figured least to figure. I'm sure by this time that Sid Simon has learned or guessed at fishy doings at 2045 Garfield Terrace. *"Been away on a trip, Lang?" "Yes, indeed, a bad one, as they say."* . . . No more booths? Where, then? I must make a telephone call. I'm only two blocks away from my old building. Dare I risk? There are phone booths in the lobby. And it's lunchtime now—executive lunchtime—chances are Rich and Ted Buchholz are out to lunch.

176

It's very likely, however, that I'd bump into someone. Abe Brenner, for sure, living his death in a busy marble tomb . . . *"I could better tell you where!"* . . . That is a lie, Dodie! How dared you discuss such things with him! You have put yourself light years beyond the hope of forgiveness. What did I ever do to make you hate me so? I did nothing—*nothing!* Books? Dear God, *books!* What unmitigated crap! As if I ever gave a good goddam if you read Agatha Christie or whomever you liked! Once you asked me, and I said that detective stories didn't interest me. That's all! Can you deny that? . . . There's another booth. . . . And the *art* business! And the *school* business! I had no intention of speaking to you, Dodie, but now I must. Either you have gone insane over a long, subtle period of time, or I have. . . . *My God, will you look at that! The whole front torn off!* . . . Is Genghis Khan occupying this city? Why this savagery? Why this insane anger? Any moment I expect a horde to come round the corner, torches guttering. . . . Speaking of anger, who just hit whom in the face? I know, but I had *reasons.* And aren't there *other* reasons? Yes, yes, no doubt, but if you don't mind I have neither the time nor the inclination for large social questions right now!

Abe Brenner is missing. In his place is a stolid, shapeless woman wearing the same buff-colored jacket over a heavy knit sweater. So the time has come, has it? Coins. I need a dime. I don't have a dime. . . .

"May I have a pack of Marlboros?"

"The soft or the hard?"

"The what?—oh, the box, please—thank you. Are you Mrs. Brenner?"

"Yes?"

"And Abe?"

"You know Abe?"

"Yes, I worked here—"

"Abe is laying already."

"Oh—I'm sorry."

"In the hospital," she says. "The doctors want to torture him

177

a little more. He's finished, but the doctors want to torture him a little more."

"I'm sorry. When you see him will you give him the regards of David Lang?"

"Thanks. I heard your name. Abe says you're a nice man. I'll give him your regards."

"Please do. I'll hope for the best."

"The best is the end."

"Ah, well . . . Goodbye, Mrs. Brenner."

She nods.

Abe Brenner says I'm a nice man. In crossing the lobby to the phone booths, it occurs to me that never once in all the years that I traded with the now finished Abe Brenner did I ever give a thought to what he thought of me. Here and there, lying in odd corners of the city, like scraps of torn newspaper carrying out-of-date history, there must be fragments of opinion on David Lang. Someday, when I have the time, it would be interesting . . .

These old-fashioned booths in building lobbies are safe from vandals. My heart is jumping again. Why don't I give myself a rest? Never mind, go ahead. What will I say? I'll think of it when I have to. How strange! I haven't dialed the old number in so many weeks. I tell you—it's almost—I'm so flooded with past telephone calls arranging this restaurant and that movie, this appointment and that cancellation, this avoidance and that obligation—I tell you that this finger poised over that circle points to me at the bottom of a roiling river where I am bumped, scraped, flopped, and raked over the rocks of years. . . . *Never mind! Dial!*

I dial.

One—two—three . . . the telephone company advises at least five rings . . . four—five—and one for good measure. Not at home. Well, why should she be? Why, after all, should she be at home?

Dodie

26.

She heard the phone in the house as she crossed the lawn on her way to the front door. She would never reach it in time. She never had, standing outside with a drunken key while the house-gagged telephone implored again and again . . . four . . . five . . . and stopped just as she managed to get the key inserted. Once she had tried to convince Lenny (whom she suspected at the time of being in love) that those determined to reach you would eventually reach you, but she was no more persuaded by that kind of logic than he was. The unreachable phone call is the message one has waited for all one's life.

Dodie Lang could no longer imagine the contents of such a message. Who could say what to her that would make the difference? There were those she wished to hear from, but they were the ones she could be sure would call again. The dream of the fabulous legacy didn't end with the end of possibility but with the end of desire. She didn't think of sudden fortunes, because sudden fortunes were not what she wanted most. She didn't think of a single, special voice, because there was none that by the touch of its magic could make everything else disappear. Still, she was annoyed. Uncaught calls made her even more jumpy than she was. There were many possibilities out there, and every one of them fraught with difficulties.

Dodie pulled off her gloves, set her bag on the dining room

181

table, removed her coat, and then went into the kitchen, where she prepared a cup of coffee. She glanced at the kitchen clock. It was almost three thirty. She was tired and irritable. At this hour anybody might have called. Lenny. Arthur. Jean. Even Ilse, with whom she had made an astonishing *entente*. Even David, from whom she had heard nothing—day after day after day. It wasn't that she wanted to hear from him particularly but that it was so mysteriously and aggravatingly unlike him to have withdrawn so completely. It nagged at her with the persistence of a mouse's scratch or a faucet's drip, his silence. It spoke to her of a resourcefulness she hadn't suspected. It spoke to her of uncertainties that had frightened her, and still frightened her, and had no right to appear in her life after almost twenty-three years of marriage.

She poured boiling water into the cup containing the coffee powder, stirred, sipped. . . . And Dr. Nathanson (from whom she had just come) had done nothing to dispel the mysteries and uncertainties. He smiled—no, he didn't smile—she had thought it was a smile, but time proved it to be simply the way his face arranged itself—he *looked* at her and nodded and waited for her explanation. . . .

"*Is telepathy, mind reading, something of that sort possible, Dr. Nathanson?*"

"*It all depends on what you mean.*"

"*I don't mean a thing other than what I said. I mean that phenomenon people call mental telepathy or mind reading.*"

"*Have you had such an experience?*"

"*Yes—no—my husband has. So it seems. Dr. Nathanson, why can't you answer me simply whether or not you believe in mind reading?*"

"*I can't answer you simply, Mrs. Lang, because there is no simple answer. I can't say with absolute certainty that it doesn't exist. Some people claim that it does.*"

Ilse and Stan had recommended Dr. Nathanson. A personal friend. "He's such a warm human being." Stan had discovered him some years ago when he was making the switch from insurance to the movie business. A period of near-paralyzing anxiety. Which was an astonishing bit of news to Dodie. She couldn't have imagined this frailty in her brother-in-law, and it was probably this more than anything else that had established the late-found friendliness between herself and that branch of the Lang family. They *were* friendly, Ilse and Stan. And understanding. And very helpful. It was they who had made the contact for her.

If only Dr. Nathanson's face were not so *Jewish!* Those thick lips. That *nose!* It was a pudding of a face, a nice, kindly pudding of a face. She knew it was perfectly awful not to relate to another human being because of his face, but what could she do? You couldn't will those things. If faces were a big thing with her, then they were, and she was sure that Dr. Nathanson would be the first to encourage her to admit it. After all, her own face . . . But about the mind-reading bit, he couldn't say. The best she could get out of him was that between people who know each other well it was always possible to have identical memories stimulated simultaneously.

"Could I have talked in my sleep?"

"Has anybody ever told you that you talked in your sleep?"

"No, but isn't it possible?"

"Yes, it's possible."

"Dr. Nathanson, is it possible that in the ordinary course of conversation you could say something and not know you had said it? That is, mention the name of a person, a place, because that was what you had in mind, but had no intention of speaking it aloud, nevertheless you did speak it aloud, unconsciously, not hearing the words yourself?"

"Is that what bothers you most, this possibility?"

"It bothers me, most or not."

"Why don't you tell me something about yourself, Mrs. Lang?"

Dully, she began to tell Dr. Nathanson about herself. Everything was ridiculously as it was supposed to be. She had read enough, heard enough, to know that she would get no direct answers to her questions, that there *were* no answers to her questions, yet she had plunged ahead and asked them, and Dr. Nathanson with pudding proficiency had handled them in the way she

183

could have predicted they would be handled were it anyone else in the world but herself in the nervous seat. How strange that after all the years of mental grooming for emotional surrender, she should find she had no talent for the game. She doubted very much that she would go on with Dr. Nathanson. Perhaps she wasn't ready. Perhaps she never would be.

But she did need help. Someone to tell her what to do. She could not afford the time, money, or attrition Dr. Nathanson would exact to arrive at an answer, if he ever did. She had to know what to do with the house. She must discuss the house with David. Someone must tell her what to do with her days. Getting a job would appear to be the obvious answer, but every time she thought of setting about to do this relatively simple thing—clothes, employment agencies, interviews—something happened which she had never even remotely experienced before. The normal center of gravity shifted in some unpredictable way, and there was set up in her mind, her stomach, everywhere, a wild gyration which threatened to shake her to pieces. Going to a department store to buy an appropriate outfit for job hunting became an eccentric wheel which picked up speed with each turn of thought—which store? what outfit? what length skirt? a dress? separates? younger? older? which store? what length? how old?—and all of this clashed with other eccentric wheels, turning on questions of advertisements, agencies, interviews, skills, jobs, and there were times she had crossed her arms and pressed into her midriff to keep the chaos contained.

It was temporary. She knew that. It would pass. She had had shocks, dislocations, and as a result she was unable at this moment in her life to go out and get a job. Not to be wondered at. If a friend had come to her with Dodie Lang's story and had ended by saying that organizing for a job was beyond her, she would have said, "Well, it's not to be wondered at. You're in no condition to go out and look for a job now."

Which left her in the house. There was no place else to be. People were busy. People had jobs. People had families. Dodie was alone in the house. On the day David had phoned her to announce that he wasn't coming home, the prospect of solitude had brushed her with the lightest of touches. She was, she felt, quite prepared to deal with the vacuum problems of solitude, but that was not the nature of the thing. What she hadn't counted on was the *volume* of silence. Each room became an enormous conch, and if in fatigue or forgetfulness she allowed herself to listen too long, her head would be filled with an oceanic roar.

Which was also temporary. It was all temporary. Something would happen, as it must, and her days would be given direction.

Jean Ferguson phoned.

"Did you try to get in touch with me before?" Dodie asked.

"Uh-uh. Not today."

"Oh."

"Why?"

"Nothing," Dodie said, her voice going flat. "I got in about three thirty. The phone was ringing, but I couldn't get to it in time. I thought it might have been you."

"No, Dodie, this is the first time I've called today."

"Okay."

"And how are you?" Jean asked.

"All right, I guess."

"Did you see what's-his-name today?"

"I did."

"And?"

"Oh—nothing. More talk."

"Heard from David?"

"No."

"Arthur?"

"Not today."

"Feeling low?"

"I guess."

The conversation was coming to its usual halt for want of impetus. Dodie wondered why Jean didn't take the hint and quit calling. What an idiotic mistake to have made a confidante of Jean. Why? Simply because she was there, a convenient alibi? No,

185

that wasn't it. It was because Jean's style had matched the color of her own excitement at the time.

"Dodie," said Jean, "I'd like to ask you something?"

"Yes?"

"Just what is happening? Ever since the business with David, you've been acting like someone under a spell. Why don't you get in touch with David if you feel so bad about it? Or is it me? Have you got something against me?"

Dodie hesitated, decided to have it out once and for all. "Jean," she asked, "did you say anything to David? I don't mean deliberately, but, you know, inadvertently—"

"You know, I could have *sworn* that was it!" Jean exclaimed. "In fact, I was going to bring it up if you hadn't. No, I haven't said anything to David, inadvertently or otherwise. And I don't know how you could think such a thing!"

"But how could he have found out?" Dodie asked wearily. "You were the only one to know."

"The only one? How do you know that? How do you know *who* might have seen you? And as far as knowing, there's one person you're leaving out."

"Who is that?"

"Arthur."

"Oh, Jean— Then I can take it that you did not say anything to David?"

"Why on earth would I want to do a thing like that? What *reason?*"

"Who knows? . . . No, I'm sorry, Jean. Of course you would have no reason, and of course you didn't. It's just that this thing has been haunting me. Please don't be angry with me, dear. I'm not myself. I know you're trying to help me, to distract me, but I guess I've got to do this in my own way, be by myself more. Sometimes just an ordinary conversation is beyond me. You do understand, don't you? Let me phone you when I want to talk. Please?"

"Anything you say, Dodie."

"You won't be mad, Jean? You do understand?"

"Sure, sure."

186

"All right, then."

" 'Bye, Dodie."

"I'll be in touch, Jean."

Jean began to sink below the surface of consciousness as soon
as Dodie hung up the phone, and Dodie hoped she would go on
sinking until she was well out of sight. But that was not to be. Jean
floated visibly, half-submerged, like a drowned woman whose
water-logged body would neither stay at the bottom nor make it to
the top. It was terribly unfair. It wasn't Jean's fault. Dodie did believe now (as she had always believed in that part of her where
real possibilities were shaped) that Jean was innocent. But this
belief affected nothing. Jean had begun her drift into the deep wa-
ters of oblivion on that fateful Sunday in October when David had
appeared from around the house with that green basket depended
from one finger and that fateful knowledge fully ripened in his
heart.

If she ever got that far with Dr. Nathanson—or someone else—
she would bring up the matter of Jean Ferguson. Not that Jean
would escape the aggravating process which turned all questions
back to their source: *Why do YOU think you made such a special
friend of Jean at the time?"* . . . She thought she had made such
a special friend of Jean at the time because Jean had had affairs
and every visiting team likes to bring its own rooting section. But
why had she *needed* it? She was not a schoolgirl. She had never
been a sharer. No, what she had needed, and got, from Jean was
the mild, necessary opiate of Jean's stylish ignorance. Jean with
her half-digested Reichian theories. Jean with her half-crazy notion about the world being a network of male and female terminals
and that men and women had a sacred duty to seek out their sexual counterparts. Jean believed that. Devoutly. Some day she
would leave her husband and become a sexual pilgrim in that belief. And Dodie had no doubt that she would, because for all her
Charles of the Ritz tastes Jean had the makings of a true cultist.
And Dodie Lang had made a friend and confidante of this casual
acquaintance because she had needed that particular unreality as

187

the reality of an affair with Arthur grew closer. And now Dodie could scarcely endure Jean's company, or even telephone conversations, because Jean was the unreality that mocked all the real fear and uncertainty Dodie had lived with since October.

At four o'clock Arthur phoned. "I had a visit from your husband today," he announced.

Dodie's heart gave a painful, terrified wrench. "David?" she said.

"None other. He hit me."

"David!"

"Yes," Arthur said. "Does that surprise you?"

"Yes! Very much! I don't think David has hit anybody in his whole life. Did he hurt you?"

"Damn right he did! If I didn't feel so sorry for the bastard, I'd teach him a lesson. I'd make him pay through the nose."

"What was the purpose of his visit?" Dodie asked.

"Well, it was my doing, really. I asked him to come see me."

A chill starting at her top vertebra spread laterally across Dodie's shoulders, to her arms, to her fingertips.

"Why did you do that?"

"Partly—principally, I should say—because of you."

"Me?"

"Yes—look, Dodie, what are you doing right now?"

"Nothing."

"How about meeting me for a cocktail? I can't have dinner with you. Rita is coming into the city. But we can be together until about seven. You could get in within an hour, couldn't you?"

"Arthur," Dodie said, "what is it that you want to say to me? Tell me now, and then I'll come downtown. I dislike very much these fake maneuvers. You know that."

"Oh, knock it off, Dodie. First of all, I wanted to talk to David because of all the things you've been telling me. You don't see yourself. You're positively spooked by this thing, whatever it is, David's espionage, telepathy, which I don't believe in the least, by the way. That's what I want to talk to you about now. But if you'd

188

rather not come into the city now, then don't. I thought you might enjoy it. You have complained about the dreariness of your days, you know."

"All right," Dodie said. "I'll meet you at five."

"The hotel?" Arthur said.

"You're not—?"

"No, no, no, no—just for a drink."

"All right."

27.

Dodie took the Long Island Expressway to the Midtown Tunnel. The city wavered before her, a vast, turreted pleasure ship afloat in its blue haze. She would come out at the other end of the tunnel and embark somewhere in the Thirties, zigzag west to the Fifties, drive to that side-street garage she had come to know so well, and then walk to the hotel.

She thought of the many trips she had made in the last year. They were all one now—the early excitement, the late premonitions—gathered together in one undifferentiated day. Because it was over. She knew that. Arthur wanted it to be over. She wanted it to be over. But even though she had been spared the real malady of love, her bones felt waxen with weariness. Perhaps it was not the end of Arthur but the end of David that made her feel this way. Perhaps it was feeling itself, the massive dose of it, after so long a period of none.

Maneuvering on the jerky, conveyor-belt misery of Third Avenue, Dodie switched on the heater. When the envelopment of hot air made her clammy and nauseous, she switched it off. She turned on the radio, but even at low volume the music only added to the general clamor of traffic. How she hated the city when it was like this—or rather when *she* was like this—caught in the fierce indifferent wash of it, a stranger to its preoccupation.

She had known from the beginning that part of the affair with

Arthur would be her re-entry into the life of the city. Not that she had been tied to the house in Long Island. She had had the freedom of the city for years—actually since Lenny started high school—but merely going into the city had proved to be a frustrating thing. She was not part of it. She, whose earliest memories were of the city, whose growth was in the city, was no longer part of it. Most of the people she had known had moved away. Those that still remained were busy during the day. There was a limit to shopping. After so many visits, her nerves began to reject the museums—or perhaps it was the museums, like the rest of the city, that rejected her with the cold eye professionalism has for the dilettante. And she simply couldn't go to the movies during the day. Coming out, she always felt like one of the city's tramps who had been ordered to move on.

Arthur was a reason and a difference and a tremendous excitement. Well, a difference, and a reason, and therefore a tremendous excitement. She had been bored sexually for years. Perhaps that couldn't be helped. So many women complained of it. But why? Why should an intelligent, virile man (and David was both), why should such a man about whom you have cared, cared greatly, begin to bore you sexually? Because he was your husband? Because he was your daily and nightly companion? She had not invented the situation. The evidence was all around. She was not by nature promiscuous. Rummaging in the dark corners of her mind, she had never spied the rat's tail of evil. There had been no perverse pleasure in betraying David. There had been only her own pleasure. But why with Arthur and not with David? And why so tremendously with Arthur at first, and then less and less?

Did nature mean for everyone to mate with as many different partners as possible before decrepitude ended everything? No, that couldn't be it. She had never felt the wayward lusts Jean talked about. Anybody. Strangers. The TV repair man. In over two decades of marriage, there had been the dependable quota of men at house parties, in shops, restaurants. PTA meetings, anywhere and everywhere, men who had signaled with varying degrees of deliberation their sexual interest. And there had been on

191

her own part varying degrees of interest and amusement but never any intention. Not until Arthur. By the time the Gersons came along, the intention existed. Arthur would have been an interesting man under any circumstances. Three years ago, she knew he could be her lover. Two years later, he was.

That was not bitchiness, to have waited two years after meeting the man, feeling more and more drawn to him, planning the act so many times before committing herself to it. She had put David on probation. That was an awful thing to have done, even in her own mind. She had never clearly defined to herself what it was that David must do, or not do, to satisfy the terms of that probation, but she was certain she would recognize the change if it ever appeared. But what a deceiving thing to do! If she had meant to give David a chance, she should have spelled out the particulars of the chance. But of course she couldn't do that. To spell out the particulars of the chance would be to destroy the chance. Like all those stupid books on sex and marriage. Clinical approaches to paradise. It was no more possible for her to have told David what to do than for David to have guessed. She had been silently demanding that David remake their lives. She had wanted David not to be David.

Why? Because David had become, fully and finally, the man he was meant to be. He would not go to plays, because he didn't like plays. Movies were better. He preferred religious music—masses and cantatas—to anything else. He read novels, books on history, religious philosophy. He kept going back to the same books, opening them at random and reading. He played outdoor tennis when the weather was fine and indoor tennis in the off season. He hated museums. He no longer cared to go into the city. He would do anything for Lenny. Sundays burned like tall pale candles. Evenings at ten thirty, David would shower, and then he would watch the news on TV, and then he would read in bed for half an hour before going to sleep. There were two ways in which he made love, he deciding according to the irregular pattern of his desire which it would be. Sexual consideration having replaced the Torah, he had trained himself to hold off his climaxes indefinitely. He would touch her in the same places, make the same noises of pleasure, and when he was finished he would sometimes say, "Darling, that was so good!" or, at other times, "Do you think Lenny's been laid yet?" The years narrowed in concentric circles to the smallest shutter opening, as though death when it came would be a solar burst. But death would not be a solar burst; it would only be the final closing of the shutter.

And that's what had happened; she had begun to see death. David lived contentedly on each day's platform as it moved through time. If he regretted, longed for, the past, he gave no sign of it. If he had hopes for, feared, the future, he gave no sign of it.

She tunneled back to her past to find in it a future she needn't fear. It couldn't be lost! There were to have been such wonderful things in her life. She was to have traveled, and she never did. She was to have had three children, and her insides were removed with Lenny. She was to have fallen deeply in love, and she did, with Bernard, who would not leave his wife. She was to have married the man with whom she was deeply in love, and she married David, who was intelligent and generous and considerate and good-looking but with whom she was not deeply in love. She had never regretted marrying David; she only regretted what had become of her life.

Perhaps regret would have been inevitable under any circumstances. She had been given to see in a ten-minute, heartbreaking vignette the regret she had been spared. This about eight years ago, when her parents were still living on the West Side, and she had gone to visit her mother during the day, taking her to lunch, as she usually did. The neighborhood was thick with the fumes that were killing it, as though beneath the surface of the streets a monstrous refuse heap of rags and bones and anger had been ignited. They went to a restaurant on Seventy-second Street, and while they were having their lunch she saw someone that memory denied and the possibilities of horror acknowledged.

Bernard Reinitz. It was he. He sat at a wall seat across the room talking to a companion who sat opposite him. Even in the awfulness of her seeing, she thought of what she had been spared. She also thought that death, picking like a scavenger among the last morsels of life, could not undo the unique thing that life had made. Bernard was still Bernard, though death had gnawed him hollow. He was dying. From across the room, she could see that. He bent to his plate in the strengthless way of a dying man. He chewed his food in the slow, blank way of the dying. His hair had turned completely white, his cheeks were sunk, and his eyes (those blue, living eyes! the seal and sweetness of his manhood!) moved dyingly among the faces in the restaurant, coming to rest at last on hers and lingering for a moment in hopeless recognition before turning away.

Were it left to her, that occasion would have passed without a word being spoken between herself and her dying onetime lover. She couldn't have brought herself either to disguise or reveal her pity properly. Always, since her marriage to David, she had hoped to meet Bernard, not thinking to resume what had once been, but perhaps to meet from time to time in some West Side coffee shop, like the one they were in, and to have restored to her through such meetings the rich anticipation that was once in the sooty air of day and in the eager air of evening—anticipation stirred by New York splendors and Berlin accents and an affair that imbued every street corner with the throbbing immateriality of her enchantment. But it was not left to her. She saw Bernard and his companion pay their checks. She tried not to look but saw anyway poor Bernard fumble away from the table. She nodded at whatever her mother was saying, listened to her own heart's funereal drumbeat, and hoped that when she looked up Bernard would be gone.

"How nice to see you, Dodie."

The voice was scaled of all living tissue—a thin, exposed wire of sound. *It was in his throat!* She said this to herself while her eyes made a thousand-mile trip to his dying face.

"Hello, Bernard," she said. "You remember my mother, don't you?"

"Of course. How are you, Mrs. Phillips?"

"Hello, Mr. Reinitz," said her mother, unable to conceal her shock.

"Yes," he said, as though a question had been asked. Then to her: "How have you been, Dodie?"

"Fine."

"Do you have children?"

"A son."

Bernard nodded, his ruined face showing neither pleasure nor regret but the merest notation of one whose growing distance from life allowed for some impersonal remnants of curiosity.

"As you see," he said in that frail, unfleshed voice, which was still miraculously able to evoke a ghost of its former charm, "I'm not in the best of health."

"I'm so sorry," she murmured.

"Yes—well—it was nice to see you again." He bowed to her, to her mother, not offering his hand, perhaps because the touch of his hand would have been too awful a memento for a former lover to take away.

Her deathwatch in the obituaries of *The New York Times* was a short one. Less than two months: *Hans Bernard Reinitz, beloved husband of Anna* . . . She hadn't mentioned to David her meeting with Bernard in the restaurant, but she did point out the death notice in the newspaper. David had looked at her, nodding compassionately, giving husbandly approval to her right to grieve.

How strange, the distinctions David made! Bernard was all right because Bernard had taken her to bed before the advent of David Lang. David had even intimated that he knew how much Bernard lived in her mind, and this too was all right as long as it remained a sexless, womanly nostalgia. While she—she had been jealous of that girl in David's novel—no, not the girl in the novel, but the actual one with whom David had lived in London, the one who couldn't pronounce her "l's." She had not been jealous of her because David had made love to her but because he remembered her with so much tenderness.

The Bernard episode had stayed in her mind as a dividing mark, the one that separated time into the great bulk that had been lived on the often-troubled but reasonably sure side of hope, and the other, shadowed, side of the recent years. The bad years. Not

195

immediately or uniformly bad, but slowly, steadily, and accumulatively bad. The onset of repetition as reality. The rumors of a different world she didn't know and could never discover. David's willingness to accept this halt and downward tilt, a little ruefully perhaps, but really with more amusement than dismay, as if after all the years he had let himself be caught in one of the silliest of practical jokes—graying hair, digestive troubles, the narrowing of interests, the realization that the look of his life was the shape of finality. Worst of all, for her, was his gentle but insistent shutting of the family door against any sudden gusts of change. It didn't happen overnight. There were summers on the Cape, and friends, and a trip to the West Coast, and generally a very busy and fortunate life. But after each summer, or trip, or evening with friends, David would return to his books and his music and his weekend tennis with a soul-sigh of contentment, certain that in a world of inexorable shrinkage and death, this was not so bad.

He began shutting the door with the proclamation of his new policy of acceding only to the dictates of his own taste. He would no longer seek to discover virtues where they didn't exist for him. He would not go to plays that neither he nor anyone else could fathom. He would not stand before a single dot of color, or a blizzard of dots, trying to mesmerize himself into the belief that something in him was moved by the sight. And once, after they had made love, after their separate trips to the bathroom, after long minutes of silence, David had said, "For Christ sake, Dodie, what do you expect? Be reasonable. There are deficiencies in life, and it isn't always the other person who has to make up for them."

But this was not the shape of *her* finality! The dots and blizzards of color might mean no more to her than they did to him, but they did speak to her of the lost street corners of her life. The meaningless plays were perhaps meaningless, but she could feel that they groped toward meaning, and that groping brought her back to the sooty air of day and the eager air of evening. She could not lose these things! She would suffocate breathing David's air of finalities and certitudes.

So she took art lessons, but she had no gift for it. And she took

196

courses at N.Y.U., but she discovered that learning without the hope of utilization was as lifeless as that shriveled mummy she had once seen in a museum, the one that had been buried with the clay pots and provisions she would need on her trip through eternity.

That desiccation was eternity!

When they met the Gersons, she knew that Arthur would be her lover. Arthur had not closed his doors. Arthur was connected to the world she didn't want to lose. He didn't love her, she knew that, but he wanted her. She didn't want to betray David, but she wanted Arthur. She had to slip through David's all-but-closed door and be with Arthur for a time, even though Arthur didn't love her, even though she suspected a cruelty in Arthur's freedom and an affectation in his style.

How could she have known that David had watched, or spied, or guessed? How could she have guessed that the room on which David was closing his door had its own private plans and interests?

28.

"Just swung at me," Arthur said. "Without a word. I have the feeling he didn't know he was going to do it until he did it."

They were sitting in the leather and wood dimness of the hotel cocktail lounge. They had met in the lobby, and there Dodie saw the discolored welt bracketing Arthur's eye. It amazed her, seeing David's violence on Arthur, as though David had kept secret from her his knowledge of a foreign language.

"I'm sorry," she said.

"Not your fault," Arthur said, shrugging. "What surprises me is that he would wait so long to do that sort of thing. Why not right away? A month ago?" Arthur shook his head and smiled. "It bothered him that *I* got in touch with *him*. The procedure bothered him. I think he had some idea of protocol in the matter. I should have waited until he got in touch with me."

"What will you tell Rita?" Dodie asked.

"About what?"

"That eye."

"Oh, I don't know. An accident. Ran into something. Something ran into me. Has David ever been violent with you?"

"Never. Not the slightest hint of it. How did he look?"

"David? Pretty much the same. I would guess he's lost some weight. He didn't look wild-eyed or anything. I shouldn't be surprised if the whole experience has done him a world of good. He seems to have lost that satisfied air."

"What did you talk about?"

Arthur considered his drink for several seconds. "You," he replied.

"Yes?"

"Well," said Arthur, shifting a little, looking off into another corner of the cocktail lounge, "after damn near blinding me, the conversation wasn't exactly friendly. I tried to convey to him that it wasn't just a matter of hopping into bed. I said there must have been some pretty bad deterioration before I ever came into the picture."

"Did he agree to that?"

"No. He didn't think so. You know David. Naturally he got literary. Rocks piled on him. The ancient death of having rocks piled on him. When he found out about us. Therefore I must tell him all. A moral duty. You know, in spite of his having hit me, in spite of everything, I have a weak spot for David. I can imagine what it must have been like, living with him, but for an outsider he has his crazy charm. Sometimes I think he thinks of himself in the third person."

"That's very interesting," Dodie said drily. "What did he mean by 'having rocks piled on him'?"

"Now don't *you* get sore," Arthur said.

"I saw Dr. Nathanson today," Dodie said. "That man is supposed to be helping me. I know he's doing what anybody else would do, but I get the feeling that the experiences of his life must leave him completely unprepared for what I have to tell him."

"Then you ought to get another man."

"I think I will. I'm sure Dr. Nathanson is perfectly competent, but I just have this feeling of talking across oceans."

"Feeling is exactly what you're dealing with," Arthur pointed out. "You've got to get yourself another man."

"What did David mean about 'rocks piled on him'?"

"Dodie, I don't know. Rhetoric. An ancient form of execution. They used to pile rocks on convicted people until they were crushed. He said that when he found out about us, that's the way he felt. Because he didn't think the relationship was that bad, apparently. He didn't think there was a reason for what happened. So I told him there was."

"Oh? What did you tell him?"

"I told him—now, look, I don't remember my exact words—I told him he'd been stifling you for years. I told him about the art school, the courses you took, your friends, your tastes. I told him he chose to be very obtuse about these things."

Dodie took a trembling sip from her glass and grimaced. "I don't know what they made this thing with," she said. "It tastes like something the dentist puts in your tooth before he fills it. Would you please order me another drink?"

"Of course. What?"

"Manhattan. A dry Manhattan."

Arthur turned to catch the waiter's attention. Dodie wondered if he had rented a room in the hotel. She would have to say no if he had. She simply couldn't. Dr. Nathanson. David hitting Arthur. Arthur's account of his meeting with David. This whole day. The thought of sex left her feeling ill. Something about Arthur contributed to that feeling. The way he was telling her all of this . . .

"Would you please take this away and bring us a dry Manhattan," Arthur said to the waiter.

. . . as if everything had taken a ludicrous turn. This talking about her life with David—*relationships*—it all had the sound of courtroom testimony—or what she imagined courtroom testimony to be: the carefully supervised process of making a half-truth whole. What she had told Arthur about David was never meant to be testimony. She didn't appreciate Arthur's making testimony out of it.

"What made you get in touch with David anyway?" she asked.

"I told you."

"Tell me again."

"Your state of mind. You were brooding constantly about what David might say to Lenny. You were worried about David's withdrawal, his silence. I thought it was stupid to go on that way when a telephone call would shed some light."

"Were you worried about yourself too, a little?"

200

Arthur sighed. He looked away again, nodded. "Yes," he said, "I was worried about myself a little too. I didn't like David's silence and withdrawal either. If he was planning to do something, I wanted to know what it was."

"Like telling Rita, do you mean?"

"I mean that—yes."

"You wouldn't like that, would you?"

"No, I wouldn't. Would you?"

"Why should she be spared?"

"Why should she be involved?"

"I see," said Dodie.

"What's happened has happened," Arthur said. "I don't see the point in spreading unhappiness."

"What about my unhappiness?"

"What do you think I should do about that?"

"Nothing," Dodie said stonily, thinking of her resolution, her heart's avowal, that if anything should happen she would immediately remove herself and the consequences from Arthur's life. Immediately! She said, "Would you believe it, I never thought of myself as a natural victim. I never saw myself on the pathetic end of things."

Without the least premonition that it would happen, she was crying. A reservoir of brine filled and spilled over. She searched for a handkerchief in her bag.

"Dodie," said Arthur.

She couldn't answer. She turned her face away when the waiter came with the cocktail.

"Dodie," Arthur said again, this time with more appeal than sympathy.

The tone stopped Dodie's tears. She blew her nose, took out cigarettes, sipped her drink. Arthur struck a match and held it to her cigarette.

"Would you really want Rita involved?" he asked.

"No."

"Seriously?"

"Seriously, no."

"I don't see the sense in it," Arthur said. "I don't see what would be accomplished."

"No sense at all," Dodie agreed.

"Stop parroting, Dodie," Arthur said, annoyed. "You know very well what I'm talking about. Would you want me to divorce Rita and marry you?"

"How do you think David found out?" Dodie asked.

"I don't know," Arthur replied. "Don't slough me off that way."

"Then don't ask questions like that," Dodie returned. "Don't ask questions with built-in answers. No, I wouldn't want you to do a thing. Let's not waste words over it."

"I don't think the words are wasted. They need to be said."

"No," Dodie insisted, "they are just wasted words. I know exactly what the words are. To do anything about it would be to make more mess to accommodate the mess that's already been made. Is that approximately right?"

"Yes."

"Then let's not talk about it. Oh, I'm bitter, all right, but it's not you I'm bitter against. Or if I am, right now, it will pass. It's not your fault. I didn't intend for David to find out. Had he not found out, it would have gone on a little longer and would have ended on its own. There's some justice in the way things have worked out. Tell me, doesn't Rita ask about me—about me and David— why we haven't been in touch?"

"What's to ask? She knew the friendship was thin to begin with. David and I had very little in common. I think we all knew that. He's quite a conservative, your husband. He doesn't think so, but he is. And you and Rita haven't much in common either."

"I'd just as soon we didn't have a thorough analysis of everybody," Dodie said. "You're right, though. It was thin to begin with."

"Not us," Arthur said, understanding her.

"Yes, us."

"No," Arthur denied. "You know it isn't true. Your sex life was lousy. You said so. As for me—you were a whole new thing, and that's always exciting. I knew what you were after when we began

202

toying with ideas about us. I'm not talking about sex, although there was that too. I hope for your sake, Dodie, you'll go on being after those things. Unlike David, you want into this world."

Dodie closed off against Arthur's way of putting it, because his way of putting it made her feel the kind of dismal impoverishment that always came when someone handed her complimentary tickets to a play or movie.

"You saw David today," she said, breaking into Arthur's good-byes—for that's what all of this was, an extended farewell. They wouldn't be seeing each other again. That's what Arthur was saying. "Did *he* say anything about how he found out?"

"No."

"Did you ask him?"

"No . . . Dodie, do you want my honest opinion?"

"By all means."

"He didn't *find out* anything. He guessed."

"Why did he guess you?"

"Because the direction of your unhappiness led to me. That he happened to be right was an accident."

"Yes," said Dodie. "You're probably right."

29.

She came out on Fifth Avenue, coasted with the southbound traffic for a few blocks, then turned east. It was night. The home-going crush was over. Vaguely Dodie was making her way toward the Midtown Tunnel. She drove automatically, her thoughts unfixed, her reflexes and the car's mechanism forming a separate intelligence. She was as far as Third Avenue before she became aware of her resistance against the movement that was taking her home. She didn't want to go to that house whose empty chambers roared their silence at her. She was afraid of the house. She imagined a criminal underground that had passed along the word of her solitude and helplessness. A dark menace closed round her in a ripening plan of rape, robbery, and murder. At night, she left lights burning in every strategic corner of the house.

She had telephoned her mother several times since David had left, but each time she had come to the point of informing her of recent events a tremendous lethargy settled down on her, like tons of weightless eiderdown, keeping her confined to the usual vaporous exchange. Had her mother known, she would have demanded that she come to Miami—*this instant!* The next plane! But the image of herself made mindless beneath a cosmetic sun and her mother's troubled partiality created for Dodie a terror greater than the terrors surrounding her empty house. To surrender to the constantly weeping child within her would be sure destruction. Her only salvation was to suffer the things she must suffer. Only in that way would she merit whatever betterment lay on the other side of this time. Despite her own wisdom and determination, however, she stigmatized her mother with the sin of not being nearer the scene of her daughter's trouble.

Thoughts of her aloneness and her mother and her parting from Arthur and David's persistent silence filled Dodie with such aching pity for the weeping child that scarcely before she realized she was doing so she had reversed her course, turned west, and was proceeding toward that part of the city where some gift of recompense could be found. She passed through the insidious park and came out on Central Park West, feeling nerve endings of memory tingle but knowing from experience that these streets could be no more than a shoddy imitation of the sanctuary in her mind. Still she drove on, across Broadway to West End Avenue, past the old apartment house that gave her no salutation from its brick-sealed senescence. She wound through streets, fearful of stopping, fearful of going home, fearful of shuttling back and forth, a lost thread on the loom of her past.

Arthur had said, "Goodbye is nonsense. There's no reason why you and I should lose each other. I wanted to help you, but I see I can't do that now. I only aggravate you. You're in a bind, and you have no patience with anything that isn't a definite answer. Okay. I can understand that. That's why I say it would be best if we didn't see each other for a time. But for Christ sake, Dodie, don't let yourself be talked back into the cocoon! You're too vital. You belong in the world."

All this on the sidewalk in front of the garage, Arthur a little impatient, because they had talked and talked and now it was late and Rita would be circling round the downtown block where he was supposed to meet her, and Dodie for the first time felt hatred because for all the truth of what he was saying Arthur was going off to his life with only a bruised eye, no complications, and just a reasonable amount of regret, while she hadn't even glimpsed the beginnings of her own future. Besides which, Arthur was being

205

surprisingly stupid if he thought that any amount of intelligence could absorb these poisons and remain unsickened by them.

Dodie had to press hard on the brake as a car suddenly bolted out from the curb and raced for the corner, tires squealing hot derision. She saw a head appear out the right window, and then a face looked back. A grin. The head ducked back into the car. One arm came out, raised upward, the middle finger signaling obscenity. Fearful they might wait for her at the corner, Dodie pulled up a car's length, then backed into the empty space. When the traffic light changed, the car at the corner shot ahead. On impulse, Dodie switched off the ignition, the lights, locked the doors, and got out of the car. She walked to Broadway—and then to the restaurant where she had once seen a dying Bernard.

She was put in a corner opposite an elderly man who looked up from his newspaper with an expression of fastidious annoyance, which he promptly corrected by inclining his head in a formal way. His manner plainly indicated that he thought these intrusions barbarous, but please to keep to your side of the table and I will keep to mine. It's the best we can do. Above all—silence!

She was hungry, but she didn't want the complications of a meal, so she ordered a sandwich. Later, she would have a piece of their delicious, fattening pastry. There was a party of four at the next table, two men and two women. Bernard's generation. They spoke in German. One of the men, the one sitting diagonally opposite her, slouched in his chair, one arm resting languidly on the table, a familiar look of enervation on his face. His lips were pursed. He was listening to the woman next to him talk. She talked animatedly, twiddling her hands, the fingers of which flashed green, diamond, and gold. The woman's high voice, the man's look of ancient boredom, the special accent pouring pauselessly from the woman's lips, all of it mixed in Dodie's mind to create a stir of familiarity. Then the man who listened with pursed lips turned his head slowly and gazed at Dodie with a directness and appeal that seemed to draw on years of the most profoundly realized intimacy. He smiled a shadow of a smile in acknowledgment of their secret.

206

Dodie felt a sea swell of time lift her powerfully and settle her once again. The man didn't know her at all. He had been listening to what his wife, or ex-wife, or friend, or lover had been saying. At last he closed his eyes, gave a half-roll to his head, and said, *"Mmyah-h, aber—"* and went on to voice soft objections to the woman's monologue.

Dodie sat at the edge of revelation, waiting for it to come, as she had waited at other times for persons and places to order themselves with a last click of adjustment into the perfect re-creation of some former time. It came at last, out of her easily summoned past —the musicians and artists and writers who had arrived from the charred corners of Europe; people who pursed their lips, nodded their heads, said, "Mmyah-h—" and looked at one another with the same bestowals and withdrawals of an intimacy that had never existed.

She recalled Bernard in a gray suit holding the hand of an old woman in both of his, murmuring German consolations. Who was that woman? Oh, yes! The mother of the pianist whose own hands had miraculously recovered their suppleness after the frostbites of three concentration camps. She recalled the massive woman with the pretty face who sang *lieder* and whose passion was to gather enough money to open a jewelry shop in New York. She recalled the one-legged artist who had offered to do her portrait "for all the kindnesses" and who had flung a charcoal across the room because her face was too "plastic," too *"American!"* He wasn't a very good artist, poor man. In the early days of her affair with Arthur, she had told him about all the broken and unbroken people she had come to know, but she hadn't told him about the artist who had attempted her portrait, and for some reason this seemed an important omission, so Dodie turned inwardly toward Arthur and experienced for the first time the loss of Arthur in the perspective of time. *He* was part of her past, too, and this knowledge made her turn to David, to whom she had told everything at one time or another. But David, she discovered, was neither past nor present. He was suspended in time, mysterious, faceless, having removed himself in a totally unpredictable way.

The waiter came with her sandwich. The bread was stale. "Oh!" she said, putting back on the plate the half she was holding. The elderly man peeped over his paper, solemn and knowing. He said, "This is one place I can tell you, my dear lady, never to order a sandwich. Something hot, yes. Pastry, yes. But never a sandwich. It is not a *spécialité"*—giving the last word the French pronunciation. Then he returned to his paper, not the least bit interested in pursuing the matter. Dodie said, "Thank you," not knowing what else to say, remaining suspended for several seconds between amusement and annoyance, deciding at last that she was more amused than annoyed.

She picked up the sandwich and ate it, and it wasn't bad, only one of the slices was stale. She glanced over at the foursome. The lady who had twiddled her fingers was still doing so, and the gentleman who had listened to it all for a thousand years was still listening. Amusement grew in Dodie. Amusement and expectancy. She had somehow wandered into a setting that was the absolute allegory of her life, although she couldn't have said how. No, though her life depended on it she couldn't have analyzed it, but she sat in a radiance of assent, confirmed at last in her response to those plays that could never be explained. Someday she must, divorced or still married, tell David of this incident. She must explain to him that the wrongness was to *reason* with those plays. Rather one must let the patterns of the play fall on the nerves, scene by scene, as this scene had fallen on her nerves, bringing recognition of that unreasonable brilliance of insight which always occurs when one is alone. Of course she would never be able to tell this to David, or to anyone else, because it was a revelation she could contain for only a few moments, and it was already passing out of her grasp.

She ordered pastry and coffee. The pastry was delicious.

"You were right," she said to the elderly gentleman. "Pastry."

"Mmyah-h," he said.

She tipped, paid, left the restaurant.

She walked back in the green, red, and diamond night to where she had parked the car. When she reached the corner of the street, two boys ran out of the darkness of West End Avenue into the streetlight of the corner, passing a basketball between them. "Hey, lady, catch!" cried one, making as if to shoot the ball at her. Dodie flinched and raised one arm. The smaller of the boys laughed. She was not frightened, only angered. She walked on, looking her futile rebuke at the boy. He was about twelve or thirteen, curly-headed, wearing a zipper jacket. He grinned at her. "Whatsa matter, lady, you don't like to play?" he asked insolently, then repeated his quick shooting movement. Again Dodie flinched and became aware that the older boy was walking beside her.

"You got something for me?" he asked.

"What?" said Dodie, becoming frightened.

"Hey, lady—" the little one called.

"You got something for me?" the older boy repeated. "How about a dollar? You got a dollar, lady?"

Dodie's heart was pounding. She seriously considered calling for help, but in that moment she thought of Lenny, and she felt she owed it to Lenny, for what reason she couldn't have said, not to be panicked.

"Oh, go away!" she said.

The older boy, who walked on her left and a half-pace behind, the distance of nightmare, said, "How about a fuck, lady? I got a big cock." Dodie increased her pace toward the car, remembering that it was locked, and that she fumbled endlessly with keys when she was upset, and that she would be helpless prey for a ghastly length of time before she would be safe in the car, so she said, "Will you leave me alone if I give you a dollar?" The older boy said, "Sure, lady," and Dodie realized that if she removed the strap of her pocketbook from the crook of her arm, that boy would grab it and run, and while she didn't care about the bag or the money, the car keys were in the bag, so she cried out in a shaking voice, "You'd better leave me alone right now!"

"Ah, don't cry, lady," said the little one, still grinning and coming closer.

And there was no one on the street! Not a soul! Furiously, Dodie whirled on the older one. "You move away from me!" she shouted. "Right now!"

He did. Quickly Dodie opened her pocketbook and took out her wallet. She didn't care if they grabbed the wallet. The keys were still in the pocketbook. But they just looked at her—curious, expectant. Dodie took a bill from her wallet, she didn't look, she didn't care what, throwing it toward the older boy. As it fluttered to the sidewalk, a wild, gleeful thing fluttered into her coat, against her groin, down, forcing the fabric of her dress between her thighs. Then the curlyheaded devil danced away, victorious.

"I touched the pussy!" he yelled, and ran toward the other, who had the bill, and they were both running toward Broadway.

Dodie put her wallet back into her pocketbook and walked to the car. She got in, started the motor, maneuvered out, and drove to the corner, waiting for whatever reaction would come. She had been frightened while it was happening, and now it was over and she was no longer frightened. She had been able to think. She had not panicked. This was what was happening in the city, and she had experienced that too.

She drove crosstown again, through the park, in the red, green, and diamond night, feeling a tranquil defiance. She had depended too much on other people. She could take care of herself.

210

30.

It was after nine when she arrived home. The wroughtiron lamp above the front door was burning, as was the dining room light, and the bedroom light upstairs. Illuminated prayers against harm. The front end of the car dipped in the declivity of the garage ramp, and the headlights splayed against the house. Dodie thought of the Hunsingers across the street and the Feinstocks who occupied the adjacent house. They were the people with whom the Langs had established a neighborly nonfriendship. Drinks once or twice a year at each other's homes, mutual concern in obvious matters (births, deaths, fires, crabgrass, marriages), but real mutuality had been trimmed over the years as neatly as their lawns. It was the Langs who had imposed the limitation. It was the Langs who felt that such friendships would complete the suburbanization of their lives. The true friends and interests of the Langs must remain in the city; or if not in the city, then at least not in the community.

Dodie's isolation was complete.

She opened the garage door, drove the car in, then closed the door from the garage side. She entered the house through the garage, passing from the utility room into the kitchen. She stood there for a moment listening for any dreaded sounds. None. She passed through the lighted dining room into the living room. After the relief of silence, she felt the usual assault of silence. She thought of David, wondered once more what source of bitterness or pride

211

supported *his* isolation. Feeling herself sliding into the sinister speculations of the past weeks, she quickly cut them off. Arthur was undoubtedly right. David had guessed. But his guessing didn't explain those terrible accuracies: that it had been going on for a year; that the first intimations were in Cape Cod—*"a gray Cape Cod light"*—no, that couldn't be explained. Yes, it could. He didn't know then, had only perceived the possibility. Then why hadn't he said something? Done something? Because he didn't believe it would happen? Because he didn't care? He *did* care. That much was certain. Because (she was letting herself slip again) David wanted to write another novel, wanted to observe his wife in this involvement, use it as material? Impossible! But why impossible? Just consider his behavior since he had left the house. Wasn't that even more unbelievable? Did she know him at all?

Dodie sat on the sofa smoking a cigarette. The battering of her thoughts made her seek protection. She cast about in her mind for distractions. What came to her was the sensation of that satanic little hand insinuating itself between her thighs. She hadn't panicked. She had behaved well. She had thought of Lenny and that had given her support. She thought of Lenny now—and her confidence turned to fear. What had David told Lenny? What did he plan to tell him? She had counseled herself time after time that it couldn't possibly matter, that Lenny was a man, an intelligent, mature man, and yet there hovered in her mind the image that would be created in her son's mind should he learn of her behavior. She knew from her own experience that every child successfully obliterates knowledge of his parents' sex life. But adultery—*her* adultery—would end that immunity. She would be left naked in Lenny's mind. He wouldn't respect her, love her. . . .

The suddenness of the phone startled her. She stared at it as if it had slapped her. Then she picked it up.

"Hello."

"Hello, Dodie."

Dodie removed the phone from her ear and held it about a foot away, trying to decide whether it would be safe to risk contact with that voice again. She returned the phone to her ear.

212

"Yes," she said.

"I've tried to reach you several times today," David said.

"I've been in and out."

"How are you?"

"All right."

"Are you managing?"

"Quite well, thank you."

"It was about one thirty the first time I phoned," David said. "Then I tried again at two, and at three. . . . Dodie, have you been thinking about our situation?"

"Yes."

Surprisingly, she was in fine control of her voice. She had imagined this telephone call many times in the past few weeks, but it had always been a dumb-show performance, her mind carrying the conversation in the form of two puppets semaphoring information. She had never listened to her own voice in these exchanges. That determining quality had been missing, as had David's. Just two disembodied emotions playing a charade. Now they were both present, and Dodie found that she was able to adjust her voice to all that had been, to all that was, even to the curlyheaded little monster who had flown off the battlements of her terrors to wriggle his hand between her middle-aged thighs.

"What are you thinking, then?" David asked. "Divorce?"

"Is that what you want to talk about?" she asked.

"I'd like to know what I've even done to make you so vindictive?" he asked.

"You saw Arthur this afternoon," she said.

"How did you know?"

"He phoned me. He told me that you had struck him."

"Not nearly as hard or as often as I should have."

"Since when do you go in for violence?"

"Since I have sufficient reason. Couldn't you have had your affair without all the usual nastiness? Did you have to jump all over me in order to jump into bed with Arthur?"

"I will not talk to you if you go on in this way," she said calmly.

"I'll hang up. I'm sorry if what Arthur told you hurt you. But did you think we were mutes? We talked."

"I didn't think I had so many shortcomings," David said.

"I'm sorry Arthur phoned you," she said. "That was a stupid thing to do. But it wasn't my fault. He didn't consult me. Had he done so, I would have told him not to do it."

"Don't you see him?"

"David, what did you want to talk about?"

"Us. I want to see you."

Again Dodie held the phone away from her. She didn't know what to say. Some inner gauge seemed to have been broken, and she was without the means of measuring her need or her safety. She didn't want to see David. Not now. Not because she was afraid but because there was a fallowness in her that mustn't be disturbed.

"I can't see you now, David," she said. "You know that I'm seeing a doctor. Naturally I've been talking to him, asking his advice. His advice is that I shouldn't try to come to any decisions at this time."

"Yes, I'm sure," said David. "That's all very well for him—and for you—but you owe me something, Dodie. I've got to see you and talk things over."

"Why all of a sudden?" she asked. "You disappear for weeks—*months*—and suddenly you're back full of emergency. What's happened?"

"Nothing has happened," David answered. "This is the time it took, that's all. Everything considered, I should be the one to judge. Dodie, I'm not going to try to persuade you to do anything you haven't a mind to do. I just want to know in which direction to start moving."

"When would you want to see me?"

"Whenever it would be convenient."

"Well, Lenny will be home in a couple of weeks," she began, then changed her tack: "What did you say to him when you were up there that made him decide to stay in school an extra week?"

"I've already told you, Dodie. Just generalities. That you and I weren't getting along. That it was serious."

"Anything else?"

"About what?"

"About me."

"That you were having an affair with Arthur, is that what you mean?"

"Yes."

"No, I didn't tell him that."

Dodie felt a catch of gratitude in her throat. A few listless tears rolled down and around the curve of her nostrils. She didn't know why she must hold this foolish mask before her, but she must. At least for the present. She would tell Lenny herself at the right time, but she must choose the right time. Right now she hadn't the resources for that crisis.

"Do you know that Lenny has a mustache?" David suddenly said to her.

"What? No, I didn't know that. He didn't tell me. Since when? A *mustache!* You mean—a *big* one?"

"Quite a size."

"But why on earth would he want to do a thing like that?" she almost wailed. "He's so *handsome*— How does it look on him?"

"Not bad," David said. "A little ragged and overgrown, but not bad . . . Will you see me, Dodie?"

"David, won't you wait a little?"

"What's a little?"

"Three months."

"No, Dodie—no. I know it would be nice to take a year or so to examine your feelings, but that can't be my schedule. Surely you can understand that."

"Yes," she said. "I can understand that. Will you wait until after Lenny goes back to school? After the holidays?"

"All right. Suppose I meet you—just a minute, I have a calendar here—suppose I meet you the first Wednesday of the new year. Would that be all right?"

"Where?" she asked.

215

He hesitated, then said: "How about the museum?"

She recoiled from the phone. All her suspicions returned. "Why there?" she asked.

"No reason. It's just the first place that came to mind. Would you rather not?"

"I don't mind," she answered quickly, impulsively.

"All right, then," David said. "It's understood that we'll meet on Wednesday—that will be January the third—say at—eleven forty-five—just inside the museum—near the art book store?"

"All right."

"Goodbye, then."

"Goodbye."

Dodie replaced the phone on its cradle. She continued sitting on the sofa thinking of Lenny with a mustache. As in a game of blindman's buff, she kept trying to pin it on his lip, but the mock mustache wandered off to one side and Lenny's face remained blessedly bare.

Dodie gathered her coat and bag and walked to the stairs. The voice that had arranged for a meeting at the museum and had told her about Lenny was still with her in its insistence that they should meet and talk. It came to Dodie as she mounted the steps to the bedroom that these past weeks of David's absence had put a new, unknown beachhead on the familiar continent of their years.

David

31.

I remember drives such as the one I'm taking now. Drives with Dodie. Not in this leather-smelling little car. Not with this music, which I have put on to oblige Kathy, who sits beside me. Dodie and I listened to WQXR, and on one such trip to the Riches', I brought to Dodie's attention the coincidence of Offenbach.

"Are you sure?" she had asked.

"Positive," I had said. "Practically every time we've gone there. And not only Offenbach, but specifically *La Belle Helénè*. Music to see the Riches by."

"Do you like it?"

"It's appropriate somehow. Gay, bouncy, overtury. Right for the Riches."

Kathy, who changed her mind at the last minute, says, "Is this going to be a middle-aged party? A husbands-and-wives thing? I mean, am I going to be the only single there?"

"You'll be with me."

"I know—but—you know—"

Her voice is a monotone of irritation. I smell a developing crisis in her life. Brian Miller. The boy with the prematurely gray hair and the preternaturally beautiful smile. It isn't that I don't care. I do. I'm concerned about Kathy, but I simply haven't got the emotional room for her just now. She knows this and resents it. I resent her resentment. A few days ago she was certain she couldn't come to the Riches', had other plans, but late this afternoon she changed her mind, asked if she could come. Yes, indeed, come along. But don't expect me to pay for whatever double cross dumped those other plans. I'm free, too, Kathy. That's the condition of freedom—that cold draft coming through a door you can't shut.

"What's that?" Kathy asks.

"What?"

"That ahead. Don't you see it?"

"That's fog, Kathy. We're in a slight valley on this road. At night, in fall and winter, fog develops."

"Do you remember the night we drove to The Powder Horn?" she asks.

"In Vermont? Indeed I do."

"Hey, how about Lenny?"

"What about Lenny?"

"Isn't he coming home at all?"

"Yes, he's coming home at all, as you very well know. You were there the night I spoke to him."

"Thought you might have heard from him again."

"And you?" I ask her. "What are your Christmas plans?"

"I don't know," she replies, gazing out the window. "I'll probably spend Christmas Eve with my aunt. Probably the next few days too."

"Your mythical aunt."

"I know you think she doesn't exist," Kathy says, "and I hate to spoil your fun. *However,* I've had lunch with her four times since I've been in the city. Her name is Elizabeth Cooper, and she lives on Fifty-third Street."

"And your parents?"

Silence. We plunge into fog. Odd sensation. I expected the fog to act like a mass of cotton covering the mouth of the car radio. It surprises me when the music continues sharp and undiminished. Giant gray amoebae swim through the headlights. Undersea travel. I slow to a crawl.

"My mother may come to New York," Kathy says—and I realize that there has indeed been correspondence.

Really I wish Kathy well. I hope I have done her no harm. I wonder why I can say to myself that this sexual living arrangement we have worked out is meaningless, an interlude with no residue. I guess I can say it because it's true. I feel sure that nothing will remain with me after Kathy passes out of my life. All that dedicated sexuality gone. And I? To her? God knows! Will she someday tell Lenny? Very likely, if they ever see each other again. I haven't tried to be a model to Lenny, but I have tried to convey a general sense of decency and limits. Is it for my vagueness and inconsistency that things have become so tentative between my son and me? Does he pity me? Dislike me? Please don't dislike me, Lenny. That would be such a fearful defeat. Insupportable. Were it not for Dodie's defection, I would have gone on constructing bombproof fool shelters against the possibility of anybody really disliking me, betraying me, much less my wife and son. But I don't believe that Lenny dislikes me. After all, why should he?

"What's your wife like?" Kathy asks.

" 'Like'? What do you mean 'like'?"

"I mean what's she *like?* Surely you understand what's meant by the word 'like.' "

"Surely I don't. Never did, to be honest, although I suppose I've tried to answer questions like that in the past. Do you mean what does she *look* like?"

"That," says Kathy, "but generally, I mean, what was she like—the whole recondite quality of her personality?"

"I don't know," I answer. "The recent history of my life could be taken as evidence that I had no idea what she was like."

"What did you *think* she was like?"

"What did I think? Well, you must let me think about what I thought. I think I thought my wife was a very fine cook—"

"Marvey," Kathy says, leaning her head against the backrest and turning to gaze out the window. Obviously she thinks I'm going to be clever about it, and she is not interested in that line. But it is true that I have always found it nearly impossible to talk

221

about what people were "like." However, I am eager to discuss it now. Kathy has no idea how eager. She doesn't know about my telephone conversation with Dodie on the day of my visit to Arthur. She doesn't know of my arrangement to see Dodie after New Year's—at the famous museum.

"You think it's not important," I say to Kathy, "but you're mistaken. Much of married life is spent preparing and eating meals. It's very important. It happens that Dodie—have I mentioned to you that my wife's name is Dodie?—from Dorothy—Dodie was—is —an excellent cook. Her specialties were French and Mexican dishes. How it worked, you see, was that she would try a new dish on me, and if I approved she would then try it on company. As I recall, once it became a company dish it never went back to being a family dish. No, that's not quite true. Once in a while, it did. . . . You're right, Kathy, I'm being trivial—although I did look forward to company for gourmet reasons . . ."

We enter another patch of fog, this one much thicker. I slow up as the headlights are swaddled in a gray density. The music cuts through clear and tumultuous. That telephone call left me with a new perspective of loss. I realized I was losing Dodie more through my removal from her than her removal from me. While I had stayed in the house and agonized, I was still negotiating with the evil that had befallen my life, but when I had moved out I had rejected the evil. The time movement had begun, slowly and hugely, as an ocean liner moves away from its berth, packed with an awesome cargo of lives and days and nights and books and music and frustration and fear and love.

". . . but I realize," I continue to Kathy, "that what you are looking for is an essential quality in a few words. Well, I'm afraid there is no such thing."

"Yes there is," she says.

"Is there? Then what's mine?"

"Chameleon."

"What?"

"Yes," she says. "There are two kinds of people—those who are

222

themselves all the time, and those who are always changing to blend in with the surroundings."

"By God, I believe you're right!" I say. "All right, then, my wife was the first kind, the nonchameleon. She didn't change. She was herself at all times. For instance, she smokes—not tremendously—not as much as I do when I'm on a cigarette binge—but consistently and without fuss. Smoking is an enjoyment to her, not a compulsion. She does it and thinks nothing of it. I, on the other hand, will stop for weeks at a time, and then go back to two packs a day. Another thing, whenever my wife would settle down for an evening, at a restaurant or a friend's house, she would take out her pack of cigarettes and the gold lighter that I gave her on our fifth anniversary. She would put the lighter on the pack of cigarettes, to have them both handy. I don't know why this bothered me so much, but it did."

"How was she in bed?" Kathy asks.

"Mind your own business."

"Oh, I see," she says, returning to the window. "I have to tell you everything, but you're not obliged to tell me anything."

"That's the way the arrangement works—but she was good in bed."

"Does she wear nice clothes?"

"It was my impression she did. I believe the description would be called 'tailored.' "

"How long did you say you were married?"

"This June would make it twenty-three years."

"God! What did you *do* in all those years?"

There's terror in that question—for me, surely—possibly for Kathy. There are times when I glance over my shoulder and see two decades shrunk to a day. I can remember in excruciating detail the minutiae of rooms and days, but I can find nowhere in my heart or head a sensation large enough to match the aggregate of those rooms and days.

"I don't think life is cumulative," I say to Kathy. "In our house, in our bedroom, there's a vanity table, and my wife would sit at that vanity table every night and apply creams and tissues to her

223

face. Every night. But all those nights of creams and tissues have not created one supreme cream-and-tissue night that will serve as the sum of that experience. Just a succession of cream-and-tissue nights that consumed so many hours of her life and mine. I'm not saying this as well as I'd like to, but it's the best I can do. And the hours that she would spend at that vanity table applying makeup when we were going out for an evening, or were expecting company. Kathy, we did most things that most people do. We went to summer places, and PTA meetings, and we voted and we paid taxes and we talked about our son, and we grew azaleas around the house."

I slow up as I approach the Connecticut toll booth. I glance at Kathy as we pass beneath a highway lamp, catching a glint of light as it slides across her cheek and silvery eye.

"Does any of this give you an idea what my wife was like?" I ask.

Kathy waits several seconds, then says, "No."

I drop coins in the receptacle and receive the green eye. I race into second gear, third—fast—pursued by the indefinable ghosts of my past.

32.

Rich lives in a house of his own designing. The northern wing of the house is a cellar-to-roof studio. "The little wop builds his dream house," Rich explained to me and Dodie when we visited a plot of ground marked with a promissory bulldozer and Rich magicked a house into being with words and airy gestures. The promise materialized. Everything in the Rich house is Rich. If Rich's wife, Vanessa, contributed anything substantial to this, I wouldn't know what it is.

Dodie never liked Rich. She didn't reject him completely, but she could never fully accept him. She felt threatened by him. She never said why, but I suspect she felt that Rich, for all his artistry and artfulness, had a Mediterranean attitude toward women. She once said that Rich could have been important if he wished. I knew what she meant, but I thought then, and still think, that she was wrong. She meant that Rich chose not to infuse his considerable talent with the seriousness that would have made him important. I think she was wrong about the *choice* part of it.

Perhaps it's because he lacks the ultimate gift that he decorates his life so cleverly. The carved antique mantle flanked by two small ship's figureheads. The lamps made of rice paper. Weavings you would expect on the walls cover the floors. Animal hides you would expect on the floors ornament the walls. All paintings and sculpture are marked by the artist: *Riccio.*

225

Vanessa admits Kathy and me, with a kiss for me and a wizard's smile for Kathy. Women have a born genius for the man-woman thing, always managing to find the right expression. Even Dodie. Vanessa's smile was quick, warm, tentative, and welcoming. A mother-courtesan with an eye for situations.

"David, I'm so glad to see you," she says in her not-so-English accent. "And—"

"This is Kathy Willens," I say.

"Kathy," says Vanessa. "I'm so glad you could come."

She takes our coats. We mount the stairs to the level above where I hear the voices. Vanessa has grown plump. She is blond. She has wistful blue eyes, a humorous mouth, a turned-up nose. I know this doesn't sound particularly well matched or English, but it does go together very well. Rich and Vanessa have two children—a boy, thirteen or fourteen; a girl, about sixteen. Mark is the boy. Laura is the girl—and her beauty has always struck me as a cooperative act of will: Rich's dark fertility and Vanessa's blond obligingness resolved into honey-colored perfection. I have known Laura ever since she was a baby. She gave me wet kisses. Only recently, in the past year, have I drawn back from her with the uneasiness that such overnight ripening can make an old, friendly, father figure feel. How many years separate Laura and Kathy? Six? A world of difference in the life of a woman, no doubt, but I am not as quick and instinctive as Vanessa. I have no handy attitude to pull out of my inventory of situations. I wish to God I hadn't come with Kathy. I fervently wish that Laura isn't at home. I wouldn't want her to see the look that would come to my face.

"How are the kids?" I ask Vanessa as we ascend. "Mark? Laura?"

"They're fine," says Vanessa. "Mark is somewhere below with friends. Laura has a date."

Thank God! Nevertheless, why did I come? Why did I bring Kathy? I haven't got that kind of cool. Perhaps I'm a changing man, but I will never have that kind of cool. My sense of exposure approaches nakedness as we reach the top of the stairs and I see Rich and his guests. There's only one person I recognize besides

226

Rich. Ted Buchholz. Rich's new partner. That accidental bidder at my postexplosion fire sale. I glance at Kathy, who has assumed a look I have seen before, a look of millennial removal her generation has established against mine—masklike face, drapery hair, eyes fastened on infinity.

Rich hurries over, glasses flashing. "They tell me the fog's pretty thick on the highway," he says to me. "Did you have any trouble?" "No," I say. "This is Kathy Willens. Kathy, this is my friend, Rich." "Hello, Kathy," Rich says. "Come on in. Let me introduce you. Let me get you a drink. What do you drink?" Rich has the good sense to introduce Kathy and me to the others as though we were two people who just happened to arrive at the same time. There are guests off in various corners of the very large, very high-ceilinged room, and introductions are abandoned with the understanding that everybody will get to know everybody in the course of the evening.

Since I have known Rich and Vanessa for so long, and since, with the exception of Ted Buchholz, none of these people are familiar to me, I assume that for all the length and depth of our friendship there has been the wish and the time on the part of Rich and Vanessa to cultivate this whole other group of friends. Childishly, I feel a pang of disloyalty.

Rich takes Kathy and me to the table of giant liquor bottles. Rich buys only the largest size going. At another time, in another country, he would have been a lord of casks, vats, great tuns of fermentation. He mixes the drinks we ask for. Kathy, after all, is female, and she can't maintain her distance in the midst of all this groovy stylishness.

"What a fantastic place!" she says. "Beautiful!"

Kathy's "beautiful," I have learned, is not *my* "beautiful." Her "beautiful" may or may not be an esthetic judgment. A satellite TV picture of a Japanese student riot the other evening was "beautiful." So was a newspaper account of a man in Ireland who had won a burial endurance contest. So is Rich's house. "Beautiful" is anything that courage, madness, or singularity has made manifest in the world.

227

"David has seen it lots of times," Rich says to Kathy, "so why don't I give you the quick, two-dollar tour?"

"Great," says Kathy.

Rich takes Kathy away. Giuseppe Riccio. Joe Richards, for American reasons. Only, as Rich once explained to me, "Riccio" did not mean "rich." It meant "curly." I also remember him saying to me at one time that a couple of hundred years ago he probably would have been a stone mason, would have carved cornices on churches, gargoyles, cherubs with little button *putzes*. "Up to a point," he once said to me, "everything is an accident. Then one morning you wake up knowing who you are. I'm an artist, and I'm a clown too. And I need money." I don't know—maybe Dodie was right about Rich.

Ted Buchholz comes over to me. He says hello, asks how I'm doing. I tell him I'm doing fine. And how is he doing? Are things shaping up?

"*Ça va,*" he says, smiling into his glass.

Then he looks up at me. He is a big man. Stout. He has thick, dark hair that forms a swell over his ears and curves opulently to the back of his head. Everything about Ted's face is large and shapely—mouth, eyes, ears, nose. His words are cheeses—mild ones —Swiss and Edam and Gouda. His eyes are unnerving, the way they look at me so steadily.

He says, "I was glad when Rich told me you were coming to-night. It gives me an opportunity to tell you how much I admire some of the material I came across in the office."

"Oh?"

"Yes. I hope you don't mind my having read some of those scripts for the educational film. Particularly the ones on music and ancient culture. Very fine."

"Thank you."

"Are you doing anything along those lines now?"

"No."

"Rich also told me that you had a novel published."

"Long ago."

"Still—think you might go back to writing?"

228

"Difficult to say. No, I don't think so. I don't know what's important these days."

Ted smiles, nods. His eyes haven't left mine for an instant. I wonder why he does that. Is it supposed to betoken a form of deference?—sincerity?

"I've always wanted to write," he says.

"Have you?"

"Yes. Plays. When I was a younger man, I was a great admirer of O'Neill. And Odets. Do you remember Odets? *Awake and Sing*. 'Awake and sing all ye that dwell in the dust.' And *Waiting for Lefty*. Still great plays in my opinion. Arthur Miller, of course. The trouble I found with the play form was that you really had to be an actor to be a playwright. That's why so many playwrights were part-time actors. Shakespeare did, you know. Act. To write a play, you really have to act each part."

"Oh?"

"Yes. The Elizabethans were the last to successfully combine language and gesture. The novel gives the writer greater satisfaction, I should think." (Watching him, listening to him, I have the feeling that my senses are being anesthetized at an infinitesimally slow rate.) "You know," he goes on, "when I was a kid, we lived in Williamsburg. I had a paper route. I've often thought of writing a novel about those days. I know you will say—"

I will say nothing. I let him do all the saying, which he does, without haste, without hesitation. His words peel off like slices of pale cheese. He tells me about the old men who befriended him and the ladies who tried to seduce him. I'm amazed at the versatility of my fellow mortals. I'm amazed at this large, sleek, pulpy, tropical plant of a man. I'm also amazed at Rich, who could have been my partner for so many years and then have taken up with Ted Buchholz without suffering some sort of emotional bends from the disastrous change in pressure.

Perhaps it is I who am emotionally unequipped for the normal range of human difference. I have created and have lived within my own atmosphere, filtering out the truth of other people. But I am by no means filtering out Ted Buchholz. His eyes follow mine with lunatic insistence. Of this I'm certain: no life is so free of dissimulation that it can bear to look into another's without occasionally averting in honest shame. Therefore Ted Buchholz is not honest. He is a liar—not just in these harmless enough fabrications —but in the private echo chambers of his soul.

Fortunately, Rich returns with Kathy. My eyes gladly pull away from Ted's and seek Rich's.

"How do you like the house?" I ask Kathy, enormously relieved to be free of the mild cheeses and shameless eyes.

"Beautiful!" says Kathy.

"Refill?" Rich asks, pointing to my glass.

"All right."

"Kathy?"

"Okay."

Ted Buchholz excuses himself and departs. Goodbye, Ted Buchholz. I don't like you. I find myself allergic to your kind of dishonesty. Not dishonesty in general, just your kind.

Rich, Kathy, and I advance on the liquor. There's a young man at the table whose vague smile particularizes as it comes to rest on Kathy. When I say young, I mean he is somewhere between Kathy's generation and mine. He wears a double-breasted blue blazer and a white turtleneck something. He is tall, fair, blue-eyed, and brutally handsome. He possesses his handsomeness the way some American millionaires possess their fortunes, not wishing it to stand in the way of democratic contact but emanating the ambience of immense purchasing power nonetheless. For reasons too vague to define, I am suddenly apprehensive. I wonder where Dodie is this evening. I wonder what she is doing.

"I don't believe you've met yet," says Rich. "Bud, I'd like you to meet Kathy Willens. And David Lang, my lifetime partner, in or out of business. This is Bud Demery. Bud is an English version of his real name. A beautiful Russian name, which I'm sorry to say I've forgotten, Bud. What was it?"

"Bodane."

"Bodane! Bodane Gregory! And Demery isn't Demery either. It's reduced from something a Russian mile long. . . . Kathy, do you think you could stand talking to this man for a few minutes? I want to show Dave something."

Rich takes my arm and leads me away. "I don't want to show you anything," he says as we walk. "I want to talk to you. Bud, by the way, is one third of an agency we're trying to crack. Let's go to the studio. As a matter of fact, I am working on a new piece. I'd like you to see it. He isn't smart, that Demery, but he isn't dumb either. Actually, he can't do a thing himself, but he has an uncanny sense of what will work. . . ."

As Rich talks, we proceed along a hallway, through a door, and down a staircase into the cellar-to-roof studio where the north wall is constructed entirely of glass. It's chilly down here, and the chill reminds me of other visits; reminds me particularly of that visit Dodie and I made when the studio was at last completed. I had bought a bottle of champagne, and the four of us—Rich, Vanessa, Dodie, and I—toasted Rich's vaulted dream in Veuve Cliquot. There are two levels here. Rich does his painting on a platform above, and his sculpture here below.

"There are people like that," Rich says.

"People like what?"

"Like Bud. Like Ted, for that matter. They have a speck of talent you could cover with a dime, but in this world of a million freaked-out specialties it's worth a fortune. . . . This is the piece."

An elongated figure. In stone.

"Looks like Giacometti, huh?" says Rich. "I don't care. I did it and then realized it looked like someone else's stuff. As far as I'm concerned, it's mine. Original. Do you like it?"

"Yes," I say. "Very much."

Rich laughs and gives my arm a deprecating shake. He's right. I don't know whether I like it or not. But then I never know whether I like a painting, a piece of sculpture, or anything in the plastic arts the first time I look at it. Or the second time either.

"Dodie would have liked that," I feel it safe to say.

"It's possible," Rich says, glancing at me.

"Arthur Gerson and I had our interview," I tell him.

"I figured if it was anything more than words, I would have

231

heard about it," Rich says. "But I should have called. I'm sorry."

"No reason why you should have called," I say. "It was more than words, however."

"Oh?"

"I hit him."

Rich rears back a little, his smile like the surprise beneath a magician's handkerchief.

"Come on!"

"I did. I'm sorry I did, but I did."

"Is he going to make a federal case of it?"

"I don't think so."

"Well, then, what the hell are you sorry about?"

"There was no emotional percentage in it for me. It was around noon that I saw him. Later in the day, the scene kept going over in my mind. It made me feel ridiculous. Such a puny reaction."

"What'd he say?"

"Oh—this and that—about me, about him, about Dodie. It's not important. Mostly lies and nonsense. Have you by any chance heard from her?"

"From Dodie? No. Why would I have heard from her? I'm pretty sure Vanessa hasn't either. She would have told me."

"Of course," I say. "No, it's not very likely she would have gotten in touch with you. Although you can't tell. Explosions make strange bedfellows. She's been steadily in touch with my brother and his wife, for instance. You couldn't begin to appreciate how strange that is. Everything is strange. I'm changing, Rich. My past is moving away from me. Each day I find myself in new territory. Somehow I manage to live in that new territory; therefore I must be changing. Or maybe I'm still in a state of shock. I don't know. Tell me, Rich, what do you make of Dodie?"

"Now?"

"Not now. I mean what did you ever make of Dodie? I know you had no reason to devote much time thinking about her—why should you?—still there must have been a time when you had a distinct impression of Dodie."

He looks at me, head cocked. "You want it straight?" he asks. "Like medicine."

Rich turns away and walks toward the glass wall on the other side of the studio. "Listen," he says, his back to me, "if you want to know what I really think, I think that you and Dodie will eventually get together again—and frankly I don't think that would be such a bad idea. What the hell—"

"Rich," I interrupt, "one problem at a time. Let me worry about my life the day after tomorrow. Just give me what I need at ten o'clock tonight."

He reaches the other side, turns around, starts walking back to me but makes a detour. I wish to God he would stand in one place and talk. All this maneuvering about. What can he possibly hit me with? Does he imagine that I've got some unbombed area left? He walks to another wall of the studio and points to the window there.

"About five years ago," he says, "we were all out there. On the patio. I was grilling hamburgers and franks. We had other people over, too. I forget who. You know, it's a funny thing, but there have been damned few times when your wife and I ever found ourselves together. Alone. There may have been an inclination on both our parts to have it that way. I don't suppose it's news to you that Dodie didn't think I was the greatest thing since crushed ice. Anyway, we were out there, Dodie and me. Just the two of us. She was sitting in a wicker chair, when out of the blue she asks me what you do all day. *You,* boychick, not me. She asked, 'What does David do with the eight hours he spends in the office?' Now I know when a woman is making conversation and when she's asking questions. Dodie was asking. So I asked her what she meant by 'do.' I told her you did a lot of things. I told her you answered correspondence, went over the films we were working on, saw people, salesmen, etcetera, and that you closed the door of your office for hours at a time and wrote scripts. I told her you had a full day, if that's what she was worried about. Well, she just sat there, the way she sits, one leg over the other, swinging, looking at me, and then she said, 'I wonder if you or David know what it means to have a full day every day of the week.' Something like that. That was all. And that's when I thought to myself that my friend, David Lang, was in trouble."

"Why in trouble, Rich?"

"Because of the way she said it," he replies. "Like water on the holding side of a dam. Quiet as a lake, but one thousand pounds of human pressure per square inch."

"Couldn't it have been simple curiosity?" I ask.

"No, David. No."

I nod. "Let's go upstairs," I say.

33.

Returning to the party, I count the number of people, including Kathy and myself. At least twenty. Perhaps more in bathrooms and other places. Evidently Kathy and Bud Demery have consulted on their mutualities, have located Rich's audio system, and are now facing each other in the kind of dance that is done these days. Bud, of course, does it well. Kathy, needless to say.

Ted Buchholz has fixed another guest with his glittering eye.

The couple who was introduced to me as Jan and Bill Anderson have drawn around themselves a circle of listeners. Bill is a rangy, attractive, sleepy-eyed man who has seated himself on the floor, his back propped against a sofa. Jan, his wife, sits on the sofa, along with two others. She is a very lovely girl. They are both deeply tanned. I learn that they have recently returned from some remote island in the Caribbean, a very small island, not accessible to the tourist trade. There is something in Bill's bland, drawling voice that informs my jumpy heart of familiar nightmares.

"We didn't notice it at first," he is saying, "but then the girl got up, and then the guy got up, and neither one of them had on a stitch. They walked into the water that way. Nobody seemed to be paying any attention. There weren't that many people around, maybe ten in all. So Jan took off her stuff and I took off mine and we went in. Later we found out that that's the way it was on that island. Everybody. Like we'd been looking for it, or it us."

"Just nudity?" someone asked.

"Everybody does their thing, whatever it is," Bill says.

"The men bring these gorgeous wardrobes," Jan added, "and they fashion in the evening. I've never seen anything like it. You couldn't call it male or female. Just fabrics and colors and styles."

"Transvestites?" a woman wants to know.

Bill shrugs. He is contemptuous of names. But Demery and Kathy have stopped dancing. They, too, are listening.

"Where is this place?" Bud asks.

Bill smiles a slow, regretful smile. "Not allowed to say," he says. "Sworn to secrecy."

"Did you join in the fun?" Bud asks.

"Yes, we joined in the fun," Bill replies, looking up at Bud, still smiling.

"What *was* the fun?" another man asks. "Just taking off and putting on clothes?"

Bill answers that the fun was doing whatever you were moved to do. He looks around at the guests with a drowsy challenge, as if asking would they dare do the same, right here, right now. I look at his wife, the lovely Jan, and she too is smiling, but she is not challenging. She is listening as I have heard birds listen to the messages of their bird life, betraying nothing of their understanding to foreign eyes. I don't understand Bill and Jan. I don't know how much of what they are saying is true. I see by the look of patient amusement on Rich's face that this is not the first time that these young and handsome people have chewed their lotus leaves in public. Perhaps it is their function at parties to suggest the intoxication of a new freedom—of which no one avails himself. Or perhaps others do. I don't know. Who am I not to believe in the fantasies of others? I move closer to Kathy.

"Is this a recondite party?" I ask.

"Is he for real?" she says, indicating Bill.

"Can't be sure," I say. "Is Bud Demery a good dancer?"

"He swings," she says, indifferently.

"Is that another drink?"

"Another? It's my third. Where were you?"

"Talking to Rich. Are you used to drinking?"

"Are you worried about me?"

"No, not worried. I wouldn't like for you to get drunk, though."

"I never get drunk," she says. "I get sick first. I get nauseous, throw up, and then I go to sleep."

Music starts up again, and Bud Demery, who had disappeared from Kathy's side, appears again. He glances over at me with a smiling by-your-leave, and then his head and shoulders begin their invitation to Kathy in miniature rhythm. Kathy sets down her glass and moves off with Bud.

I look around for Vanessa. She's not in this room, so I walk down to the floor below and find her where I expect to find her, in the kitchen. She is arranging platters of food. She smiles at me.

"Would you believe that Bill Anderson is a hard-working, dedicated man?" she asks.

"If you tell me he is, I believe it."

"He is," Vanessa asserts. "He runs some sort of human relations clinic. Isn't that odd? He and Jan have no children. I've never been able to find out whether it's a matter of choice or biology. I don't understand this other thing."

"You mean the magic island?"

"Yes. I suspect things haven't been going well for them in bed for years. They're always trying to promote some sort of communal orgy. Bill is, really. Women have less patience with that sort of thing. Who is that girl, David?"

"Kathy?"

"Yes."

"I don't know who that girl is, Vanessa, except that she's sharing my apartment. I visited Lenny at school early last month, and Kathy came back to New York with me. Asked for a lift, and when we got to New York she stayed with me."

"Oh, David!"

"Yes, I know. I couldn't begin to trace the motives for that imbecility. I was scared, alone, vengeful, and more than a little out of my mind."

"She's so young."

237

"I know. You and I grew up at a time when such disparities were important. They don't seem to be now, Vanessa. I am assured endlessly that they are not. I don't understand Lenny's generation. I doubt I ever will. But I'm beginning to see that there is a difference. I refused to believe that for a long time, but I was wrong. I guess when you reject something very deeply, you must do something about it."

"Oh, yes!" Vanessa palpably agrees.

I examine her face for a few seconds. "What is it that you reject?" I ask her.

She motions with her head. Upstairs. *"That,"* she says.

"The people?"

"Everything. I love Rich. God knows there's nothing wrong with our bed. But I'm tired of that nonsense up there. I'm sick of it, but I think Rich is addicted, and that scares me. They make me feel that the world is coming to an end, and I don't want to feel that way. I've got such lovely kids. I think I would like to go back to England and live in the country for a while. I don't want fashion and cleverness anymore. I'm not that way. It's awful. I do love Rich, he's so full of life, but I'm afraid I don't want what he wants."

"And I thought that at least *you*—you and Rich—"

"Yes, I know. So did I. For a long time."

"How bad is it?" I ask.

"Bad enough for me to know that it can't go on indefinitely," Vanessa says. "I don't know what will happen eventually. Please don't say anything to Rich about our speaking. He knows what I feel, but I think it would upset him terribly if he thought I was talking to others about it. I tell it to you because you're such an old friend. He'll probably tell you himself one day."

"Probably. Vanessa—"

"Yes?"

"About Dodie. Have you spoken to her?"

"Once. Several weeks ago. After I learned of your breakup. I don't think she really wanted to talk to me."

"Quite possible. I'm trying to find out something about the

woman I lived with for over twenty years. Do you think you understood Dodie? Now? Ever?"

"But not at all," Vanessa replies emphatically. "The first thing to put me off about Dodie was her dislike of animals. What I remember of your visits is having to tie up Flip for all the time you and Dodie were here. I didn't dislike Dodie; she just mystified me. Her internal geography was made up of city streets and buildings. We just didn't have the same points of reference. But, you know, David, I did think that you and she had worked out something wonderful between yourselves. Ridiculous, in view of what's happened, but there it is—I actually thought you could read each other's minds. Not literally, of course, but something that came to that. And that's not the way it was at all, was it?"

"No, that's not the way it was at all."

My gaze is caught and held by the little rectangular blocks of hard wood that make up this solid kitchen counter. Each block is slightly different in grain and color. Something moves in my mind —another arrangement—the days and thoughts that pieced out my life with Dodie.

"No, that wasn't the way it was," I say again, "but I'll tell you something strange, Vanessa. You keep my secret, and I'll keep yours. When it was much too late, I *was* able to read Dodie's mind. Not read exactly, something else, I don't know what—*access!*—I was given access to her mind—or my own, which is more likely. When it was all too late, I was given access to my own mind. . . . Here, let me give you a hand with those plates."

"Please," she says.

34.

I realize now that I have never liked house parties. I lack the attributes that make for a good time at a house party. The first and most important is liquor. My tolerance varies, but not by much. If not two highballs, then three; if not three, then four; but sooner or later the quick happy sun dims, and I am left with a headful of haze and a small hammer striking the painful position of two o'clock in my skull. And even if I do manage to keep my drinking below the critical point, I eat the nuts and cheese and toothpicked niblets until I am crapulous and cranky. And even if I am faithful to my resolve to open my mouth only for talk, I invariably find myself following the swing of other hobbyhorses until I am dizzy and full of rancor.

Rich's party is no different. The drinkers drink and according to their constitutions become loud or mute. Conversational islands form and break apart. Kathy comes over and sits down beside me.

"What do young people do at parties?" I ask.

"Smoke, drink, fuck," she replies.

I examine her profound expressionlessness. "Where is Bud Demery?" I ask.

"I don't know where Bud Demery is," she replies, her words passing over arctic wastes of indifference. "Talking to somebody. How should I know?"

"Tell me, Kathy."

240

"Tell you *what?*"

"What you're thinking."

"My mind's a blank. Completely."

"I don't believe that."

"That's too bad, Mr. Lang."

"All right, Kathy."

"Look," she says, "I'll be going to my aunt's on Christmas. I'll take my stuff with me, and that will be that—okay?"

"Okay."

"Where's the john?" she asks.

"Through that hallway. Second door to the right."

"Excuse me," she says, getting up and walking in that direction. She pauses to rest the glass she is holding on the perilously narrow railing at the top of the staircase.

I turn to the conversation on my left. A stocky man with a grizzled beard is describing an auto trip over an old railroad bed through the Rockies. At one point, it seems, you can get out of your car and peer straight down for a thousand feet. This reminds a woman of her trip to Italy last spring. I see Rich standing with Ted Buchholz and two other guests.

Some turn of interest or boredom rearranges the human pattern around me. Grizzled Beard has turned away to light a thin cigar and take up conversation with a mannish-looking woman with cropped, grizzled hair. I have the feeling that the two of them have finally yielded to the affinity proclaimed by their hair. The woman who traveled to Italy last year turns toward me. She is wearing a short skirt, and I can see the variety of fabrics encasing her thighs. They look, the fabrics, like components in an intricate program. Her stockings are one shade of nylon, the tops of her stockings another, and the elastic garment that overlaps that swelling display is still a third. She has dark hair and dark eyes and probably was quite beautiful once. She tips her head and looks at me as though she has at last decided to give me the compassion that has taken root in her heart. She asks me if I have traveled abroad, and I tell her no, not since the war. She asks me if I wouldn't like to—and I realize that something has indeed stirred her pity. Yes, I say, I

241

would like to. I tell her that I would very much like to go back to London and see the city that for some years was the bleeding center of the world's history.

As I talk, I cast glances about the room. I don't see Kathy. I glance at my watch. It lacks at least an hour before my leaving will not be thought peculiar. Vanessa is passing around platters of food, and as I nibble and talk to the lady with the programed thighs I project myself into my little Swedish car traveling on a dark road. . . . There is that lapse in attention when you are talking to someone, or listening, and the mind tilts in its own direction, tilts away from the conversation, and then picks up with a start of guilt the last word. . . . I am about to ease my conscience and reward my companion's cheerful solicitude with a lengthy statement when, like a snarling accusation, a glass shatters on the floor.

I am on my feet so quickly that one might think it was my arm, or an extension of my subconscious apprehension, that had brushed that glass from the railing. I am the first one there, and I begin to pick up the pieces. Rich is at my side. "No problem, Dave," he says. "Just leave it. You'll cut yourself. I'll get a broom and shovel. Was that your friend's glass?" I let fall the ragged piece of glass I am holding between my fingers. Why, I wonder, "my friend"?

Again I look around the room, and there is Kathy standing at the liquor table. I continue to look, and I find Bud Demery in another corner, talking to a woman, a woman I have seen him talk to before. By the way that woman averts her head, half-closes her eyes, I gather she is positioning herself to receive some dreadful lie or irony that Bud Demery's words will futilely try to conceal.

I walk over to Kathy and stand beside her. "Are you having another drink?" I ask. She shrugs one shoulder but doesn't turn to me. I notice that her hair has been freshly combed. "Kathy?" I say. "No," she says, shrugging again, "I'm not having another drink." "Kathy," I say once more. Now she turns slightly and gives me a sideward glance. Her eyes appear abnormally large and luminous—an effect, I make out, achieved by the warm suffusion in her high cheekbones. I turn away from her and look at the lady

242

with the thighs. Her solicitude. Rich's "my friend." The fresh comb
marks in Kathy's hair. Kathy's eyes. Her flush. The glass . . . the
crash . . .

"I'm ready to go," I say.

"Okay by me," says Kathy.

We turn away from the table and begin the awkward process of
saying goodbye.

No fog on the road on the trip back. Kathy is silent. There is a
program at midnight that plays chamber music. I turn to that station and catch the slow movement of a quartet.

"You like that?" Kathy asks.

"Yes," I say.

"Why?" she asks. "I don't believe you. Nobody could really
like that. There's no melody or rhythm or anything."

"You just don't hear it," I say.

"You know," she says, "there's one thing that I *really* despise,
and that's the kind of person who's always pretending to like something because it's supposed to be highbrow, or deep, or—"

"Recondite?"

"You're terribly funny," she says.

"What's troubling you, Kathy?"

"Nothing's troubling me."

Anger seizes me so suddenly and furiously that I'm shouting
before I have a chance to consider. "Yes, something is troubling
you! And it should be troubling you! You've got to stop this, Kathy!
For your own sake! You can't spread for every man who takes
your fancy! It's sick!"

"What the hell are you talking about?"

"You know goddam well what I'm talking about!"

"I do not!"

"Then forget it!"

"No, wait a minute!" she exclaims. "This is good! I'd like to
know what business it is of yours what I do? You don't give a
damn about me!"

"Then you admit it," I say. "Where, for the love of God? Where

243

did you and he find the place to hump like a couple of animals?"

"Are you jealous?"

"No, I'm not jealous. I just think it's sickening, that's all."

"But not with you," she says. "That isn't sickening."

"I thought you cared for me."

"Maybe I do. But you don't give a damn about me."

"That isn't so. I don't know where you got the idea that I didn't give a damn about you. I do! At least you knew me for more than twenty-four hours before you went to bed with me. And you claim to love this boy, Brian. How do you manage all this chaos, Kathy? Tell me what goes on in your mind when you—"

She slides down in the bucket seat and turns her head away from me. Her sobs are deep, racking.

"Leave—me—alone!"

"All right."

A dead creature—woodchuck or dog—appears on the road ahead. I speed past the mash of fur and blood. Kathy cries so sincerely that I begin to hear in her abandon familiar echoes. It seems to me that her crying is my crying; that I have wanted to cry like this ever since that fading afternoon on the lawn. The hopeful affirmation of the last movement of the quartet contradicts Kathy's tears and my share in her tears, so I switch off the radio. I want Kathy to go on weeping. There's a solvent in her tears that is loosening feelings that have congealed in me. I want to put my arm around Kathy and comfort her. I want to kiss her hair and her face and taste on my lips the salt of her tears. But she is a very young girl, and the emotion which compels me stands confused before the years that separate us.

"Kathy, why are you crying?" I ask her.

She doesn't answer but goes on crying for long minutes. After a time, I am aware that she has stopped. We drive in silence. Kathy keeps her head turned to the window as she speaks:

"It was a girl's room. I don't know where. *He* seemed to know the house very well. There was a window and a curtain. There was a light from outside the house that came into the room, and I could see a whole shelf of Fresca cans—you know, the soft drink. The funny thing is that I used to do that, collect soda cans, make a display of them in my room back home. And there were books, and a typewriter. Somewhere below there were kids, boys, I could hear them. They were yelling and playing records. The Beatles. I don't think we were in there ten minutes. Nobody saw us. Then we went outside and walked around the house. God, it was cold! . . . I swear, Dave, I think I'm going out of my mind. I'm only twenty-two and everything is so crowded in my head. I don't know what's happening to me. I don't know where I'm going to find room for the next twenty or thirty years. Do you know what I mean?"

"Yes," I say. "I know what you mean."

She is silent again for a time, then she says, "Dave, will you please see Brian, talk to him, for my sake?"

"Yes," I say.

35.

I began by saying I was alone. That was true in the sense that I meant it. Kathy was part of the sudden landscape that had come into view as a result of the turn my life had taken. It might have been somebody else, no one at all; just my days utterly alone, without my former life, would have served equally well as the new terrain into which I had wandered with my baggage of new pains and old memories. Now Kathy is not here. Apparently she does have an aunt. At any rate, she is no longer in this apartment with me, and I see that I have been mistaken.

She bought me a Christmas gift. I bought her one too, but that was different. Considering our ages, it was natural that I should have bought her one. I have bought Christmas gifts for Dodie, and then for Lenny, for so many years. The amputee, I have heard, goes on wiggling absent limbs and fingers; but sooner or later there is the problem of turning the page of a book, or kicking back to a child the blue-and-white ball that has rolled within reach of a foot that isn't there, and then the meaning of impairment stretches from earliest memory to distant death. Lenny's Christmas gift will be the snappy little foreign job he will drive back to Vermont. The Christmas gift I couldn't buy Dodie was the page I couldn't turn, the ball I couldn't kick. So I bought Kathy a gift. I bought her—not knowing her sizes or, really, her tastes—a large, glossy, illustrated book on the dance. It was partly reflex, the gift, but it was more because I am so much older, and Kathy is away from home, and for all her Maillol thighs and yogi flexions and five hundred dollars and sexual pioneering, she is only twenty-two, and I have seen her cry.

But in the exchange of gifts, I was not the first. Kathy was. She couldn't have known I had bought her something. She handed me a box handsomely packaged in black and gold, saying, "Merry Christmas, David." It was a lamp, one of those dome-shaped, slender-shafted, high-intensity desk lamps. I'd been using a very unsatisfactory floor lamp for light. It was meant for a room, not a typewriter. Kathy must have noticed this. I don't know which affected me more, her noticing the need or the gift itself.

"Gosh, thanks, Dave," she said, when I presented her with the book.

"You're very welcome. And Merry Christmas. And now tell me how much you spent for that lamp. That was silly, Kathy. You can't afford to be buying me such gifts."

"Cut it out!" she said. "How come you bought *me* a gift? I mean—well—Christmas is not a *Jewish* holiday."

"True," I said. "But I've always liked Christmas. I didn't know it belonged to anybody until it was too late to get over my infatuation."

That was true. I've been a celebrant since my third or fourth grade. I believe it was in the third or fourth grade that the teacher placed a small evergreen in a corner of the room, laced with silver tinsel and hung with the deep-hued Christmas bulbs which wrenched my unsuspecting heart with longing. My mother turned away with hard rejection when I pointed out my bright desire in the Woolworth store, immediately imparting to those rich colors the deeper hue of illicitness.

"You have your own," she had said.

I didn't have my own. My mother was a believer, not a practitioner. No seven-branched candelabra ever glowed in the Lang home. My father visited temples on the high holiday only, moved by some gloomy atavism. I suspect that he had been forced early

247

to swallow a burning dose of Yahweh, and it silenced him for-ever on the subject.

"Well," I said to Kathy, "I won't insist. I do appreciate this. Very much. Tell me, Kathy, what are you going to do after your aunt? Where will you be going?"

"I don't know," she said.

"Can you stay with your aunt?"

"No."

"Why?"

"Reasons."

"Brian?"

"I don't know," she replied. "Listen, you don't have to be con-cerned about me. I can take care of myself."

"I know you can," I said, "but I would ask these questions of any friend alone in the city. We *have* become friends, Kathy. I don't know what else to call it. Someday I'll look back on our campout, and perhaps I'll be able to give more accurate names to my actions—I can't speak for yours—but for the present I feel much concerned about you, and I'd like to know how you are and how you're faring. I want you to come back here if you have no-where else to go. Will you?"

"Okay."

She looked at me from between the narrow stage of her hair, and I believe that what I saw in her eyes could be called self-sufficiency—and something else—perhaps concern for *me*. After all, she has lived with me for some weeks. Something of my lost-ness must have become apparent.

"But you will see Brian?" she asked again.

"Yes. Have him phone me. Or you phone me. I can meet him here, or wherever is convenient."

"Okay. Take care, David."

"You, too, Kathy. Remember, I'm a phone call away."

I must confess that I haven't in the least missed Kathy these two days. I'm not glad that she's gone; I'm just unaware of her absence. Oh, I think of her from time to time, but the thought is stillborn. Kathy. The three-phase exercise. A leap. The hair. Those underground connections. I hope she is not now, or ever will be, in serious trouble. I know I will hear from her again, see her, not because of love or dependence, but because of Brian.

There are three days to the new year. New Year's Eve, for me, is a fearful time. I hate it. The false gaiety pumped into the occasion inflates its striped carnival skin to a huge balloon. I long to puncture it, to have the preheated, synthetic air come leaking out. Last year Dodie and I spent New Year's Eve at the Riches'. A large party, including the Gersons. Dodie danced with Arthur. Several times. Her hand on his shoulder—their cheeks? . . .

I get up and go to the window. I look below at the wide street where one evening, a week ago, I had seen two men with their hands on the roof of a car, the police, the revolving red light splashing fear on the buildings. . . .

Dodie? For the love of God, *Dodie!* I have a photograph of her in my wallet, but to *look* at it? To *remind* myself? Of course I know her face! Her jade-green eyes, the fleshy nose, the full lips, the auburn hair. Then what? Then this: In the last few moments I seem to have lost the unity of her face. I'm compelled to piece Dodie's face together—eyes, mouth, nose, chin. Kathy's face leaps in my mind whole. Not Dodie's. I've had a premonitory feeling all day. Naturally I didn't start moving toward the phone before it began to ring, but it seems as if I did.

"Hello." My heart is banging crazily.

"Hi—Dad?"

"Lenny! How are you?"

"Fine. Say, would it be convenient for you to pick me up at the terminal about five tomorrow?"

"Convenient? Yes, it would be convenient. Did you have a good time?"

"Yeah. Swell. I really did a lot of skiing. How are you?"

"I'm fine. I've been looking forward to your call. Have you been in touch with Mother?"

"Sure."

"Where will you be staying?"

"What do you mean?" he asks, puzzled. "At home. I mean—unless—what did you have in mind?"

"Nothing, nothing. Of course you'll be staying at home. Did Mother say anything to you? We haven't been much in touch, you know."

"Yes, I know. It's so damn ridiculous—"

"What is, Lenny?"

I hear his sigh. It angers me foolishly, powerfully.

"This not being in touch," he says. "It's kind of self-defeating, isn't it? I mean, there must be things you've got to talk over. You've got to make some sort of arrangement, don't you?"

"Yes, we do," I say. "There's no point in talking about it now. Look, you'll be arriving about five tomorrow, you say. I don't know if Mother has made any plans for the evening, but if it's all right with you, if you're free, perhaps we could have dinner together."

"Sure. That will be fine."

"Is there anything you'll be needing?" I ask. "Money?"

"I have some."

"All right then. See you at five tomorrow."

"Right. So long, Dad."

"So long."

But he will be needing money during the holidays. Dodie has the passbook to the savings account. I've been drawing money from my checking account in the downtown bank. How long has it been? The end of October, the two ghastly weeks that followed, my trip to Vermont—say, eight weeks. But why say anything? I have only to look at the calendar to be precise. I don't want to look at the calendar, however. I don't want to be precise. What has she been doing? Going to museums with Jean Ferguson? Seeing Arthur Gerson? Was she surprised to learn that I had struck Arthur? Of course. She knows I'm not the sort who goes around striking other people, even when provoked, even when greatly provoked. That was untypical. She must surely know that I'm curious to know whether almost twenty-three years of conjugal living hasn't left some slight residue of curiosity or concern, particularly when rumors of so much untypical behavior must have seeped back to her.

Now that I've experienced the thing I wouldn't have believed possible, that I would have to assemble Dodie's face, feature by feature, in a mind that held it so inviolably whole for so many years, I see, indistinctly, among scarcely perceived changes, the possibility of other disintegrations. I begin to see that I may not have been whole to Dodie for years. I begin to see that the size of Dodie's rejection may not have been so immense.

36.

Since Kathy left, I have lost interest in shopping. There's almost nothing left to eat in the refrigerator or cupboard. A can of sardines. A box of Saltines. A jar of peanut butter. And I haven't the slightest desire to get dressed and make my way through the muck left on the streets after last night's snowfall. The radio talked of a blizzard, but apparently the worst of it has moved out to sea. Enough fell, however, to make a mess of the city.

It began as I was driving over to the West Side bus terminal to pick up Lenny. He looked fine, with his ski tan and his mustache and his oatmeal-colored Loden coat. My son, the skier. Even though something of Dodie's immediacy and wholeness have been lost to me, I can imagine her reaction to these evidences of the latest Lenny—a Lenny bursting with springtime force from the private soil of his private life. I know what puzzled impotence she will feel, because that is what I felt, and we do share in our feeling toward Lenny.

I didn't get much of a chance to talk to my son. I drove back to the apartment from the terminal, weighing the feasibility of dinner with Lenny, and deciding against it. An hour or so of the snowfall we were having and the chances of his getting out to the Island that evening would be very slim. My vision of Dodie's wretchedness was physical in its force. I turned over my little sport car to Lenny and sent him on his way.

It's eleven o'clock in the morning now. I go to the window and look out to the Jersey Palisades, which are patched black and white. Then I look to the New York side, where the snow covering the banked areas flanking the West Side Drive still has a freshness whose imminent doom is burlesqued by a dog galloping slow-motion and pausing to piss on the snow with urban contempt, then galloping on. The city will easily prevail over the storm, which in a way is disappointing. The only weather extreme that can paralyze the city is a hefty, no-holds-barred blizzard, inches deep, and as a matter of principle I welcome such falls. Once a winter. For twenty-four hours. The raging avenues struck dumb, white, motionless.

But that wasn't the case this time. Lenny arrived home with no trouble. He phoned me from the house, as I asked him to. . . .

I look down through the window to a still closer scene. I see smartly booted New York housewives going to and from the expensive market across the street, shopping for the little delicacies in glass jars they will serve to the celebrants who will convene between nightfall and midnight, the annual cell meeting of a desperate Dionysian cult. What nonsense! Why can't people have a perfectly glorious time on New Year's Eve? They can, I suppose, but I just can't imagine it. Anyway, I have a jar of peanut butter, the smooth kind, and I have a novel to finish reading. It was given to me last night, in manuscript form, held together by one of those black, steel-spring folders whose ferocious clamp provides a perfect symbol of its owner. I had been forewarned of its coming. Kathy phoned me yesterday about this time.

"Hello, David," she greeted him. "How are you getting along without me?"

"These walls weep for you," I said. "But I'm getting along. And you?"

"Still at my aunt's. I think I may look for a job after New Year's. Got any idea what I can do?"

"One or two."

"Not that, mister. Seriously."

"Are you serious, Kathy? How about school?"

253

"Oh, shit! I have my B.A. What would I do with an M.A.? I'm bored with school."

"Have you been in touch with your parents?" I asked her. "Is your mother coming to New York?"

"Yes, I've been in touch with my parents, and no, my mother isn't coming to New York. I think my father's afraid to let her go. He's afraid she'd never come back, and he's probably right. Come on, Dave, are you going to help me?"

"But what can you do, Kathy?"

"I can type a little. No steno. I can read the English language with recondite understanding. I can dance."

"Look, Kathy, if you really want a job, you'll have no trouble getting one. I can ask Rich, if you'd like. He has many contacts in the advertising field. In fact, I understand that Mr. Bud Demery—"

"Don't be smartass."

"All right."

"You're being smartass anyway," she said, sounding aggrieved.

"What do you mean?"

"You know very well what I mean. You're sitting there waiting for me to ask. Why do you have to make me ask?"

"Ask what, for heaven's sake?"

"About Brian. He called you, didn't he?"

"He did not."

"Didn't?"

"Not today. Not yesterday."

"Well, he was supposed to," she said. "I gave him the phone number, and he said he was going to phone you."

"He hasn't so far. Listen, Kathy, I'll be picking up Lenny at the bus terminal at five today, and I'll probably be spending some time with him. I may not be home until nine or ten in the evening, so if you're going to be in touch with Brian you'd better tell him that."

"Okay, I'll tell him. Listen, Dave—"

"Yes?"

"Would it be all right if I phoned you later, say about eleven?"

254

"Sure. Why?"

"I want to know what happened."

"All right, Kathy."

"Talk to you," she said.

It was about nine thirty when Brian phoned. He introduced himself, said I might have heard his name. I said indeed I had, knew the purpose of his call. He said he'd sure like to get a professional opinion on what he'd written. I told him my professional standing had lapsed a long time ago but that I'd be glad to read his novel, for whatever value my opinion might have.

"I sure appreciate this, sir," he said. "I know it's a drag to have to read some shitty first novel, but there's this consolation: it isn't very long, about two hundred pages. That isn't very long, is it? I mean as novels go?"

"No, that isn't very long."

"I read your novel," he said.

"So I heard."

"I liked it. It's not exactly my bag, but I respected what you were trying to do. I think I ought to warn you I'm more experimental in my writing."

"Oh?"

"Yes. My kind of writing may not be your bag, but I think one person can respect what somebody else is trying to do."

"I agree."

"Look, I'll bring it over right now."

"What! Tonight? In this snow?"

"No problem. Just give me the address, and I'll have it over in thirty minutes."

I was about to argue the hour, the condition, the folly, but I realized that the folly was mine to counter my reason against his burning impatience. I gave him the address, and within thirty minutes the buzzer sounded and the doorman announced I had a visitor.

He wore a belted coat of rainwear material with a fur collar.

255

Something prompted me to look down at his shoes (perhaps the many times I have done so when Lenny came in out of the rain or snow), and I was confirmed in my suspicion. He wore a pair of suede shoes soaked to the ankle.

"Well, come in," I said. "I'm pleased to meet you."

"Thanks," he said. "I won't take up your time now. I'll just leave this with you."

He handed me a bulky manila envelope. He was not tall, perhaps a shade over average. He was hatless, and he had, as Kathy had described, prematurely graying hair, kinky, grown thick, making me think of sheep's wool. He had blue-gray eyes, perfect teeth, perfect smile, perfect everything. He was a stunning young man. Poor Kathy, to be competing for this cup bearer against such mad gods.

"Well, if you're sure you haven't got five minutes for a cup of coffee," I said. "Those shoes don't offer you much protection."

He looked down at his shoes, then up at me, then shook his head slowly and mysteriously, as if I'd informed him in some cabalistic way of the very sympathetic reading I would give his novel.

"My shoes," he said, smiling, still shaking his head. He looked up, waved, and began to move off down the hall.

"Just a minute," I called. "When will you be in touch with me?"

"How long will it take you to read it?" he asked over his shoulder.

"I should be through by tomorrow," I said. "Late afternoon, early evening."

"Six?" he said.

"Yes. I'll be done then."

Nodding, he continued to the elevator.

Kathy phoned promptly at eleven.

"He was here," I told her. "He's a very handsome young man."

"Yes," she affirmed dully. "Did he leave the thing with you?"

"He did."

"Do you think you'll get a chance to read it soon?"

256

"He'll be returning here at six o'clock tomorrow evening to pick it up."

"Oh, Christ!" she whispered.

"What's the matter?"

She sighed, "I'm scared. I don't know why, I'm just scared. I hope to God you find something to like in it."

"Kathy," I said to her, "this novel means nothing to me. I mean it *may* mean something to me, but I have no special stake in it. And I have no special scruple about this sort of thing. I'm not a teacher or an editor or a keeper of the flame. You tell me what you think it would be best for me to say to Brian, and I'll manage to say it convincingly."

"No matter what you think of the novel?"

"No matter what I think of the novel. You just tell me what would help him. Or you."

"I don't *know!*" she moaned. "I swear I don't know! Tell him the truth. Tell him what you really think."

"And suppose what I think is hurtful?"

"It won't make a difference," she replied.

"To him?"

"To either of us," she said.

I began reading that evening.

37.

I read in bed and fell asleep before finishing the first chapter. I wasn't bored—on the contrary—I was fascinated—but I was sleepy, and I knew I would have an uninterrupted day before me.

I go on reading as I have my breakfast of frozen orange juice, Saltines and peanut butter, and instant coffee. I try to place the strange colors coming off the pages of Brian's novel, but I can't, quite. The boy who wrote this is a contemporary of my son. This is the world that I don't understand. This is the world that claims to have a new view on life, love, and history. The title of the novel is *Burning Glass,* and it is about two Midwest college boys who hitchhike east to spend a hot summer in New York. They find a pad in the East Village, and the sustaining elements of the story are rock music, pot, head shops, sex, conflict between blacks and whites, male and female, and the boys themselves. There's a girl with whom both boys fall in love. (I looked for a resemblance to Kathy but could find none.) This conflict becomes the testing ground between good and evil. To give up the girl to the other is good, to want her exclusively is evil. Perhaps I'm interpreting it all wrong, but it strikes me as a very familiar kind of romantic sentimentality.

I think it's a bad book. I don't think so, I know so. The boys and girls in the book are not young people but young attitudes. The race attitude. The drug attitude. The sex attitude. The anti-establishment attitude. Frank and Josh (the two boys) do not talk to each other as human beings—as, for instance, Brian and I talked to each other last evening; as Kathy and I have talked to each other; as, for another instance, I have heard Lenny talk with his friends. Everything is put in a cryptic, aborted way. But I can't be sure that what appears to be a lack of talent is not a means of getting at something either above or below my threshold of response. Perhaps my life experience has rendered me incapable of understanding what Brian is attempting to say. I don't believe it, but I must hold it aside as a possibility.

In spite of my rejection of Brian's style and story, I continue to read as though I had come into possession of the pages of a lyrical genius. Somewhere in these pages may be a clue to my son's life, which, I must confess, my own demonstrations of love and concern have failed to reveal. Perhaps if I can become one in spirit with the fears and needs of these boys (*I* have been fearful; *I* have been needful) then all of this will not seem so clumsy and unbelievable.

So I read on to the inevitable violence. I eat more Saltines and peanut butter, knowing that this still, portentous day will be saved forever from anonymity by the mingled flavors of Brian's prose style and Skippy peanut butter. One of the boys—Josh—holes up in a cellar after killing a Negro. Frank tries to persuade him to give up to the police. Josh refuses. More shooting. Josh is killed. Frank writes a letter home, saying that he is going to stay in New York and work for a better world.

It's almost four o'clock in the afternoon when I finish Brian's novel. The day, which began with the vestiges of yesterday's near-blizzard, has turned clear and cold. I feel the cold on the window with the palm of my hand, and it transmits itself to my stomach which shivers in sympathetic nervousness. Looking out, I see exhalations of city smoke feather in the freezing air. The slush in the street below had been fashioned by the cold and traffic into sculptured filth. A lowering sun coats the snow along the banks of the West Side Drive with a pink lacquer. I feel hungry and nauseous. I imagine myself sitting here the rest of this day—hungry, unshaven, nauseous—perhaps adding to the general seediness by a couple of hours of solitary boozing—but instead, within ten minutes of putting down Brian's manuscript, I am in the bathroom showering and shaving. I will dress and go down into the darkly refrigerated afternoon and buy basic provisions like bread, meat, eggs, milk, fresh oranges, and also some of those expensive little delicacies in glass jars to serve to Brian as we talk, because my whole life has been a conditioning in that kind of bourgeois hospitality.

As I shave, I experience a revelation. Brian's is a new voice! He had something original and powerful to say, and the language he used was the language he needed. I contain this happy knowledge for ten seconds, and then it evaporates. Brian's novel is nothing of the sort. It's a mess of sophomoric junk. No, it's not. It's just badly written, but there's a story there, and perhaps even a significant story. I begin to appreciate Kathy's pendular distress.

But I will have to say something, and I had better prepare that something rather than depend on the inspiration of the moment. I will say what I think Brian wishes to hear. I will say that he has written a novel of promise; that the trademark of talent is on every page— No, I won't go that far. I will say that there is unmistakable talent, but that this should be looked on as a first effort. Good God, who wants to hear that! No, I will say that—I don't know what I will say. I *shall* have to depend on the inspiration of the moment, and whatever I find in Brian's eyes. It will be praise. I know that the only honesty for a writer is the honesty of praise. I may include a comment or two about the ideas—perhaps a little strengthening there— No, better to suggest the blue pencil; the blue pencil compromises no one.

By four thirty I am shaved and dressed. By five thirty, I have returned to the apartment with two large paper bags full of groceries. By six ten the buzzer makes that tearing sound. The damn thing hasn't sounded that often since I've been here, but every time it has it has shredded my nerves. I go to the brass speaker on the wall.

"Yes?"

"A Miss Willens and a Mr. Miller to see you."

"Yes, indeed. Send them up."

So! Brian *and* Kathy!

The doorbell.

"Hello, hello. Come in."

Brian is smiling. Kathy, hooded and booted, has on her millennial face.

"How are you, sir?" says Brian.

"Well, thank you. And you?"

"Just fine."

"And you, Kathy?"

"Frozen."

They enter the apartment. "May I—?" I say, and Kathy unbelts her mottled coat and appears to walk out of it, leaving me to capture the soft pelt and hang it away. Brian, too, removes his coat, and tosses it on a chair.

"Yes, it is cold," I say. "I did some shopping earlier and stupidly forgot my gloves. My hands were frozen by the time I got back to the apartment."

Kathy surveys the room casually and then goes to the bathroom.

"Well," I say to Brian, "I do have several antidotes for this kind of weather. How about a drink?"

"Yes, sir," Brian says, sitting on the chrome-and-foam sofa. He doesn't make himself quite at home but sits forward, rather, knees spread, elbows on thighs.

"Scotch, bourbon, or rye?"

"Bourbon's fine. With some ice and a little water."

I go to the kitchen. There's mutual humiliation involved in moments like this. I mean moments during which one human being holds secret that information capable of giving great pain or great joy to another. The job, the love, the accolade to be given or denied. It's the most miserable kind of playacting.

I hear Kathy come out of the bathroom, and I ask if she would like a drink.

"Scotch, please," she says. "Some soda, if you have it."

261

I prepare the drinks and bring them in. Kathy has seated herself in the armchair. She has combed her hair, and in taking the glass I hand her she gives me the briefest of glances from that narrow stage. No clues. I'm strictly on my own. "Bourbon," I say to Brian, handing him a glass. Then I sit down at the other end of the sofa, the space of one seat between Brian and me. We are, the three of us, a tense triangle.

"I'm a little surprised," I say to Kathy. "I wasn't expecting you."

"We're supposed to go to a New Year's party later," she explains, "so we figured I might as well come along. I hope you don't mind."

"I couldn't think of anything nicer."

She is wearing her usual short skirt, and her Maillol thighs invite the male eye as sumptuous food invites gluttony. Is it possible that this impressive girl and I have copulated as frequently and as dedicatedly as I recall? And that she is now sitting here with her "boyfriend"? And that all three of us are acquainted with this recent history? Yes, all this is known, but it is known as a single landmark is known to travelers moving off in different directions—visible, differently seen, and increasingly distant.

"Have you been working exclusively on this novel?" I ask Brian.

"Pretty much."

"I ask," I say, "because I've always wondered how others manage financially in this city when they're trying to get something done—a book, a play. Any city, for that matter, though I know it's tougher here."

"I have some money," Brian informs me, smiling pleasantly and reflectively. He has such blue eyes. I feel he has come prepared to put up with a certain amount of patronizing. "I have an inheritance from my father," he says, "but my mother controls it until certain conditions are met. She spoon-feeds me from time to time, if I'm being a good boy. I'm from Michigan. A small town. We have a house there. I'm not doing the starving-artist routine."

I wonder if Kathy has drawn on her experience with me and

262

advised Brian to get the biographical crap out of the way first: *"He's that kind of guy—you know, fatherly, nosy. . . ."*

"Did you finish Brian's novel?" Kathy asks, looking toward the window.

"I did," I say, glancing at Brian.

"What I'd like," Brian quickly interposes, "is to get a book on the street as quickly as possible."

"On the street?"

"Published."

"Oh—I never heard that expression."

"Yes," he says. "I thought maybe you could help me."

"I? How?"

"I thought maybe you could help me get this into the hands of the right person."

"I'm afraid you're mistaken about that," I tell him. "I know no one in the publishing business these days."

Brian closes his eyes briefly and shakes his head. Obviously he has come prepared for minor obstacles. He smiles. "A publishing house knows the books it's published. And the names of the authors. I thought if you would write a letter sort of recommending my book—that would be a great help." Having defined the purpose of his visit, he leans back and clasps a knee in the sling he makes of his interlaced fingers. His handsome face radiates good health. Kathy, too, looks her usual glowing self. They do make an attractive, vigorous pair. The smile Brian continues to form with his lips exposes the white tips of his teeth, and their glint bites sharply into the soft flesh of my prepared good will. He wears a double-breasted jacket of a striped material, a solid blue shirt, an enormous tie. I wonder why I haven't noticed before the strength and assurance of this young man.

"Brian," I say, "I found some very interesting things in your novel, but I really couldn't say whether it's ready for publication or not. In any event, you can do just as well by sending it to any publisher on your own. My recommendation is worthless."

"Did you like the writing?" Brian asks.

"Why—yes—yes, I did. I—"

"The story?"

"Now, the story was really interesting. I found—"

"Let me tell you something, Mr. Lang—"

"For crying out loud!" Kathy interrupts him. "Why don't you give Dave a chance to talk?"

"Why," Brian returns, without looking at her, "don't you mind your own fucking business?"

"Now wait a minute—" I begin.

Brian keeps his eyes on me, his diligent blue eyes, which blink from time to time, as if to keep meticulously adjusted his fraudulent show of deference.

"Sorry, Mr. Lang," he says. "Don't take it seriously. That's the way we talk. What I was going to say was that I knew beforehand that you wouldn't dig my story. This is a different world I'm talking about. I wouldn't expect you to understand it—"

"That's a lot of crap!" Kathy puts in.

"Now wait a minute—" I say again.

Brian looks across at Kathy with his bright smile. He shakes his head. I notice that he shakes his head a lot—a familiar gesture; I wonder where I've seen it before.

"What the hell would you know about it?" he says to Kathy, in a voice that places itself somehow in the same area as the smile, the head shake. Familiar and unreal. "I mean what the hell would you *know* about it? You're practically illiterate."

"That's what you'd like to think!"

Brian holds up both hands, shakes his head again, grins. "Christ, baby, I don't have to think anything. You said so yourself. I mean you *said* it!"

"Look—" I say.

"I said a lot of things to save your goddam sick vanity, if you want to know the truth!" Kathy flings at him, angrier than I ever saw her in our brief stay together. She gets up. "Do you mind if I get another drink, Dave?"

"Help yourself."

Brian gets up too. He looks down at me. His naturally ruddy face has taken on a deeper hue. Another head shake, more slowly

264

this time. He stands limber and pretends amusement—and at last I recognize this pantomime. This is the latest Hollywood hero, the head-shaking, smiling, mumbling lout who handles these situations in fearless, violent style.

"You mean you're a liar, is that what you mean?" he asks Kathy.

"Yes, I'm a liar." Kathy returns from the tiny kitchen. "I've been lying a long time. I know why you won't give Dave a chance to talk. You're afraid of what he might say."

"Baby, I don't give a shit what he might say, or what you might say."

But he does give a shit. Young Brian Miller is finding himself suddenly exposed and vulnerable. And I also believe that Kathy has discovered something in our brief stay together that has thrown a new light on her Brian. Or on herself. She comes in from the kitchen holding a glass with both hands.

"Then why did you want him to read your stupid book?" she asks.

"Cut it out!" I say, raising my voice. "The two of you!"

But they're not cutting anything out. This is an old fight, one well soaked into their systems, and like alcoholics they need only a touch more to be blind drunk. Who says you have to be married to enjoy this bitter fruit?

"Because," Brian answers Kathy, leaning forward, teeth gleaming, "you told me he knew all the big-shot publishers in New York, and that he was such a sweet old fart even if he was a lousy lay, and he was just *dying* to do you favors. Why the hell else were you putting out for him?"

"*You goddam liar!*" Kathy screams, drawing back one arm and letting fly, girl-fashion, with her glass.

I see the amber liquid erupt festively, see the glass shatter against the wall, just below Ralph Friedman's Feininger print, thinking to myself: *Oh, my God, a riot in Ralph's place!* Then I see Brian shaking his Hollywood head once again as he starts toward Kathy.

"Now just a minute—" I say, putting myself in the way.

Brian looks at me as if for the first time, and I see what I should have guessed before: that brightness in the eyes which is the condensation of anger; the sour frustration behind all the head shaking and smiles; the hate against me, if not for what I am, then for what he imagines me to be. I began what I hoped would be a placating gesture, a placating word, when that unexpected object was suddenly loosed, striking the left side of my face with such outrageous force that I had no choice but to fall toward the indicated darkness.

38.

I came to in a timeless trough. I was merely warm and relaxed. I distinctly recall trying to remember out of what circumstance of sleep I was awakening. I tried to incorporate the annoying patch of cold I felt against my face into the dream, but the dream—if there was a dream—had receded too far. The need for explanation became urgent, and I opened my eyes to see Kathy's large, frightened eyes, and conspicuous freckles, and the ceiling beyond. I was on the floor. Kathy was on her knees beside me, a wet washcloth in her hand. I remembered everything.

I get up and go directly to the bathroom. I'm feeling remarkably little pain from a blow that managed to knock me out. I look at myself in the mirror and see a red contusion on my face, a little forward from my ear. Several things occur to me at once. I think of reporting Brian to the police, but immediately I remember Arthur Gerson, and in a quick adjustment of conscience I count all three of us—Brian, Arthur, myself—quits. I touch my face. It hurts, but not much. It feels as if an excess of fluid has been injected beneath the skin. So, I think, this is what it is to be knocked out. Not too bad. There will undoubtedly be a swelling there, and perhaps some discoloration.

I return to the living room. Kathy is sitting on the sofa, looking very pale.

"I'm sorry," she says. "Does it hurt?"

"Yes," I say, feeling testy toward her. "How long was I unconscious?"

"Not even a minute. I'm sorry, Dave. Brian is sick."

"Then why did you encourage this meeting?"

"I didn't know he would do that. I swear I had no idea he would flip. And he was *lying!* I hope you didn't believe those lies. I never said any of those things."

"Where did he go?" I ask.

"I don't know. He just left. He grabbed his damn manuscript and left."

"Has he ever hit you?"

"Yes."

"*Yes!*" I bellow. "Good God, Kathy! He *hit* you! Why in God's name did you have anything to do with him after that? I don't understand you."

"He's sick," she says.

"Yes—well—you've said that. I'm not too confident of that kind of sickness. Too many crimes are tolerated in the name of sickness. What's the matter with him?"

"He's full of hate," she answers, telling me what I already know. "He pretends it's love, but it's hate. He wants to be a writer. He once told me that love wasn't worth a damn to him if it didn't improve his style."

"And yet you stayed with him," I say. "Kathy, I'm sorry, too."

"Dave, you better keep something cold on that," she says. "It's swelling up. I'll get some ice cubes from the refrigerator. I'll put them in a small towel, and you can keep applying it to your face."

She makes the ice pack. I take it and apply it gingerly to my face. Now I'm beginning to feel the effects of Brian's fist from the base of my neck to the top of my head. By clenching my teeth, I can measure the full thickness of the swelling. Kathy is wearing a simple blue dress, midthigh. It has some sort of white trim around the collar. She sits down again on the sofa.

"Will you let me stay here?" she asks.

She doesn't mean right now, I know. She means in the days

268

ahead, and understanding this, my heart is wrung with pity. She looks so nice, young, dressed up for a party, and there is such a clot of disorder in her life. I wish I could do something to dissolve that. But she cannot stay with me. That is out of the question. There's physical and moral horror in the idea. Whatever her life-style has made of sex, mine cannot make of it the easy solvent of every mood and misalliance. We've gone beyond the newness of the first few weeks, and what we do now will have in it the con-sciousness of change and regret. We've lived with each other, seen each other through crisis, and to keep sex meaningless after that would be a depravity. At least for me it would, and therefore I cannot allow her to stay with me.

"No, Kathy," I say. "I know I said you could, but it would be the worst kind of folly."

"For a little while," she pleads. "A few weeks."

"No, Kathy."

"I like you very much, Dave. It wouldn't be just a matter of convenience."

"I like you, too, Kathy. I'd be glad to give you money for a hotel room, if that's what you need. But I couldn't have you come back here. I feel differently toward you now. What I feel should lead to love, and it can't."

"Why not?"

"Because I'm too crowded with other lives. You're too young. I'm too old."

"We were good in bed," she says.

"We wouldn't be good any longer," I say. "I just don't feel the same about things. You think in terms of years to correct and for-get and begin again. I can't do that. . . . Kathy, I must know, what are you going to do?"

"When?"

"Tonight. Tomorrow. Next week."

"Tonight I'm going to the party I told you about. Don't worry, Brian isn't going to be there. He wouldn't want to be anywhere near me."

"And after that? Are you going to remain in the city?"

"I guess not."

"Will you go home?"

"Uh-uh! No! I think I'll probably go to San Francisco."

"What will you do in San Francisco?"

"Stay with a friend. She just got a divorce. She's been asking me to come out."

"But what will you *do?*"

"Christ, I don't know, Dave. Get a job, I suppose. Maybe I'll go to school out there. Get my M.A. Teach. How do I know? You want everything nailed down, don't you?"

"No, I don't, Kathy. Please forgive my old habits. When will you leave for San Francisco?"

"Pretty soon, I guess. Maybe in a couple of days. The truth is, Dave, I spoke to my parents on the phone, and my father said he wouldn't give me a dime. I'm going to need some money."

"And you shall have some money. How much? Five hundred?"

"You're crazy! I don't need that much."

"Yes, you do. Fare. Clothing. Something to tide you over once you get there. Listen, tomorrow is no good, tomorrow everything is closed, but the next day you must meet me here, and then we'll go to my bank. I want to buy you traveler's checks. I want to make sure you've got some safe form of currency. And then we'll have a nice lunch. We'll go to a French restaurant. I know you like French food. Meet me here day after tomorrow at ten o'clock. Will you do that, Kathy?"

"All right, Dave."

270

39.

At eleven that evening, Lenny phones me. We have rarely cele-
brated New Year's Eve together. When he was young, he would
be asleep at the raucous hour. When he was older, Dodie and I
would be having our adult parties while he was at his much
livelier, I'm sure, adolescent ones. But always Dodie and I had
our exchange with Lenny before midnight. We would phone him
wherever he was, or he would phone us, and at least once in that
strained evening we would exchange a "Happy New Year" that
was without embarrassment or qualification.

"Happy New Year, Dad," he says.

"And a Happy New Year to you, Lenny. Where are you calling
from?"

"Some apartment in the city. We're having a party. Some kids
from school."

"Good. Have fun."

"And you?" he asks.

"Well, you know how I feel about New Year's. I'm quietly
celebrating my absence from the festivities."

"Listen, Dad, we thought we might come over tomorrow and
say hello, if that would be okay."

"We?"

"My girlfriend flew in today. Marie. Marie Covillo. I picked
her up at La Guardia. I thought you might like to meet her. We

did some sight-seeing today. She hasn't been in New York since she was a kid."

"I see—well—Marie—yes—that's very nice—would love to meet her—"

"How about early afternoon?" Lenny suggests. "Like one thirty or two."

"Fine. Lenny—"

"Yes?"

"Have you been home? With Marie, I mean?"

"No. We're going home after the party. Mom's expecting us. I told her we'd be coming home late."

"Then Marie will spend the night at the house?"

"Yes."

"I see. Fine. Please wish Marie a Happy New Year for me in advance of my meeting her, will you?"

"Sure thing—and we'll see you tomorrow."

"Yes, indeed. I look forward to that."

My face hurts. I've been applying cold compresses all evening since Kathy's departure. Undoubtedly I will have a face. An eye as well.

I go to the window and look out, seeing other windows aglow with Christmas decorations. I recall that in the instant of Brian's fist I thought that something had been flung at me from a corner of the room. I couldn't believe that Brain—or anybody—would *hit* me. There have been very few fistfights in my life. The ones I recall present themselves to my mind in the image of two small trees angrily embracing. Once, a million years ago, a boy flung a piece of coal at me, hitting me on the side of the head. I went down to my knees, a ring of darkness closing in. But I remained conscious, the unbelievable pain notching up my rage until I cried weak obscenities into the concrete street. My mature life has known no violence. I don't count the war. The war was not personal violence. Perhaps if a German soldier had run at me, it would have been, but none did. Now, within a few weeks, I have struck and have been struck. The left side of my face is taking

272

full account of the blow it received. The sensation is throbbingly personal. But somehow I feel that the antagonism that inflicted that blow had been lying in wait for me for years.

I wonder what Dodie is thinking—particularly about the girl she has not as yet seen. This is the first New Year's Dodie and I have spent apart, but I know we are thinking of each other through Lenny and his girlfriend, Marie. . . . Marie Covillo—"my girl-friend"—I play with the vision of Lenny walking shoeless in an unknown room, saying mustached things to a faceless girl out of his other life. . . . On a summer's day, in a shimmer of time, Lenny poured milk from a container, added a viscous glob of chocolate syrup, stirred, the sun pouring through the kitchen window. . . . Oh, my son! I couldn't imagine the transitions that would bring him to manhood and independence.

Marie. Marie Covillo.

She is dressed in brown. She wears a fleece-lined leather coat and brown leather—or plastic—boots. She has long, pale-blonde hair. I make out brown eyes behind metal-framed, octagonal eyeglasses. When Lenny introduced her to me, she put out a slim hand and caught her lower lip between her teeth. There's a quick outward play of personality, but I can't make out exactly what it is. Geniality? Reserve? It may merely be the expression that came to her on saying hello to the father of her boyfriend. It may be the first time in her life she's done that.

My impression is that Marie Covillo feels no urgent need to seek Lenny's father's approval. I'm quite sure that Lenny has said nothing to her to indicate that his parent's good will was of no account, but in the presence of this girl and my son I am made to feel the externality of my existence. It is not that Lenny doesn't care what I think, but that finally it wouldn't matter.

"Lenny tells me this is not the first time you've been to New York," I say.

"I was born in Pompton Lakes," she says. "We moved to Cleveland when I was two years old. But I visited when I was younger. We have relatives in Sheepshead Bay. All I could remember of New York was the ocean."

"What's that on your face?" Lenny asks me.

"Oh, that. Ridiculous. I was looking in one direction and talking in another."

"Talking?"

"Did I say talking? I meant walking. Banged into that doorjamb in the kitchen."

"You must have been walking fast," Lenny says. "It was quite a crack."

"It's a pity you don't have nicer weather," I say to Marie. "How long are you planning to stay in the city?"

"Until it's time to go back to school," she says. "We'll be going back together."

"I see. That's fine."

Lenny is sitting where Brian sat yesterday. He is dressed in a blue suit, yellow shirt, blue tie, luxuriant mustache. Marie's skirt intersects her thighs more or less at Kathy's level, but Marie doesn't have the beginnings of Kathy's amplitude. Nevertheless, she is fully shaped to man's need. I ask questions about school, and I learn that Marie is majoring in English, too, but that she's mainly interested in theater, in acting. Lenny says that she's very good, could easily turn professional if she wished. "And do you wish?" I ask. Marie says that she isn't sure. She knows that she likes to act, but she hasn't given much thought to how far she will take it—or it will take her. She is sure that she isn't interested in *big* theater. What she means is that she is more interested in *what* she acts in than in merely acting.

I wouldn't call Marie pretty. No doubt Lenny thinks she is. She has a narrow face and a small mouth whose corners apostrophize when she smiles. Her eyes, as I make them out behind the oversized glasses, are perfectly circular. Her skin is pale, delicate, a tincture of amber. Perhaps I don't think she is pretty because in reality she is beautiful. I have always been at odds with female estimates of beauty. Suddenly I remember where I have seen this face before: I have at home—former home—the house

274

on the Island—a book on the Italian Renaissance. At the back of the book are many photographs of Renaissance portraits. One of them is of a young Florentine lady who must surely be the physical ancestress of Marie Covillo. For some reason, my thoughts switch to Rich, *his* dark Italianism, and I am avid with curiosity.

"Do you have brothers or sisters?" I ask.

"Oh, yes. Plenty. Three brothers and a sister. We're Italian."

"And are you the youngest?"

"No, I have a younger sister. I have a brother who's three years older than me, and he teaches American Lit at a small college in California. He and I are the mavericks in the family. My other brothers are big and square. They shoot animals and march in parades."

"I see. I don't know if Lenny told you, but my business partner —former business partner, I should say—is Italian."

"I know," she says. "Joe Richards."

"Riccio, actually. A gifted man. We've been friends a long time."

"My father," Marie says, as though I'd asked, and I guess I had, "owns a fleet of garage trucks. He's a private contractor. Industrial waste. The money's in resale, not in removal."

Lenny, I notice out of the corner of my undamaged eye, is now sitting as Brian sat, hunched forward, elbows on thighs, his gaze downward on the carpet. If there had been any conscious irony in Marie's description of her father's business, I think I would have detected it. I don't think there was any conscious irony—perhaps the unconscious kind that slips into remarks intended to oblige. Of course I've been trying to find out about Marie and her family. Isn't that only natural? Lenny has "brought home a girl" for the first time. I have long anticipated this scene, but it was never part of my anticipation to be sitting in a New York apartment while Lenny's mother occupied a house in Long Island. I see myself proposing an acceptable order for my son's life out of the shambles of my own. I see what *they* see, and I am seized with the need to prevent further foolishness.

"Lenny," I say, "what did you want to talk about? I have the feeling you came here to talk about something. You and Marie?

275

Are you planning to get married? Or are you already married?"

"No, we're not married," Lenny says. "We probably will get married about a year from now, if we still feel the same. I did want to talk to you about something, though—"

"Yes," I say—feeling that I can't love Lenny in any other way than the way I have always loved him, but knowing that that way is ruinous. I know that I must give up the pursuit of his life. It has gone so far beyond me, or in a direction that I can't follow, and I must give up the pursuit of it or I shall lose everything.

He says, "Would you be very upset if I transferred to another school, a bigger one, a university? Actually I'm interested in urban studies, and I'd like to get to a school where they have good departments in that field."

I'm not quite sure what he means by that, but I must begin acting on what I now understand about Lenny's life and mine, so I say, "No, I wouldn't mind. I think that's fine." I'm not sure whether it is or not, but the important thing for me now is not to pursue his life any longer. Therein lies the terrible, futile foolishness. I turn to Marie: "And you?" I ask. "Are you going to stay where you are?"

"No," she says. "I'm going to transfer, too. We're both making applications to the same schools. I want to get with a good drama department."

"I see. That's fine. The important thing is to know what one wants."

This is not at all as I envisioned Lenny's life, but my life is not as I envisioned it either. I never knew exactly what it was I wanted for Lenny, but whatever it was I wanted it to be distinct. I saw him achieving distinction for qualities which were uniquely his own. A lawyer, a teacher, a research scholar, perhaps a writer. Something individual. Separate. In other words, I saw his success in my terms. It seems I have barely set myself to wait for these developments, and here they are—Lenny spoken for, not separate, not individual, but part of the world as he sees the world, as he wants the world. It doesn't look at all like the vision I had for him, but there must be an end to foolishness and pursuit. I must

276

withdraw my life from his if I am to salvage anything of all that love.

So we talk for another half-hour of plans and possibilities. Lenny tries to find some clue that would account for my damaged face. Obviously he doesn't believe my explanation, but that's too bad. I already see it will be just as well if I leave certain areas of my life unexplained. I see that it is possible that he will seek to know something about me when I cease wanting so desperately to know about him.

When they are preparing to leave, Marie goes to the bathroom.

"Are you all right?" Lenny asks me.

"Yes," I say. "How did you find Mother?"

"I don't know," he replies. "All right, I guess. She looks a little thinner. Dad—"

"Yes?"

He looks at the window. He wants very much to say something, but he has gotten out of the habit of saying personal things to me. I don't think this is my fault, but I'm grieved that he should find a moment like this so difficult. Dear God, why should this be so when I have been so open with him! He is looking for encouragement from me to say what he wants to say, but I won't give it to him. I've accepted his maturity. He must see that I have.

"You and Mom are going to see each other, aren't you?" he says.

"The day after tomorrow," I say.

Still looking at the window, he blurts out, "I wish you'd be nice to her! I'm not trying to tell you what to do, one way or the other, as far as you're both concerned, but I do wish you'd be nice to her, because—well—because I think she's taken a hell of a beating."

"Why, Lenny, of course I'll be nice to her," I say.

40.

Kathy and I go directly to my bank, where I purchase five hundred dollars' worth of traveler's checks for her. She has to sign them at the desk of one of the bank officers, a man whom I have seen and who has seen me for years. I feel an urge to explain to this stranger-acquaintance that my niece is setting off on a cruise, the promised gift of her graduation. Thank God, I do no such thing. He sits, Kathy sits, and I stand. While Kathy is signing, the man looks up at me, at my eye, and I pleasantly stare him back to his own business. A small but significant victory for me. Walking out of the bank with Kathy, I take with me another proof that I am subject to the ordering of experience. Not giving a damn what the man thought, I had conquered an old Lang reflex to explain irregularities.

After the bank, Kathy and I go to the French restaurant I had selected. I had been there before. The style is flamboyant. Red and gold. High ceiling. Chandeliers. We order drinks—she, a Daiquiri; I, a scotch and soda. Everything is sumptuous—the linens, the silverware . . . .

"How was the party?" I ask.

"Okay," she replies, shrugging.

"Brian, I take it, didn't show up?"

"No."

"Heard from him?"

278

"No."

"Do you think it's finished?"

"It's finished."

"I'm sorry."

"No, you're not," she says.

"True," I say. "I'm not. Brian is a very dangerous young man to know. Not because he hit me. He's an ordinary person with a lust for accomplishments. Combine that with his violence, and you've got a walking time-bomb."

Kathy looks away. I'm not telling her anything she doesn't know. I notice that she's wearing a dress I haven't seen before—the kind of dress, I choose to think, that a young lady might wear to lunch with an older man who is neither her lover nor her father. That's a highly arbitrary description, I know, but I'm seeing things with unusual clarity today. That may be due to my eye, my left eye, which has taken on a pigeon's-breast iridescence. Looking at myself in the mirror this morning, I was reminded of that battered wreck who approached me some weeks ago as I was leaving the old office building after my visit to Rich. I'm not claiming affinity, but I know now that he and I are living in the same world. It's a matter of circumstance, that's all. Anyway—Kathy's dress—which I find very becoming, very suitable.

"Is that a new dress?" I ask her.

"I bought it just this morning," she tells me. "Just before I came over to the apartment. I had seen it in the shop window for days, and I knew I wanted it. The store opened at nine thirty. I had to sweat them out. It was reduced in price, but I still can't afford it. I don't care. I'm entitled to one nice thing from my adventurous sojourn in New York City."

"You certainly are," I agree.

I believe she bought it to appear in something new and nice for our last lunch. I don't know if my response to such gestures is disproportionate or not, but I doubt it will ever change. Dodie, too, never failed to touch off soft explosions of poignance when she would do, wear, or say anything just for me. Perhaps it was the

279

gradual withdrawal of these presents that prompted me to start poking around in the dump heaps of my brain.

The waiter brings our drinks.

"Here's to you, Kathy."

"And to you," she says.

"Will you write to me?" I ask.

"If you want me to."

"Wouldn't you want to on your own?"

I can't imagine her saying no, and actually she doesn't say it; instead she tips her head slightly and lifts her broad shoulders.

"I'm not good at letters," she says. "If writing letters was my bag, you'd be the first one I'd write to, but, I don't know, either you're with a person or you're not. I've written to friends, and after a while it gets so damn *silly*. You're inventing things to say. You're asking questions when you're not really curious. Do you know what I mean?"

"Perfectly. Kathy, please drop me a card when you get settled. As for the future, if you're ever moved by something—need, nostalgia, or money—to drop me a line, do so. Forgive me for asking one last time: What about your parents?"

She shakes her head. "I've made the break," she says. "It's best. If I were to go back, even for a visit, the old agony would start all over again."

"But surely you don't mean you'll never see them again?"

"Oh, I'll see them again, but only after certain things have happened. I'm not sure what. I'll know it when it's happened. Christ, Dave, that *eye!* . . . I don't know—maybe marriage—but whatever it is, it'll be something to keep my father from getting at me again."

I suppress a desire to ask yet another question. It's something other than my conscience-ridden wish to bring Kathy together with her parents. I'm curious to know what items in the voluminous catalogue of parent-child difficulties has brought about this break and this courage in Kathy to be on her own. But even as I toy with the notion of asking, I realize that it would be just as foolish for Kathy to attempt to explain as it would be for me to ask. The occasions of conflict are simple enough, and simply enough described, but how to describe the silent sessions between one conflict and the next, the sour silent sessions in which rejection is born?

Another waiter is at our table handing us the outsize menu cards. Kathy orders fish. I order veal. And vegetables? Yes, vegetables. I am reminded of something—Dodie—who would never return a menu she was holding directly to the waiter, but would let it slide from her fingers to the table and then would survey the room in which she sat. A harmless enough mannerism (the waiters never seemed to mind) but one which always left me wondering what girlish dream of style was repeated in that foible. Again I experience the inability to see Dodie instantaneously and whole. Parts again—mouth, nose, eyes. And have there been changes? Lenny says she is thinner. Has she adopted a new hair style? I am to see her tomorrow, and the prospect of confronting the myth, the reality, the immensity that has grown in my mind awes me.

"What are *you* going to do?" Kathy asks.

"Do?"

"About your wife? That setup?"

"I was just thinking about my wife," I say.

"I thought you were."

"What made you think so?"

"You were quiet. I figured this must be a place you've been to before. You and your wife."

"The possibilities are not that numerous, are they?"

"What possibilities?" Kathy asks.

"What a person might be thinking."

"That depends," she says.

"That depends," I agree.

"Dave—"

"Yes?"

"Why did you want to know what I was thinking? I mean when we were back in the apartment?"

"To see what the truth really looked like," I tell her.

"And what did it look like?"

"Like nothing in particular. It was all a mistake. I guess truth

281

lives in its own element, like deep-water fish. Beautiful colors, fantastic forms, but when you bring it to the surface, the colors dim, the movement ceases, it dies."

"I could have told you that," Kathy says. "Not that way, but pretty much the same thing. Whenever you would ask me I would tell you the truth, I really would, but the only trouble was that while I was telling you the truth I was already thinking of something else."

"I know."

After lunch, which Kathy enjoyed thoroughly, we walked to the corner of Fifth Avenue and stop there, near the display window of a foreign airline. The weather has turned mild—a soft, chemical haze. I feel lulled by the food and the air and the sonorous thrum of traffic. I turn to Kathy, who surprises me by resting her hand lightly on my arm and leaning toward me to kiss me on the lips.

"Goodbye, Dave."

"Goodbye? Where are you going?"

"I'm leaving the day after tomorrow," she says. "There are some friends I want to see yet. I want to spend some time with my aunt."

"Yes," I say, suddenly awake and panicky. "Of course. But I thought we would still have some hours together."

"It would be heavy," Kathy says. "Sad and heavy."

She's right. Time wouldn't pass, it would accumulate, sad and heavy.

"All right," I say. "Listen, Kathy, do you have absolutely everything you need?"

"Everything."

"Well, then—goodbye, Kathy. Take care of yourself."

"You, too, David. Thanks for everything."

She turns from me and joins the human traffic going south. I begin to walk in the opposite direction, not because I have a destination, but simply to complete Kathy's action. I look up and see gauzy light glint off the metal trim of buildings. I feel powerfully susceptible. Somewhere behind me Kathy is moving toward the West Coast. I shall never see her again. Shall I turn around and run to find her? Shall I tell her that I love her and will take care of her? It's possible for me to love. I can feel it. The taste of it is in my mouth like the taste of some exotic fruit—persimmon or pomegranate—sweet, harsh, clinging. I don't turn around and run after Kathy, of course. I have gathered too much momentum in another direction.

David and Dodie

41.

Another mild day, sooty and blue. Approaching Columbus Circle from the north, David Lang was reminded of another life when he had experienced a clairvoyance close by the monument to the sailors of the *Maine*. He and Dodie had been saying good night to friends (concert at Carnegie Hall, coffee, a stroll; it was early autumn) and there came to him the sure knowledge that Adlai Stevenson would lose. He had had many premonitions in his life, but this was the only occasion he could remember when he had given up thinking about a coming event because of his certainty of the outcome.

Then the interim before the encroachments of a new era. David wondered if it had been given a name yet, this new era. Probably it was still too new, its calamities too fresh. But something had ended for him with the Stevenson defeat. Stevenson's sincerities would sound foolish today. The worth of the individual. The young didn't sing of the individual. History had separated from David Lang while David Lang had played tennis and listened to cantatas and waited for these fashions to resolve themselves into an acknowledgment of true value. Well, he would wait a long time. Stevenson's world had died with him, and acknowledgment was the problem of survivors like David Lang.

Time-conscious, David looked at his watch. It was only eleven o'clock. The one gain in all of this—time. Only he couldn't think of it as a gain. He had been walking for years out into time as into an ocean, deeper by tiny degrees, up to his waist by the end of the war, up to his chest by the time of Stevenson's defeat, up to his armpits by the death of Kennedy—and suddenly the ground began to rise, a sandbar way out here, and he was again only ankle-deep in time. He felt foolish in his exposure to so many hours of the day. He knew it couldn't go on this way indefinitely. There would be a precipitous drop shortly, and he would be once again armpit-deep in his progress to total submersion. But right now, today, and for the many days of this untoward season, he had walked from morning to afternoon to night on this sandbar of time.

He entered the museum without hesitation. There was the art book room to the right—there the display racks—*the very display racks!*—he had seen so clearly in his vision. He stood in the vestibule looking at the room, matching its real dimensions against the image that had floated into his head one October afternoon. This was different. The arrangement of the book displays along the wall. The telephone booths in one corner that hadn't appeared in his vision at all. And the counter where purchases could be checked out. But these discrepancies pointed up, if anything, only the error of his vision. This was the real room, the one his uneasy soul had abstracted. This one was devoid of terror. This was only a room full of books.

David took off his coat and folded it over his arm. The checkroom was to his left. He thought of checking his coat but decided against it. Dodie might not wish to stay. He looked at his watch again. It was still fifteen minutes short of their arranged meeting time—if, that is, they met at all—if Dodie showed up. There was the possibility she might not. He tried to imagine himself into the coming meeting, but his imagination was equal only to the stillborn scene of Dodie's entrance. He conjured her through the revolving door, and there she would stay. Then through the door again, and the second revenant would replace the first, the third the second; but the ghost would not advance toward him, nor he to the ghost.

He clasped one hand with the other behind his back, his coat draped over his left arm. He was wearing a brown tweed suit, a white shirt, a diagonally striped tie. He squared his shoulders from time to time. Good posture did not come easily to him. He tended to slouch. He was aware of it, and therefore he gave a compensating lift to his head. This made him, at times, look contemplative, at other times aloof, and at still other times he looked vacant. The gray that had come into his hair had given the brown a more interesting texture. His brown eyes were normally underscored by pockets of a deeper brown, but the discoloration of his left eye gave sensational focus to a face that normally arranged itself against any possibility of the sensational. That longish face tried for the normal arrangement, but it had to contend with an eye whose swelling had constricted its normal field of vision. It also had to struggle with a motor of apprehension that kept going on and off, on and off, subjecting it to distressing changes of current.

So it was not the usual David Lang who stood, hands folded behind his back, chin tilted, in the vestibule of the museum. This David Lang looked like a man who might have endured some of the things David Lang had endured. And the hand of his watch had barely advanced since he had last looked at it, so David bought a ticket of admission and entered the exhibition hall where various forms of abstract expressionism were displayed. He could stroll around here and still keep an eye out for the real Dodie.

He stopped before a piece a sculpture—brass or bronze—feeling a long-dormant throb of hostility. It was a squat thing, no higher than his thigh, hewn or molded into orbicles, from which extended lateral bars, from which depended verticle connecting rods, to which were welded other orbicles, other bars and rods. Some of the surfaces were smooth and shiny, some deep-pitted, black, as though eaten into by acid. It was disturbing, ugly, brutal.

David sighed. Why? he wondered. No doubt he was supposed to be affected as he was affected by the sight of it, but what was the point in being affected this way? Could he live his life better for having seen it? Could he reconcile the fact of death for having seen it? It was disturbing and ugly and irreducibly its own brutal self. Sighing again, David moved toward a panel where, one after the other, he looked at paintings that were less brutal if no more communicative. He moved to the end of the panel and found himself confronting the glass wall that gave out on a courtyard where statuary stood beneath expensive apartment windows and an innocent sky. He looked at the swollen loins of the familiar figure in the center. He thought of Kathy, daughter of the American heartland, who thrust her loins at life in similar fashion, and for an instant David was flooded with a refulgent idea. If he could make it whole, articulate it, why—why that would be the beginning of a new golden age! It would be the end of war, the brotherhood of man, the gateway to mortal happiness! It had to do with Kathy—with Kathy and the statue—the sameness of all human desire—and it needed to be turned up just one pitch more to make it to a permanent, glowing revelation—but David wasn't able to turn it up just that one pitch more. He breathed his freshest hope and sensibility on the fire, but it was already dimming. He failed of the inspiration that would have made an ordinary idea into a miracle, and so he turned away from the window, walked over to the next panel of paintings after pausing to look over the vestibule for a sign of Dodie.

She wasn't there. Despite the numbers milling around, he would see her if she were there, looking for him. And he would want to see her as soon as she arrived. He would want to pay for her ticket. Not that he wanted to be obviously attentive, but neither did he wish to seem callous or indifferent. He was not that way. No, no matter how much or in what way he changed, he would never be that way. He had been pushed in directions and with a force he never could have foreseen, and he had discovered what he would do under such circumstances, but certain instincts remained. He would always show the same considerations, even though his allegiances had been shattered. His longing to live was flavored with the same Lang seasoning, even though the world had become an unfamiliar place and his personal landscape was as nude as a desert.

He moved along another panel of paintings. The old affront.

The insistent demand on his attention with qualities he disliked. Like this piece of sculpture, which he found himself confronting again, a thing long in the making and inexpungeably *there*—like Arthur Gerson, or Ted Buchholz, or Bud Demery, or—Brian! The sudden recollection of Brian shocked David. His eyes remained on the heavy piece of metal, but he was seeing Brian's azure-eyed enmity, and it seemed to David that this enormous shell fragment—palm-smooth and acid-gouged—had been blasted straight from Brian's angry dream. He liked it no better, but it seemed to him he understood. For the first time! He believed that there were people who would deliberately choose to say this, and that there were other people who would understand what it said and why it was said. He had seen it. He had the evidence of it on his face. It was not dishonest. It was the way things were, and David knew that this was the end of his belief that the world could be like him if only it tried. His wife, his son, his friends, the daily newspaper, this museum, the scope and variety of the world which did not take its cue for being from David Lang. There was separation, and perhaps it was separation itself that was the reason for love, the need of it, the despair of it.

"Have you been waiting long?" the voice asked—and in the spell of his new understanding and distraction, David went past the hopeless complexity of this meeting and simply said as any man expecting someone would say, "No, not long. Besides, there's the exhibit to look at."

"My God!" Dodie exclaimed. "Your eye!"

"Yes," David said. "I'm afraid I got socked by an angry young man. How are you, Dodie?"

"I'm all right. Did somebody really hit you?"

"Yes."

"You're leading quite a violent life these days."

"It would seem so. What shall we do? Would you like to have some lunch?"

"It makes no difference," Dodie said. "Why don't we just walk around?"

"All right."

There were changes for David to see, and he had been marking them off as they spoke. There were scorings on Dodie's face he had never seen before; lines bracketing the corners of her mouth and repeating themselves outward once or twice before being intercepted by the angle of her jaw. Her hair was different—differently done. The same color, but more full in the crown and fastened in the back. She was wearing a suit that David didn't recognize. She looked thinner, younger, older—he wasn't sure. Her eyes, the jade-green eyes, were the same, but his annotation of her eyes only gave new measure to a face that had concealed and revealed and had been the agent of its own emotions for the many years he had assumed its absorption into his life. He was seeing *this* Dodie for the first time—the one who had lived with him; had aged; and who had had an affair with another man for reasons having to do with all the samenesses and changes he was observing in her now.

They walked around the same area that David had covered before. They looked—or pretended to look—at paintings, listening in their silence to the vibrations of their meeting after so long an absence. David kept glancing at Dodie, taking in the green bow of some fluffy material that fastened her hair in the back. He tried to recall if she had ever worn such a bow in all the years of their marriage. Was it something in their separation that accounted for that bow? Was he the inhibition that had prevented that bow from appearing before? It was youthful, that bow, a fillip of the new Dodie, or the Dodie he never knew, and because of this David felt regret as sharp and deep as a dagger thrust.

And Dodie, eyes fixed determinedly on the canvases, carried with her the green-blue and jaundice-yellow image of a bruised David like a pulsation in her optic nerve. The nervousness jiggling behind her breastbone held equal promise of laughter or tears should she give way to it. It was comic, David and Arthur wearing almost identical badges, as though they'd both undergone the same initiation rite. Several times Dodie had to catch her underlip between her teeth to keep the threatening jiggle under control. Then

David said, "Is this where you met?"—and the comedy ended, the jiggle ceased, and instead of seeing David and Arthur, she was seeing herself in the kindly admonitions of Dr. Nathanson's kindly pudding of a face. It wasn't funny.

"No," she said.

"I thought it was," David said. "I thought you said the museum."

"*You* said the museum," Dodie reminded him.

"You were going to a Matisse exhibit the Sunday you met Arthur."

"David, is this what you wanted to discuss?" Dodie asked.

"Yes. I'm curious."

"To know if your informant was right?"

"There was no informant."

"Oh, David!"

"Truly, Dodie, there was no informant."

"Then how did you find out?"

Now that the moment was here, David knew. He had known all along, of course, but he had had so much else to contend with that late afternoon in October, and for weeks after. He had had the explosion, and the debris, and the injuries, and the past, and the future, and the smoking present all charred and splintered. Now he was recovered and looking back on it. He told Dodie this, told her that he had had to recover first before he could know how he knew. He told her that when he saw her there on the steps of the house, he knew he was about to lose her. He told her that for all his knowledge of their difficulties and differences, he had had no premonition that he was about to lose her. It came to him as a certainty as she stood on the steps that October afternoon in her white turtleneck sweater and heather-colored suit, her hand reaching for the doorknob. "I didn't know how you had gotten that far," he said, "but I knew how far it was." He told her that he feared she was about to disappear before his eyes. He reminded her that he had asked how she had enjoyed the Matisse exhibit and that she had said it was lovely; and when she said that, he saw Arthur Gerson standing near the rack of the book store there in the vestibule. "Because I knew that much about you, Dodie," he said. "You're

293

not the woman to take unhappiness to museums and find solace in pictures. I understood there must be someone, and I didn't have far to look in our lives to know who it might be. That's how I knew, Dodie. Nothing mystical. If you were leaving me, you were going to someone. And if it was not here that you met Arthur, then I don't care to know where it was."

"It was not here," Dodie said.

"All right, then," said David.

"We met at a bar, at a hotel," Dodie said. "I didn't meet Arthur that Sunday. I did go to that exhibit with Jean Ferguson. I met Arthur on other occasions."

"All right, then," David said. "That's finished. I hope you believe what I've told you. It's true."

"I believe you," Dodie said. "But not about that eye. How did you get that eye? Did Arthur hit you back?"

David smiled and shook his head. "That's the truth, too," he said. "I was punched by an angry young man. Let me tell you one more truth, Dodie. I've been living with a girl at Ralph's apartment. A student who came back with me from Vermont when I visited Lenny early in November. She asked me for a lift, and when we arrived in New York she stayed with me. She's gone now—gone from the apartment. She's leaving for San Francisco. I almost fell in love with her. I think I did fall in love with her for about an hour. Were you in love with Arthur?"

"Not even for an hour," she said.

They walked round and round the panels, gazing blindly at the paintings, and now they came out again to the center where the sculpture of Brian's anger sat squatly on its pedestal. David looked at it lovelessly for a few seconds, and then he told Dodie about the boy who had wanted him to do something about having a bad novel published, and the altercation that followed.

"His name was Brian Miller, and he was the boyfriend of the girl who was living with me. That's the way it was, Dodie."

Dodie believed him, completely, because only the truth could come dressed in such motley. Fantasy has its own costume.

While she accompanied David across the hall, Dodie dealt with

294

the information that had been given her. She found it all too easy to imagine David shacked in with a college girl (the girl took the form of the girl Lenny had brought home, Marie, that pale-blonde thing with too much eyeglass and too much ego) because no one had to point out to her that David was an attractive man, and the damnable thing was that a man was attractive for so *long* while a woman faded and faded. Dodie felt a different sensation behind her breastbone now: a hot stab of jealousy and outrage that she had worried and wondered about David, feeling regret and remorse, while David, who hadn't her reasons, who was merely getting back his own, had eased himself so quickly in young, careless flesh.

"Where are you going?" she demanded, stopping.

"I thought we would get a bite to eat," he said, stopping too, looking at her.

"Look, David, I thought you wanted to settle something," Dodie said irritably.

He continued to look at her, and Dodie was forced to turn away because she could see that he understood. She stood for a moment in perilous need of some assurance. She wanted to hear David say that it didn't matter, that the girl didn't matter, that he hadn't been in love with her for an hour, not for a second, and she was terrified lest she say something that would reduce everything she had felt and thought and resolved to a sodden mass of futility.

"I don't think I like that girl," she said, continuing in the direction they had been going.

"You probably wouldn't," David said, following her.

"I'm talking about Marie," Dodie explained. "Lenny's girl-friend."

"Oh?"

"Do you?" Dodie asked. "I know you met her."

"I don't know," David replied. "She's not what I had imagined for Lenny, but then Lenny himself is not what I imagined he would be. He's better, perhaps, but not what I had imagined. So how can I tell? Marie may be the right girl for him, whatever that means. And who are we to talk?"

"She's ambitious," Dodie said.

"She says not."

"Yes, I know. But she is. And someday her ambition will hurt Lenny."

"Someday something will hurt Lenny no matter how much we wish for it not to happen."

"Does that mean we should stop caring?"

"Oh, I care," David said. "Very much. But Lenny is launched in his world, has been for years. There's nothing we can do *except* care."

Dodie knew this to be true, but the amazement of hearing David say it made her turn to him, and she saw with a fresh shock the blood colors some stranger had stamped on his face. It was real, that eye. So was the little demon who had wriggled his hand between her thighs. The outrage and jealousy dropped away from Dodie.

They inched along the cafeteria line. Dodie selected a salad. David chose the fried fillet of sole. They found a table from which they could look out on the garden with its statuary. David gazed on the garden, and he recalled a time of his life when he hoped to be sitting like this, looking out on such a scene, enough money in his pocket to buy the discriminating leisure of a week, a month.

Dodie too looked out on the garden, and beyond, to the world Arthur told her she should enter, that she *must* enter.

"I'm going to get a job, David," she said.

"You should," he said.

"And I can't go on living in that house," Dodie said.

"We'll sell it," David said. "I can't live in it either, and Lenny no longer needs it."

"I must do something," Dodie declared. "The important thing for me is that I do something for the rest of my life."

"Of course," David agreed.

They finished their food, drank coffee, and then left the museum. They turned as if by agreement toward Fifth Avenue. It seemed proper to David that they should be walking toward Fifth Avenue.

That was the city, all right, and they had walked on Fifth Avenue twenty-three years ago, after coming out of the department store, and the sun had glinted off the metal trim of the buildings, and he had seen the interior room of Dodie's castle where she had spun not gold but grief. He had loved her then—Dodie—who wanted to be more beautiful than she was. Now they were more than two decades older. This world would never match their hopes. It would grow less and less familiar. Yet they must live in it. Where else could they go? With whom?

"Will we live together?" David asked Dodie, when they reached the tumultuous avenue.

"Will you help me?" Dodie asked in return.

"Of course," David said instinctively, because it was his habit to help, and because he knew what a sorry thing it would be to have to share with anyone else his late and difficult coming of age.